Absolute Zero

by Ireland Gill

Copyright © 2015 by Ireland Gill

All rights reserved. No part of this publication may be reproduced, stored in a retrieval system, or transmitted by any means – electronic, mechanical, photographic (photocopying), recording, or otherwise – without prior permission in writing from the author.

Printed in the United States of America
ISBN: 978-1517297046

To Brian – my husband, my love, my knight. Without you, all of Hayden's most admirable qualities that I adore would cease to exist. Thank you for occasionally humoring me with agreement, even when I am utterly wrong. Thank you for always having my back, even in moments when I have clearly lost my mind. Thank you for loving me unconditionally, and for your limitless patience.

And most of all, thank you for accepting me for me – even the darkest parts. You are my life, my haven.

Chapter One *Haven*

The thirteen-hour drive to Georgia did a lot of things for me. I'd run through a lot of music, unable to elude the emotional roller coaster on which my mind insisted on taking me. I'd come to terms, a bit more, with the new life that awaited my arrival in Georgia, but I'd also over-analyzed every aspect of it. I tried not to think of the dismal feelings I'd had for the first Seeker, as I couldn't help wondering if those feelings would continue while I met others just like her. It was inevitable, the fact that there were more souls stuck in their own deserved hell waiting for me to save them. And these thoughts, without fail, made my outlook bleaker. I was a vessel for the dead who were trapped in the dark realm with the devil; the dead who, I believed, didn't deserve their peace. Ever.

I'd gotten to know my new Mustang like the back of my hand during the long drive; every button, dial, light, and switch. I melted into the driver's seat and sometimes became very distracted as I let my mind wander. Luka, my guardian angel's best friend, would occasionally pop in from time to time into the passenger side. Well, it was more of a "disappearing" and "reappearing" act he'd gotten down to a science twice an hour. I'd caught on to the pattern after the third round.

And then, there was Hayden, my angel and the object of my unspoken affection, following behind me in the moving truck. He kept sending Luka in to tell me the next set of directions even though my state-of-the-art navigation system was working just fine. Either that, or he'd call me for the hundredth time, and we would talk hands-free through my bluetooth. Honestly, I think it was killing him that he wasn't in the car with me and the fact that I wasn't up for stopping more than the one time we found a twenty-four hour IHOP right off of I-77S in Charlotte. A stack of pancakes and Southern charm at three A.M was definitely a good choice. After the stop in Charlotte, Luka became a permanent fixture in my car.

"So...." Luka trailed off as he bobbed his head, looking out the window without continuing with his thought aloud.

I put the pony in gear and headed back to the highway, slightly averting my eyes to see the illumination of the green ambient lighting on the angel's face. "So?" I inquired curiously.

"That was a nice dinner-lunch-breakfast meal, er,

whatever you want to call it," Luka declared.

I smiled at him, playing along. "Can't beat IHOP, Lukster," I said as I thumbed the search button to find a new playlist we could listen to. Despite the massive yawn that escaped me, I felt good and awake after eating. I was especially buzzing after the gigantic chocolate shake I'd downed, but I wanted to stay charged, so I made sure to play music that would keep me pumped for the rest of the drive. I kept the volume low because I felt there was something more than just "pancakes" that Luka wanted to talk about, but I had no clue what was on his mind.

"Cookie?" Luka stalled by holding out the tin of chocolate chip cookies from Ms. Makerov. It was her for-the-road present to me when I'd gone to visit her for our last goodbye.

I smirked at the angel. "No thanks, buddy. I'm stuffed till next Tuesday."

"Okay." He placed the tin back on his lap. Then, finally, out came his true agenda. "You know, Evigreen, if you're tired, I don't mind taking the wheel for a while," he offered.

I didn't have to turn to look at him to know he was flashing his teeth in a cheesy grin, but I glanced at him anyway and caught his crooked smile. "You just wanna drive my car," I accused with a laugh.

"Okay, so maaaaaybe that is an incentive, but I'm only looking out for you." He shifted in his seat. "Hayden's orders, you know."

"Right." I rolled my eyes and smiled at him. "I had a feeling something was up."

Luka sighed. "So, you're not going to let me drive, huh?"

I looked at him apologetically. "This beautiful contraption is my baby."

"Ha!" Luka guffawed. "And you wouldn't trust *me* with your baby?" he asked playfully. I was happy he didn't take my comment too personally.

"I trust you with my life, Luka," I assured him. "But," I paused for a moment in order to really figure out the best way to explain how I felt behind that wheel, "this is the one place, right now, that I feel like things are normal." I could tell I was about to make the conversation turn down a serious road once I'd said that. I continued. "Sitting here in this Mustang, operating everything from this seat, shifting the gears to make it go at whatever speed I want it to go, like slowing down when I realize I'm going too fast, it's the only way I feel like I have a sense of control, and I kinda need that right now." I took a side glance at him and saw him half-grinning at me. It gave me a sense of relief.

"You know, Evika," Luka started, "as perplexing as you can be sometimes, I think I hear you loud and clear on that one." He reached up and gave a couple of light tugs on my pony tail. "You're gonna be okay," Luka comforted me in his most serious tone. "You've got the best angels in history looking after you."

I smiled genuinely at him. There really was a lot of meaning to what he said, and I felt content just knowing that he understood me.

"I already knew that," I said to him.

"Good," he said with a head-bob. There was a long pause before he continued. "Then you'll know that the one day you finally *do* break down and let me take this thing for a spin, it's in great hands. Just sayin'." I caught his wink at me as he turned up the music.

Just like my own angel knew me so well, Luka was beginning to understand me without question. He smiled and scooted lower in the seat, making himself comfortable, and silently indicating he would be staying in my car for the rest of the trip. I didn't mind; next to me, was the quirky sidekick of mine who gave me a warmth in my heart like no other.

I shook my head and smirked, keeping my eyes on the road as we drove down the unlit highway. The darkness of the route ahead was almost eerie, but I looked in my rear view mirror to see the headlights of the moving truck full of, well, my *life*, driven by my Guardian with whom I felt safe.

The sun was just starting to rise after a few more hours of driving, breaking up the clouds of the still sky when we'd finally turned down our new home road, Chatham. The navigation gear couldn't keep up with my speed as it recited "five-hundred yards, three-hundred yards, one-hundred yards," and then finally, "you have reached your destination."

I turned into the long, cement driveway and gawked at my new house, the purchase I'd made without seeing in person first. It stood tall and proud, waiting for me. Beige siding, white shutters, a red front door and the greenest of all grasses laid out like a canvas all around it, stretching out in all directions. The closest neighboring homes were visible, but the privacy we'd have was outstanding. Seclusion without the solitude. The house was framed with a giant stone walkway that led around either side of it.

I pulled up to the top of the driveway and parked, simultaneously flinging the door open to get out. I couldn't move fast enough. With the slight turn of my head, I could see beautiful blue ocean. I stumbled to the side of the house in awe along the stone walkway. My neck craned as I scanned the house from the bottom up, my mouth agape, and then I looked past the massive structure. I gasped with every other step.

I ran up to Hayden, who was stepping down from the moving truck cabin. "Omigod! Omigod! Hayden, it's huge-mammoth and absolutely perfect!"

"Told you she'd like it," Luka said, getting out of the pony.

"Well, I sure hope so, cuz we kinda bought it." Hayden laughed.

"Where's the key? Where's the key?" I jumped around my angel, patting him down.

"Oh," he said slyly, "you mean....*this?*" He whipped the key out from the back pocket of his jeans, dangling it from his index finger accompanied by a small, metal key chain with a silver shamrock, a reminder of my Irish blood.

I slid the key from his finger and smiled at him. "You are so good to me."

He gave me a smug look as we started walking to the front door. "You just better remember that." He chuckled.

I leapt onto the porch and dashed to the door, shaking with so much excitement that I could hardly get the key to work. As I pushed the front door open and stepped onto the granite floor of the foyer, I fell in love all over again, but this time it was with three thousand square feet of architecture. The house was twenty times bigger than I thought it would be, and the pictures I'd used to decide on the purchase didn't do it justice. My new house was, without a doubt, the cream of the crop. Every corner turned was a moment of awe as I'd walk into a room bigger than before. My imagination ran wild as I thought of the décor that I'd lay out in each room. A huge mansion; a canvas for my creativity, and the home in which I'd be spending the rest of my life....with my angel.

Considering most of the furniture was left in the house for us – compliments of Hayden's master negotiating skills – I only had to bring my miscellaneous junk. Not that I had much to begin with, anyway. Between the three of us, we were able to get all of the boxes in the house in less than an hour. The boys didn't let me carry anything too heavy, despite my stubbornness. It seemed as though the heaviest box was the last out of the truck, and it was full of all of my art projects; unfinished, of course. Luka was the lucky winner of that one. He carried it all the way to the master suite on the top floor where my room would be, then huffed his way to the living room, slamming his body into the cushions of the red, suede couch and letting out an exasperated "*phew!*" I laughed at him.

"Well, that's the last of it," Luka said, putting his feet up and over the side of the couch.

"I thought you guys didn't get tired," I teased him. "Shouldn't I, the *human,* be the one who's panting and out of breath?" I plopped on the couch next to his head.

"Hey, kiddo," Luka said, "that last box was a nightmare. Next time we do this, you're payin' for movers. I'm not cut out for this."

I laughed. "I would have, but Hayden didn't want to." It was true.

Hayden came walking over, bringing a box to the living room. I noticed he'd taken his shredded leather jacket off – the item that reminded me of my first encounter with a Watcher – and was unpacking in his dark gray t-shirt. My eyes averted to his twitching arm muscles as he set the box down. *Holy angel.* "Because I'm a tank and we won't ever need movers," he chimed in. He gave his left bicep a few smacks and grinned at us.

Both Luka and I rolled our eyes and laughed.

"So, are you gonna take a nap before unpacking? It was a long drive for you, you know, since you didn't let me drive.....*at all*," Luka jeered, nudging me in the arm.

"Nah," I waved my hand, "I've got a second wind." I looked out the window. "Besides, I don't like wasting the sun. It's such a beautiful morning. I'll sleep later."

"Don't feel bad about the Mustang, Charmin, Hayden comforted Luka. "She hasn't even let *me* drive it yet."

"Jeez," I guffawed. "What is it with this car?"

"Hey, we may be angels, but we're still dudes," Luka retorted with a chuckle.

"Ev, you really should get some rest," Hayden said. "I told Elka she could swing by later."

"What? We just got here and you're already inviting people over?" I teased.

"Sure, why not? Oh, and Elliott will be here later on, too, for the whole castor thing. We've got a busy day."

I slouched at the mention of *castor*. Elliott was the angel techie at the House of Counsel, the one who designed all and any tools I would need. "Oh," I said. I was disappointed that Hayden couldn't have just let me have a day or two to enjoy my new home before getting down to business.

The thought of castors made me cringe. I was to create my own with Elliott, just like my father had. Once I had my own, there was no turning back; I was officially the new Soldier of Light for all those wicked souls. Although I wasn't thrilled that Elliott's visit meant I was one step closer to having to deal with the saving of the dead, I was still excited to meet him.

"Well," Luka stood to his feet, "I've got things of my own to take care of, Evigreen. I'm gonna hit the road, er, air, whatever."

"And what could *possibly* be more important than unpacking with *me?*" I poked.

"Oh, you'll find that out when I come back tonight with your housewarming gift." Luka winked at me.

I shook my head and smiled. "Full of surprises, aren't you, Charmin?"

"Good ones, though. I promise." He grinned, leaning his head toward me and offering his puffed out cheek, expecting a kiss.

"Thanks for the help, Luka." I planted a peck on the angel's soft cheek.

"See ya, Evigreen." Luka spun on his heels to face Hayden. "Be back later, Darkwing."

"Later, Luka," Hayden responded. "Thanks, again."

Then Luka was gone, shimmering out of sight. I was starting to get used to the way angels came and went.

I dragged myself to the kitchen, realizing I was a lot more tired than I'd let on. I knew Hayden was right. I should have lied down for a while, but I was eager to get everything unpacked. I was trying so hard to be organized, especially with such a great, new place. I *had* to keep the place clean. No more messes. I vowed I'd make that change. The mess from my previous apartment-living would not follow me.

"Here's a box that should have made it to the kitchen," Hayden came around the corner, setting the heavy box onto the tile floor. "If you're up for it, we should probably get kitchen stuff put away first."

"My thoughts exactly," I concurred.

Hayden pulled a box cutter from his back pocket and started cutting the duct tape placed over the seams of each box. It was unnerving how quickly he was slicing each seam. I started unloading and unwrapping the contents of the first box while he continued with the slicing until the cutting came to an abrupt stop, followed by a quick hiss forced through the angel's teeth. I turned to see that he'd stopped to examine his hand for a moment. I knew instantly what had happened.

"Oh, God." My immediate reaction led me to grabbing one of the towels from the first box I was still unpacking. "I saw that one coming a mile away, slick. You okay?" I rushed to his side.

"I'm fine. Just stings a bit," Hayden admitted with a shrug.

I took his hand in mine to look at the damage and apply the towel only to find nothing but a small, pinkish-white line running across the side of his left palm that showed no signs of a fresh wound. It was as if it were only a scar left behind from the healed skin. I could have sworn it was the hand that he'd cut, then I looked up at his unforgettable smirk as I recalled the reason for the lack of blood.

"Angels don't bleed, remember?" he reminded me.

"Humph," was my reaction. "You're lucky. That could have been a bad one."

That winning smile gleamed across his face. He just stood there in a stupor, staring at me. I had no choice but to let out a nervous laugh.

"What?" I asked, embarrassed.

"You were coming to my rescue," he answered. "It's kinda cute."

I blushed, feeling the heat rise to my face instantly. "Protective instinct, I guess."

"I'm flattered," he said with a slight bow of his head.

"Good. You should be. Don't do it again." I confiscated the box cutter from his hand.

Hayden laughed. The doorbell rang when I'd just started cutting the tape off of the rest of the kitchen boxes.

"Early," Hayden muttered, shaking his head in disapproval. "I knew she'd do that."

"Elka's here already?" I asked him as I followed him down the hall to the front door. "I thought you told her 'later.'"

"I *did*." He chuckled. "But she doesn't take direction very well."

I knew Hayden had invited Elka over so we could officially meet sooner than later. She was one of the angels of the Guardian Council, the head angels. I'd imagined that she would be stunning, just as the boys were handsome. And she didn't disappoint. I watched Hayden open the front screen door and saw the morning sun illuminate her silhouette as she stepped into the house; a tall, petite body dressed in a light pink summer dress, white blazer and pink ballet shoes. And that long, blond hair, with its beautiful, loose curls bouncing with each, quiet step she made through the doorway; she was as graceful as a feather in a light breeze.

"Got a thing for pink, Elk?" Hayden said.

She stretched her full, pink lips into a playful smile and patted Hayden gently on the cheek. "Why does this seem to surprise you, silly angel?" She glanced past his shoulder, and our eyes finally met. Hers were a dark, chocolate-brown, framed by an oval-shaped face with a light, olive complexion. Her smile widened.

"Evika!" she squealed as she extended her hand, her curly, blond locks bouncing as she flitted over to me. "So nice to meet you....again. And this time, you're awake!" She giggled.

I took her hand, and we shook as I looked at her curiously, until I realized where we would have met before. "Oh, right!" I acknowledged. "My apartment. I was unconscious." I laughed as I thought about the first day I'd met Hayden. I'd passed out on the curb after getting wounded by a Drone. I woke in my room wearing my pajamas and smelling of soap. Hayden explained to me that he'd called Elka for help while I was still unconscious.

"Yeah," her smile started to dissipate as she paused. Then her face suddenly brightened. "But, no worries," she waved her hand at me, "I saw *nothing*. Kept my eyes closed the whole time and just felt my way around to get you cleaned up and into those clothes," she explained innocently. Then a look of horror washed across her face. "Oh, *jeez!* That sounded horrid! Evika," she attempted to redact her previous comment, "I just meant---"

"Elka," I put my hand up and laughed heartily, "it's fine. I get it." I liked her instantly. It was hard not to. Her perkiness and innocence was refreshing. "And thank you for your help that day. I'm glad Hayden called you," I assured her.

She smiled at me with that purely innocent face of hers. "Quite the gentleman, this one," she nodded to Hayden. "He called on me right away for help."

From the corner of my eye, I caught Hayden staring at me with a crooked smile, arms folded while he leaned in the doorway.

"What?" I humored him.

He flashed his alluring grin. "Oh, come on. You know you want to ask her." I looked at him, confused, then realized what he was referring to.

"Ask me what?" Elka turned to me with an inquisitive stare.

"Uh...." I gave her a sheepish smile. "I'm kind of fascinated with the whole color spectrum of angel wings now," I admitted.

Elka's high pitched laughter filled the room. The echoes of her voice chimed melodically throughout the foyer, giving me no choice but to join in with her song.

"I see," she said as her laughing dwindled down to a slight giggle. "Well, I think I know where this is leading." She scoped the right and left sides of her shoulders and stepped back, giving herself more room.

"Hey, hey, hey, Blondie. Not in the house. You'll break stuff." Hayden chuckled, waving his hand to the door.

Elka wrinkled her nose while sporting her flawless, pouting lips. "Jeez, Hay-bird, you are just no fun," she jeered. "As if I don't know what I'm doing." She shook her head.

"Why don't you just *tell* her, for cryin' out loud?" Hayden asked. "It makes it so much easier."

"Ugh!" Elka guffawed as she put her hands to her hips and cocked her head. "Now, where's the excitement in *that*.....Darkwing?"

Hayden rolled his eyes lovingly. "Touche, Miss Herring. Touche."

My laughter continued, of course. Their bantering was quite amusing, and he and I both knew his approach was the same as Elka's just a short time ago; I was dragged out behind my apartment building without any warning before Hayden unveiled his wings. Forever memorable.

Elka grinned my way, showing her perfect, white teeth again. "I'll show ya later, when Hayden can't suck the fun out of everything," she promised me with a wink.

"I'll hold you to it."

"So, you ready to take her out?" Hayden asked, nudging Elka in the arm.

"Out?" I inquired.

"Oh, yeah. Out. You're going with Elka to the mall and bringing me home a new leather," he leaned into me with a smirk, "pursuant to our previous agreement, if you've forgotten." I remembered, all right. I owed him a new jacket after the last Drone attack. The only reason the monster had been lurking was because I'd darted out of the apartment in a fit of rage and ran around the city's dark alleys. "I'll be taking care of some household matters while you're gone, anyway," he added.

"And these are matters I am not to be a part of?" I tightened my lips.

"Only because they would bore you."

"Oh?" I perked up. "Then, it sounds like a good deal to me."

Elka laughed. "Well," she said to Hayden, "that was easy."

"Hey, if I'm lucky, he'll have everything unpacked by the time we get back." I gave Hayden a playful nudge.

"Don't hold your breath, Pony-girl. I have a lot to do. Setting up appointments for utilities, satellite---"

"You're right," I interrupted. "Not my cup of tea. I'd rather be shopping."

Hayden laughed at me.

Elka locked her arm with mine. "Hence, the reason I'm stealing you away this morning, so go get your purse and make sure you have your bank card. We have a mission."

"Ah, yes," I said as I walked over to the couch to grab my purse, "the mission for a new leather. He won't let me forget."

"Oh, believe me. He'll never stop. Be glad you're getting this done today," Elka assured me.

I looked at Hayden, who was nodding. "It's true," he said. "I'll never stop."

"So," I smirked, "you're trusting me to pick something out for you, huh?"

"Absolutely," he bobbed his head. "Total trust." He paused, and I waited, looking at him incredulously. Then finally, he grinned widely. "Just be sure to bring home the receipt."

"Ha!" I pointed at him with a laugh. "I knew it."

"Ugh!" Elka grunted exasperatedly. "You and those leathers. I swear they have a name for angels like you," she poked with a smile.

"Yes. It's called *bad ass*. Take notes," Hayden boasted as he dug into one of the boxes in the living room.

Elka rolled her eyes. "I have to wonder, Hayden, if that ego will ever fade...should *you* ever decide to," she teased. Hayden belted out a hefty laugh as Elka tugged my arm. "Come on, girlie. We're burnin' daylight here. See ya, Hay-bird," she called behind her shoulder as she flitted to the front door with me in tow.

"Have fun, you two," Hayden called to us. "Oh, and Ev," he winked at me, "try not to miss me too much."

I smiled at him and gave in to my urge to rush to his side and plant my lips on his cheek. "I'll try not to, Angel-man." But no more than two steps out that door with Elka and I already did miss him.

Elka and I got into the pony and looked at each other. I had no idea where I was going and wondered if she even knew, but she just held a girlish smirk on her cute face and folded her arms, staring back at me. "Holy Moses." She laughed. "Luka wasn't kidding; the match between you two *is* impeccable."

All I could do was blush. "Uh," I felt the heat in my face instantly, "yeah, well....I care about him," I admitted with a nervous laugh. "A lot," I added.

"Sweetie," she placed her hand on my shoulder and smiled, "there is no doubt in my mind that you two were made for each other. I'd bet my wings on it."

I smiled back at her, hoping that the subject would be dropped, and we could just go shopping. I wasn't really up for any more "bets" with angels.

"Anyhoo," she locked in her seatbelt, and I mimicked her, "Oglethorpe Mall isn't too far from here and they have over one hundred stores and tons of restaurants. You can take me out to lunch." She winked at me playfully. I couldn't resist her charm. It was impossible. She grew on me, indefinitely.

"The mall it is, then," I agreed as I plugged the info into my navigation system. I started backing the pony out of the driveway and looked up to see Hayden waving goodbye at the screen door, holding his ripped leather in the other and waving it around. I laughed heartily.

"Oh, that boy is relentless. Seriously," Elka muttered. "Just look at him," she said with a giggle. Elka didn't have to tell me twice. I was already staring at him. "He'll probably be popping in a Coltrane CD any minute now."

"Coltrane?" I gave her a quick glance.

"Oh, yeah," she said. "Huge fan. It's all he'd listen to during his entire trial at the House of Council." She looked at me solemnly. "I kind of figured you already knew about that by now, his trial?"

I nodded as we drove down the street. "Yeah, he told me," I answered in a sad tone. I thought about that bittersweet night; Hayden revealed something so personal and upsetting, yet it was the night that I felt the truth in my heart about my feelings for him. "At first, he didn't want to tell me because he thought it would show him in bad light," I told her.

"That's because everything is so hard on you already, Evika. He takes great pride in being your Guardian, and I'm sure he just didn't want you to think any less of him. Or worse; for you to be afraid of him."

I turned to her as I braked the car at the stop sign. "I could never be afraid of him, and I could never see him as anything differently than I do now. He's....I'm...." I couldn't think of how to describe my feelings to her without needing to resort to words like "in love." I hadn't even said those words out loud to myself yet and I wasn't about to belt it out to Elka. I needed a good word for Hayden; something to explain what he was to me. "He's like my---"

"Haven." Elka finished for me with confidence.

A smile of satisfaction grew on my face as I felt myself agreeing with her, entirely. "Yeah." I nodded. "He's my haven."

Chapter Two *Right as Rain*

    Elka and I made it to the mall in less than fifteen minutes and headed in to find Hayden's new jacket right away. I wanted to find something different for him, not just the typical black leather he'd had. I sifted through so many racks of coats in so many stores until I spotted the most bad ass leather I'd ever seen. It was dark brown with four pockets, zipping up the middle and worn at the fold and hem lines. The first thing I did was pull it off the rack to smell it. I imagined Hayden's scent blended with the scent of the leather. The thought of it intoxicated me as I finally held it out for Elka's approval.

"Holy, masculinity. Now, *that* is our Hayden," she approved with enthusiasm.

"I'll take that as a yes, then." I laughed and walked the jacket up to the register, completely satisfied with my purchase.

Elka and I strolled around the mall, going in and out of every store, talking as if we'd known each other forever. It was just like we were a couple of old friends. Elka was so easy to talk to, and I admired her honesty and her poise the most. I was fascinated by her graceful step and her gregarious personality. She seemed like a girl who wasn't afraid to be herself.

I learned a lot about her "gift," and I found it engrossing. It was similar to my father's gift, only she could see a full picture; glimpses of life-changing events caused by nature, and the Council relied on her to report these glimpses as it meant a better chance of survival for humanity. A lot of these events needed more than just the usual one-angel-to-one-human setup. It took a whole group sometimes. Nature would always take its course, as the Creator intended it, but as Elka explained to me, nature does not choose sides, so the Council is there to keep that balance in the best way they can.

She told me that fate can change in one second, and even the smallest detail can throw off the future. She often had problems with her gift, in the beginning when she was first created, but was soon able to decipher the importance of the information in her visions. I was shocked to find out that, even though many lives were lost during certain eras, without Elka's help they would have been even more tragic. Hurricanes, earthquakes, floods, fires, volcanic eruptions; these were all things she'd seen over time. And whatever next, big thing was going to hit was going to be near Los Angeles. She wasn't allowed to tell me about the next event in detail because it was, of course, against the rules for her to share outside of the Council. However, she did explain that "details" aren't exactly what she gets all of the time. Sometimes, the glimpses are very vague, and the only hint given to her is the "where" and "when." And occasionally, even part of those details are omitted.

I'd asked Elka why it was only glimpses of natural disasters she could foresee, and why it was not world wars or acts of genocide. She told me she didn't know for sure, but she thought it was because anything like war or mass murder is all done by man, decisions by humans. Guardians are always there to guard their own humans, but that is all that is given. Nature does not know right from wrong like human kind, it only exists. As much as I'd have liked to disagree, I knew she was right. And as much as I wanted to gripe about how unfair that fact was, I knew in my heart that it really wasn't.

"Oh, Evika! Look!" Elka pointed to the costume store. It was one of those Halloween set-ups that only lasted for the month of October and there, in the display window, was a mannequin in a black dress sporting black-feathered angel wings. "You have to get those. You just *have* to," Elka demanded.

I looked at her curiously. "What, the wings?"

"Absolutely!" she exclaimed as she jumped, curls bouncing.

I laughed at her excitement. "For the purpose of....?"

"Are you kidding? Savannah has tons of hot spots for Halloween events and I happen to already know that Hayden plans on taking you to one," she told me.

I smiled at the thought and looked back to the mannequin to observe the wings more closely. They were hanging on the mannequin's shoulders by black ribbon so elegantly. Black feathers layered every inch of them while a strand of fluffy boa material aligned the thick of wings along the top. They weren't even close to replicating the angel wings that I came to know, but I had ideas of my own that started brewing in order to make them even more fabulous. A few of my tweaks, and the wings would be extraordinary. I turned back to Elka, who had been watching me eagerly and biting her bottom lip as she awaited my decision.

"Oh," I said with a shrug, "why not?" No sooner did I give in than I felt Elka's petite hand yank my forearm through the store's entrance.

"I knew you'd comply," she said smugly.

About eleven stores and five shopping bags later, we were hungry. We decided to leave the mall and drive down a ways to the Big Boy we passed. I had to laugh at myself. There I was, walking around with mad cash and able to eat wherever the hell I wanted, and all I could think of was the comfort I'd left in Cleveland. But Elka didn't seem to mind at all. She seemed to have an appetite much like mine, and she certainly found joy in that double cheeseburger. We sighed simultaneously, sank into our booths, and stared out the window.

"Wow, I haven't had one of these in years," Elka said.

"I used to live on this stuff until Joel started becoming all chef-y." I giggled at the memory of Joel using me as his guinea pig for new recipes.

"Ah, yes." She grinned and nodded. "The best friend who adores you to no end." She winked.

I laughed, blushing at her comment, then felt my expression grow serious. "He really got me through a lot a few years ago." I shrugged. "Still does."

Elka studied me for a moment. "I don't know much about him, but Joel is a good person and a good friend to you from what Hayden has always told me." She smiled. "He would dive into on-coming traffic if it meant saving you." She was right. Joel would do anything ridiculous like that if it meant saving my life, which made me remember how fragile a human life can be. One irrational decision, and sometimes, that means the end. I'd already seen it first hand in my own First Death, when I met Hayden.

I half smiled at Elka's comment. Every human had a Guardian angel. Even Joel. "Elka, do you know all of the Guardians and their humans?" I couldn't believe I hadn't asked Hayden the same question before.

"I do." She bobbed her head with a smile, but her expression turned incredulous. "But you're prohibited from knowing who they are due to conflict of interest, *especially* those close to you; Joel's, Ms. Makerov's, even your mo---" she cut herself off. Her lips tightened, and her hard blink was indicative that she'd regretted her words.

I sighed. "Even my mother's," I finished for her.

She looked at me apologetically. "Listen," Elka said solemnly, "I'm an angel, so I can't condone the joy of what I'm about to show you. But," she pulled out a folded up newspaper article and handed it to me, "I do know that this may give you some sort of closure on the matter of your mother."

I looked at her inquisitively, reluctantly taking the folded article from her hand and unfolding it. The headline of the Cleveland Plain Dealer read: WELCOME BACK, CARTER. I read on: *A Cleveland man by the name of Anton Carter hanged himself on Friday evening after his incarceration. Carter was dragged back home after attempting to flee the country to Mexico, less than a day after his last murder in Newark, Ohio. His crimes range from May, 2007, up to his most recent only weeks ago...*

I read the rest of the article as it went on to describe the details of each of the murders and the victims' names. The beat of my heart came to a stop as my eyes scanned over the name: Nora Stormer. The lump in my throat grew bigger, and I felt my eyes filling with tears. The tingling in my nose started, and I looked up at Elka, speechless. Her big, brown eyes gazed into mine.

"They found him," I declared with a whisper.

She nodded slowly, pushing her plate away and folding her hands together on the table. "I thought you should know, even though the police will be contacting you soon."

"Th-thank you, Elka," I choked out. The hurt was brewing in me all over again, an unsettled mass of pain that never went away. I looked down at the article once more, flipping to the next page showing Carter's mug shot. I felt sick to my stomach as I looked at the color photo of my mother's killer; a man in his thirties with a round, shaved head, and dark circles under his dark eyes. That brewing hurt turned to anger, as it always did, and I felt my eyes glaring at his image as my palms clutched to the edges of the paper as if he could feel my wrath. I was glad he was dead. He deserved death. I reveled in the idea that he was going to be with Alysto, tormented in his own hell.

Just then, a distraction lured our heads to turn and look out the window. The rain was pouring down, pelting heavily against the glass. Soon there was commotion within the restaurant, and the double doors swung open as more people flooded in for shelter, some mumbling profanities and others just gazing at the rain as if it were something they'd never seen before. I looked around at the soaked citizens of Savannah, wondering why the rain that fell was regarded as such a bad thing, wondering why people sought cover from it. It was only rain.

My attention reverted to Elka, who sat patiently with her hands still folded, looking at me with a half smile. "Kind of off-season for this, isn't it?" she questioned.

The tubby, gray-haired man in the booth behind her turned and grunted. "Well, it sure as hell ain't supposed to come on like a hurricane," he said in a raspy, smokers voice.

Elka contorted her face for a moment, looking out the window, once again in thought. And I did the same. We watched the rain pour down for a few minutes in complete silence. It seemed as though Elka enjoyed it as much as I did. I found comfort in that.

Finally, the downpour started to settle, and the low mumbles of the people started to quiet as they filed out of the restaurant, carrying on with their interrupted day. Then, as if clarity set upon her, Elka locked her eyes with mine and gave me a stunned expression.

"Holy. Freaking. Appalachians," she finally said. "I can't believe it."

I froze, looking at her worriedly. "Elka, what's wrong?"

"We have to go. Like, now." She grabbed all the bags, then my hand and we went up to pay the bill.

We ran to the car hurriedly, and I questioned her all the way out to the parking lot. "Elka, please. You're scaring me. What's so urgent? What just happened in there?"

She slid into the passenger seat and just smiled at me, which gave me a bit of relief. "Just get us home, girlie. Don't you worry about a thing. Nothing to be scared of. We just need Hayden A.S.A.P. because I think I just figured something out."

There was no time to turn my head at red lights to ask her more questions as I hit every one of them on the green. Although, I wouldn't have gotten in one word anyway. She kept going on and on about how she "knew she was right about this." About what, I still had no clue.

I pulled into the driveway and parked, following Elka into my own house. I had to laugh. It was as if *she* lived there. We walked briskly through the front door; she, with such urgency and determination, and me, with curiosity, just trying to keep up.

Hayden was walking from the living room, turning down the jazz music he'd been listening to. Elka had been right; it was Coltrane playing on those speakers. "In a Sentimental Mood," if I'm not mistaken. I'd recognized it since Joel had played it a few times while he prepped our dinners.

Elka stopped in the foyer, placing her hands on her hips. "Jeez, Hay-bird, since when did you become such a blockhead?"

"Huh?" Hayden spun on his heels to face us.

"Her *gift*!" Elka flailed her hands in the air. "Are you blind?"

"We've already established her gift, Elka. It's better known to Evika as her curse, by the way."

"Ugh!" Elka grunted. "No, no, no," she argued in frustration. "I'm talking about an entirely different thing here. I can't believe you haven't even noticed!" She looked back and forth between the two of us. I just stood there, clueless like Hayden. I looked over at him and shrugged.

She shook her head as if still in disbelief that Hayden wasn't catching on, and looked out the window in deep thought. "Okay. I have an idea," she said to Hayden. "You always seem to be the one to piss her off, so do something that will piss her off," she demanded.

"What the hell do you want me to do?" Hayden was baffled.

"Jeez!" she muttered in frustration. "It figures that you can rile her up any other time, but can't do it on the spot when I really need you to," she said. I laughed at her, and Hayden did the same. Elka pursed her lips. "I guess I'll just have to handle this one myself," she said. The tone in her voice almost indicated her words as a threat. Then she turned to me. "Evika," she said with a sigh, before a long pause, "I'm so sorry. You'll have to forgive me for what I'm about to do, but it's absolutely necessary."

I looked at her curiously and had no time to even formulate a question in my mind before my bottom jaw dropped. Elka wrapped her arms around Hayden's neck and planted her luscious, pink lips on his. *My* angel's lips! Okay, so they weren't really mine for the taking yet, but still, the nerve! I couldn't believe what I was witnessing. I started to think it was a joke until she wouldn't let him go, then proceeded to lace her fingers through his hair and moan quite audibly.

Hayden's body became rigid, as if the realization had finally hit him. His hands rose to Elka's arms to peel her away from his face, but she didn't relent. She squeezed his neck tighter and ignored his obvious discomfort. *Omigod! Omigod! Omigod!* What the hell was wrong with her? Was she out of her God-forsaken mind? What was she trying to prove?

I felt my blood start to boil and my jaw clench, my fists tightening as I dug my nails into my palms. My eyes narrowed at Elka's perfect angel face like a pair of daggers, and my nostrils flared. All in one, abrupt movement, she pulled away from Hayden and turned to look at me. She stood casually, folding her arms while observing my hateful glare.

"Yup," she bobbed her head. "That worked like a charm," she said with a smug look.

Hayden stared straight ahead and out the window with a look of shock. What the hell was wrong with him? Did she mesmerize him so much that he was that awestruck? It figured; I'd finally found the one that I'm in love with, and my place in his life gets trumped by a blond angel bombshell.

"What the hell did you do *that* for?" I squealed at her.

Elka smirked at me, then at Hayden. "*Now* do you see what I'm talking about?" she asked him.

I glared at her with such intensity, but I was filled with curiosity just the same. What *did* she do that for? Was she trying to get me to spill my heart out to Hayden right in front of her so she could stomp on it in victory? Or did she mean to cut me so deeply that I'd just crumble before her eyes? I looked at my angel again, starting to deflate as the shock subsided and as millions of questions continued to brew.

"Evika," Hayden said distantly, still staring out the window. "Look."

I pursed my lips and looked out the window, as I was told. I saw the rain falling hard and plentiful. I heard it hitting the wooden porch heavily, coming down so rapidly, angrily. I couldn't believe I hadn't noticed the rain starting up once again, a force that came on so strongly. Then, the realization hit me like a cold stoned brick.

"Omigod," I whispered in disbelief.

Hayden finally looked at me, still holding his awestruck expression. "Did....you do that?" he asked me.

Elka laughed and shook her head. "Of *course* she did! That's what I'm trying to convey here." Her laugh trilled throughout the foyer again. She stood shoulder to shoulder with Hayden, looking at me proudly. "She's our little rainmaker."

"No." I shook my head in denial. "That's impossible."

"Oh, really?" She raised an eyebrow. "You fell from a nine-story building and died once already, yet you're walking around like a normal human, all in one piece." She started ticking things off on her fingers. "You've met most all types of creatures of the dark realm and you've even gotten attacked by one. You're a millionaire because your father could predict the future, and you've been hanging out with angels for the past month who've even taken you for some flying lessons. You can also see and speak to the dead, and you're standing there, telling me that *this* is impossible?" I nodded, still in disbelief. Elka just giggled and shook her head again. "So stubborn, this one. Just like her father."

My eyes reverted to Hayden as I watched him approach me slowly. It seemed he was in a bit of a state of shock as well. "Evika," he raised his hands to my shoulders cautiously and looked into my eyes intensely. "Do you think you can make it stop? Do you feel as if you can control it, the rain?"

"I.....I don't know. I don't even know how I did it in the first place," I admitted.

"Can you try? Just," he paused for a moment, "clear your mind of everything and concentrate on whatever you are feeling. See if that works."

I looked down. What I was feeling was exhaustion from how angry I'd felt just moments before. I then looked at Elka, who was still smiling proudly at her victory. She laughed as she took in my expression. "Trust me, babe. He is *not* my type," she assured me. "I swear it was only for the purpose of getting you to do what I thought you could do. Cross my heart," she said as she drew an X over her chest. "You can stop hating me now, I promise."

I half-smiled at her, then glanced back at Hayden, who was biting his bottom lip trying desperately not to smile.

"What?" I asked defensively.

"That really bothered you, didn't it?" he whispered to me with a smug look.

"It only shocked me," I lied.

"Yeah, you and me both." His expression turned serious. "Will you please just concentrate? It's still pouring out there. Do you want me to help you calm down by---"

"No!" I cut him off immediately. I knew what he was asking. He was offering to use his gift, to sedate me; the drug in his touch that he'd used on me before. I didn't want that. "I mean, I need to try this on my own," I explained.

Hayden nodded with understanding.

I sighed and kept my eyes on his, getting lost in those deep, emerald pools, thinking about how his lips would feel against mine and wishing that I could have been Elka for just those few seconds of bliss. I understood what she'd done and I trusted that it was only to prove a point, to make me see. I saw much more than what was planned though. I realized the passion I had for Hayden was much stronger than what I already knew I felt for him. I felt a fire within me that would rise to any occasion just to claim him as my own. It made me see that I really had more than just love for him, but a yearning to be only his, and him only for me.

He never took his eyes from mine as his half smile slowly grew into his five-hundred watter. I listened to the sounds around me and heard the rain was already quieter and lighter, coming to a stop. The sun shone through the bay windows, shining its warming rays upon us. The soft skin of my angel's face brightened along with his expression.

"So this is why it rained so much in Cleveland since you've Crossed," he declared with a light laugh.

"A little work, and she can get this down to a science!" Elka said excitedly.

"But I don't even know how I did that," I said, gesturing to the window.

"Well, we sure know what triggers it to start!" Elka guffawed. My face flushed instantly. She flitted over to me and grabbed my hands, lightly bumping Hayden out of the way with her hip. He obliged and moved aside with a laugh under his breath. "Evika, this is fantabulous!" She jumped up and down a few times. "I mean, okay, it completely defies the laws of nature, but still!"

I looked at her inquisitively. I didn't really see the excitement in it at all. "What's so great about making it rain? If this is my gift, then what's the point? What good is this?" Clearly, I wasn't struck with the same thrill that Elka possessed.

"What *good* is it?" she repeated in shock. "Are you kidding me? Rain is an element of nature. And besides, whatever gift is bestowed upon you always has a reas---"

"A reason," I cut her off, nodding and rolling my eyes. "Right. There's always a reason."

"You seem disappointed," Hayden chimed in.

I looked over at him. "Well, it's not like I can see the future or anything cool like that," I answered, recalling my father's gift.

"True," he agreed, "but no other Soldier of Light has ever been granted two gifts, either. That's a huge deal."

Two gifts. I was appalled that Hayden was still even considering my ability to see dead peoples' worst sins as a gift.

Elka sucked air in excitement. "Oh, this is so great!" she squeezed my hands once more before finally letting them go. "Now, we'll just have to practice."

"Practice?" I asked in disgust.

"Of course. I mean, you need to learn how to control this before it gets out of hand," Elka said matter-of-factly. "Who knows the hysteria you may cause in this town if you're making it rain all of the time. These people would think it's the Apocalypse or something. Just imagine some of the nutjobs out there who are already preparing for a dooms-day." Hayden laughed at her. "What, Hay-bird?" She turned and snarled. "You think I'm kidding?"

"No." He shook his head. "I just find this rather entertaining. Usually your incessant bubbliness is infectious to others, but Evika seems to be immune to it at the moment."

I turned to Hayden again. "I'm sorry," I said, "I just don't see the purpose of this. It's like God hates me or something. I see all the crap that put the souls in the dark realm and now I cause it to rain. Yippee," I said sardonically, throwing my hands into the air. "Rain is the thing that keeps kids from going outside to play, the reason people buy umbrellas to shield themselves from getting wet, the reason---"

"The reason the earth is cleansed wherever it falls," Elka interrupted me with a smile.

I glanced at her, opening my mouth and ready to retort something about mud, but I was stunned that she came up with something to say to me that was so simple, yet so profound. And enough to make me shut up. Rain cleansed. It was as simple as that.

"She's right, you know?" Hayden said to me. "And this is so....you. You love rain. You have all of your life," he reminded me.

"Just wait till the Council hears about this!" Elka said excitedly.

I walked over to the bay window and pressed my nose and hands against the glass. My angel was right, I loved the rain. Always have for as long as I can remember. The wooden porch was soaked, along with the grass, the flowers, my Mustang. But as my eyes followed the cemented driveway toward the street, I saw where the line had been drawn, where the rain had stopped. It was about six feet from the street; six feet of dry cement remaining. I started to wonder about the parameters; how far I could make it rain, how long I could make it last, and how hard I could make it fall. Maybe I could find some good in this after all. Just maybe.

Chapter Three *A Little Bit of Past*

"Pink?" I asked Hayden as I walked back into the house after saying goodbye to Elka. He looked up at me with a curious expression. He was sitting at the dining table making out a grocery list. "I mean, *really*, Hayden. How could you possibly forget to tell me angels can have pink wings?"

After the whole rain discovery, Elka had to head back home. But before she left, she dragged me outside, as promised, to show me her wings. It was something of a thing with her to show them to me rather than just tell me. We went to the back yard, as it was a bit more secluded, and she sprung those feathery things out in the open, shocking me out of breath. *Pink!* It was the first thing I saw; a soft, cotton candy pink, almost the same color of her sun dress. All I could do was smile and breathe out a long-winded "*wow.*" She curtsied and giggled, coming up to give me a massive squeeze. "I knew you'd like them." Then she was off, shimmering into the air and disappearing before my eyes.

"Oh," Hayden chuckled, "sorry about that. She's the only one that I know of. That color must have slipped my mind."

"Hmm." I raised an eyebrow and gave him a playful glare. "Elka slipped your mind? How could *that* angel slip your mind?" I sat down next to him.

"It was my subconscious' way of keeping it a surprise, I guess." He laughed. "Don't worry. No more surprise colors."

I looked at him incredulously. I imagined an angel springing tie-dye wings. "Are you sure?"

He looked up, as if in thought, and concentrated for a moment. Then he met my eyes again. "Yup. Covered 'em all." He grinned. "But, isn't the element of suspense so much fun?" he teased, pinching my cheek gingerly.

"A blast," I said sardonically.

I watched him while he continued with the grocery list. I admired that he was taking over the responsibility of so many things, taking care of me. It always seemed that once one person in my life was gone, another would step in and keep my head on straight for me. It was as if that role was always filled, so I never officially had to grow up.

I thought about telling Hayden about the article that Elka gave me. I wondered if he'd known about Anton Carter yet. I wondered if Elka told him she was going to give it to me. And I wondered if he was waiting for me to say something first.

"Are you doing okay?" He must have been looking at me for a while as I was deep in thought, because the pen lay on top of the table, and Hayden's hands were folded in front of him.

I looked at him, wondering why he would ask me that particular question with such attentiveness, until I felt my fists clenching. I loosened them and sighed, pulling out the article from my pocket. "Elka gave me this today." I handed Hayden the article and watched him unfold it.

He looked at me curiously, then back to the paper, changing to a look of concern as he read. Finally, his expression became apologetic as he sank further into his seat. "Evika, I'm so sorry." He shook his head. "I didn't know," he said quietly.

"She didn't tell you first?" My voice sounded so small.

He sighed. "No, she didn't. And to be honest with you, that really pisses me off. I'm sure she meant to tell me first, but with the events that took place when you two returned from the mall, she probably forgot about it completely."

"Oh," was all I muttered as I looked down at the floor.

Hayden folded the article back up, scooted his chair closer to me and placed the paper on the table. "Is this how she figured it out, your ability to make it rain?" he asked as if he already knew the answer.

I looked up at him and nodded slowly, but I felt numb then. I turned my head and concentrated on the emotions, awaiting the ones that took me over in the restaurant when I first saw the article, but they were non-existent in me at that moment. Instead, a fear overtook me as I thought of Anton Carter and his death. A coward. A killer. Another enemy. He was now a Seeker, and it would be my duty to save him once his time had come. If his time came.

"Evika," Hayden's voice pulled me back, "I know what you're thinking, but you don't have to worry about that," he assured me, grabbing my hands.

I studied his eyes for a moment, hoping he would give me a definitive answer if I asked the right question. "How do you know this?"

He paused, looking over at the folded paper, then back into my eyes holding a determined expression. "Because, for the things he did, you will be well into the next life before his time has come. There are way too many ahead of him and there is no way you'd get to him in your lifetime."

I felt prickling in my eyes. "I don't want to see those things, Hayden. I can't live through that day again. Not again," I choked. "I won't save him."

The angel wiped away my tears with his thumbs. "I know," he said softly. "And you won't have to. It won't happen, Evika."

I looked him dead in the eyes. "You promise?" I wanted assurance. I wanted an iron clad oath from him in order to convince me for good.

He returned my gaze and, without hesitation, he replied, "Cross my unbeating heart."

I half smiled at his comment. It was true about his heart. I sighed in relief, relaxing my muscles and letting out a deep breath. "My heart can't deal with any more surprises," I tried to joke. "It's aging me quickly."

Hayden studied me for a moment. "Huh," he said as he leaned closer to me. His eyes focused on the top of my head. "Must be where that gray is coming from," he pointed to my hair.

I glared, playfully, feeling a little more like myself again. "You've become quite the comedian, lately." I shoved him lightly in the arm, making him chuckle.

"Further growth on you, I suppose." He winked at me.

"Well, nonetheless, I had fun with Elka today," I told him. "She's sweet."

Hayden's face grew suddenly serious, and he blew out a long-winded breath. Was it something I said? I could tell something was on his mind as I watched him curiously. "Listen," he started with slight hesitation "about Elka today....."

Hayden apologized for Elka's unexpected boldness and assured me that he had no idea she was going to kiss him like a crazed maniac, but the conversation only made me blush. It was funny that he thought that he had to explain himself to me as if he'd done something wrong, but I guess he was starting to get the subtle signs regarding how I felt about him. On second thought, the hard rain that came down while

Elka planted her lips on his wasn't exactly subtle in the least bit. As I thought about the severity of the precipitation I'd brought on, I *really* went red in the face. He had to have known my embarrassment.

"You don't have to apologize for what happened, Hayden. It was weird for Elka to kiss you like that, but, like she said, she was aiming to prove a point." And I was completely convinced that, by the time she'd left, that was all it was, a point she needed to make.

He smiled and nodded, then looked at me admiringly. "You know, I know that you're not really that gung-ho on the whole idea, but this new gift of yours is pretty fascinating."

I shrugged. "I guess it's better than the first one I acquired." I tried not to say it too scathingly as I thought of it as my curse.

"So, where are all the bags from your fun day of shopping with Pinky?" he asked. "Or did those get all ruined from the rainstorm?" He chuckled.

I rolled my eyes at him. "They're still in the pony."

He nodded. "*And?*" he asked with a raise of his eyebrow.

A smug grin started growing on my face as I realized what he was getting at. "Hayden Crow," I said facetiously, "are you implying that you'd like to see the new leather I bought for you today?"

He leaned toward me and grinned. "Am I that obvious?"

I sighed dramatically. "Isn't the element of suspense so much fun?" I mimicked his earlier comment..

He laughed. "Okay, *Rainmaker*, I get it. But it won't stop me from going out to that Mustang to get those bags."

We both sat there silently while studying each other for a few seconds. Smirks slowly grew on our faces. I had a feeling that Hayden would spring at any moment to run out to that car and get into those bags. Then, simultaneously, we both darted out of our chairs, running out of the kitchen and into the hallway where Hayden grabbed my waist and slid me to the side gently, just to jet past me like a bullet. At first, I didn't care about letting him win, but then I thought about those angel wings I'd consented to buy and I wanted those to remain a surprise.

"No! Wait!" I yelled at him as I caught up and leapt onto his back. I threw my legs around his waist, one arm around his neck, and my remaining hand across his eyes to block his vision. It was an instinctive move. "You cannot get into those bags yet, Hayden!" I squealed and giggled simultaneously.

He bellowed a laugh. "*Ooooohhh,* are we hiding something?" In one, quick movement, Hayden pulled me off of his back and placed me in front of him, my back against his body as he held my arms crossed over my chest. I looked down at his arms as they embraced me. *Oh, dear God, I could let him do this forever.* "You're hiding something, aren't you?" he said playfully into my ear, his breath tingling the side of my neck.

"Yes!" I confessed. "Now, stop right *here*!" I planted my heels into the hardwood floor, pressing my body against him to get him to stop scooting us toward the front door. I panted, trying to catch my breath. "I'll go get your new, *bad ass* jacket." I tried to recoup myself. "Hold your wings."

"Hmm," Hayden loosened his grip. "Now, that's more like it."

"You're merciless." I shook my head, grabbing my keys from the coffee table.

He flashed his five-hundred watter at me, making me melt. "And you love it." Ugh. Of course I did.

"You're obnoxious, too," I added as I walked past him, poking him in the gut with my key.

"And yet, you're still going to bring me my present," he pointed out with a smug smile.

"Gotta pick my battles with you, Darkwing," I snickered as I walked out the door and to my ride.

I opened the trunk, and grabbed all of the various bags, making sure I kept the Halloween bag hidden between the others. It was bright orange and so obvious, but I really did want to keep the wings a surprise, especially after the ideas I had running through my head for the costume I would wear. It made me giddy to think that Hayden already had a little "plan" for us to go do something for Halloween together, whatever it was.

I shook off my daze, shut the trunk and turned to head back inside when I instantly jumped at the sight of a little body standing not three feet from me. My heart jolted as I squealed at the boy. He stood there with a radiant smile on his pale, round face, his hazel eyes staring into mine. His dirty-blond hair was disheveled in various, spiked points.

"Hello," he said with a smile as he adjusted the over-packed book bag hanging over his shoulders. "I'm sorry. I didn't mean to scare you." He held out his hand to me. "I'm Elliott."

My eyes widened. "*You're* Elliott?" I felt guilty for thinking he was at my house to sell candy bars or something. "Uh. It's nice to meet you, Elliott." I shook his hand and tried to play down my shock.

"Sorry that I'm early, Miss Evika," his young voice said apologetically. "I was eager to meet you."

Miss Evika? I laughed nervously. "Really, it's okay. You wouldn't be the first today. I'm getting used to the new company." I assured him.

He smiled. "Well, it's great to finally meet you. I trust that Mister Hayden has advised you that we are designing your castors today?"

I nodded slowly, still intrigued by the little angel. "Yeah, he's inside. I was just...." I trailed off as I looked down to try to remember what I'd been doing, "grabbing my bags. Elka took me out for a while this morning."

He chuckled. "Ah, yes. Miss Elka said she would be visiting. She made quite a discovery today, from what I overheard."

"Hmm." I half smiled. "News travels fast with you guys, huh?"

"Yes." He laughed. "In *our* world, it does."

We were quiet for a few seconds. I still couldn't elude my bafflement over the little angel. I finally shook it off. "Well, come on inside, Elliott." I gestured to the cement walkway that led to the front door.

"Here," he held out his arms and grabbed all of the bags effortlessly. "I'll get these for you."

"Oh, no," I contested. "You really don't ha---"

"I insist," he said, effortlessly carrying all five bags along with his own as if they consisted of nothing but air.

As we made it up to the porch, I let the mini angel go first. I looked up to see Hayden swinging open the door.

"Elliott," Hayden greeted him with a wide grin, "welcome to the new casa."

"Good afternoon, Mister Hayden. I was hoping I wouldn't be a nuisance coming this early." Elliott stepped inside, walking past Hayden to set everything down in the foyer.

"Nonsense," Hayden assured him. "We got hit early today. The pink one just left." They both laughed as if it were some long-running joke between them. "You can set up right over there if you'd like. I'm assuming that coffee table will be sufficient?"

Elliott turned to observe the living room furniture. "Sure is," he bobbed his head, grabbing his bag and heading into the room.

I stepped through the door and gave Hayden a scrutinizing stare. "*That's* the angel techie?" I whispered, pointing to the little boy in my living room. "Would it have killed you to warn me that he was, oh, I don't know....*a ten-year-old kid?*" I said quietly through my teeth.

"He's not ten," Hayden whispered back. "He's a hundred and forty-two years old."

I rolled my eyes. "Whatever." I grabbed all the bags to get them up to my bedroom. "Your new leather is so off limits until further notice."

He chuckled. "You know, one of these days, a little surprise of mine is going to make you undeniably happy. I just know it."

I shook my head, unable to keep from grinning as I headed up the stairs with the bags. "You are impossible."

"That may be true, but I'm still getting my new leather before the day is over," he called to me up the stairwell.

My body shook with laughter. "We'll see."

When I came back downstairs, I went straight to the living room. The angel techie had blue sketches, paper, pens, rulers, colored pencils; his book bag was like a Mary Poppins' purse. It made me laugh down to the moment I saw the old diagram of the castors that belonged to Jack. I pulled them out from under the pencils.

"These were my father's?" I asked, staring at the sketches.

Elliott nodded. "You recognize them?"

I looked into his hazel eyes. "I've used one already."

"Oh," his face grew solemn with regret. "Yes. I forgot that you've already conducted your first save." He paused for a moment. "Miss Evika, I'm truly sorry for the burden that has been bestowed upon you. I'm sure that my visit here today only solidifies the destiny that awaits you." He sighed with a look of guilt. "I'm probably the last angel you wanted to meet."

My heart sank for him. I could see that he honestly felt horrible. "Elliott, that's ridiculous," I retorted. "It's your job to get this done. I may not be happy about continuing down this road or my new role, but I would never fault you for it."

He gave me an innocent smile. "We are all here to help you," he said. "Every one of us, we'll always be by your side. And I'm always here for you, with whatever you need from me."

I smiled at him, finally getting used to the overly-wise, adult-talking ten-year-old on the couch next to me. "I'll need every one of you, Elliott." His face beamed. "I don't know when, or for what, but I know I will."

Elliott and I worked on the designs for about a half hour; everything from the size and shape down to the indentation of the keypad, bulbs and inhaling mechanism. He drew the outlines first so I could get a better feel for my ideas to make them more unique, and then it hit me.

"Hey, Elliott?" I asked. "Are you able to make them any other color besides that silver my dad had?"

He cocked his head and looked up in thought for a moment. "Hmm. It would take a few trials and errors to get the vapor metal to agree with the substance that made the colors, but I'm pretty sure I could do it. What did you have in mind?"

And that was when I chose four colors. I actually had a good time watching someone else with a knack for drawing. Elliott was quite the artist as he drew out my ideas, even coloring them in with the hues I'd chosen; black, silver, red and orange were the colors I wanted as I thought of the dragons on the hoodie that Luka bought me. It was a fun salute to him, just to let him know how much he meant to me. It also meant a lot to me as well, that design. The dragons were symbolic to me, the way they were unified, but also played against each other. The way I felt inside, a battle of confusion.

"These are definitely going to be more creative than your father's." Elliott chuckled.

I smiled with a shrug. "Gotta make my mark somewhere, I guess."

He briefly looked up at me in thought. "Speaking of marks," he looked down at my right wrist and pointed, "I see that you have the same birthmark as Jack had."

"Oh," I looked down at the negative zero, rubbing over it with my fingers, "yeah, his was on his other wrist though, from what I remember, anyway....which isn't much."

He nodded, admiring the mark. "Did Luka give you the necklace I made?" he asked me with a proud look.

"He sure did." I pulled it out from under my t-shirt. "I wear it every day. Thank you."

He grinned as he finished up with the last part of the sketch on which he was working. "Do you know what that symbol means?"

I shook my head, looking at him curiously. I had a feeling I wouldn't have to wait long to find out the answer.

"Well," he started, "while the zero representations behave as equal under numeric comparisons, they are different bit patterns and yield different results in some operations, like software developing, for example. But, in mathematics, signed zero is still zero; negative or positive."

I gave him a blank stare. "Uhhhh," I muttered.

Elliott giggled. "I'm sorry. I can get a little carried away with numbers and such." He sighed. "Basically, the negative zero isn't really *negative* at all if it doesn't want to be. It can represent a positive as well. Zero is zero. It's a filler for whatever it wants to represent. The answer is always the same."

"Oh." I smiled, somewhat understanding his point. "So I'm not marked by the devil or anything creepy like that, right?" I asked jokingly with a nervous laugh.

Elliott chuckled innocently. "Not if you don't want to be, Miss Evika." He shrugged with a smile. "It's just a birthmark."

"Well," I gestured to the sketches he held, "I hope I haven't made these too complicated for you."

"Absolutely not," he said. "Your wish is my command, you know, as far as angel-techie stuff goes?" he nudged me. I felt my face turn beat red, making Elliott bounce with his childlike laughter. "It's okay. I'll take that over the other stuff they call me. And I've been called worse. Your father used to call me 'Runt.'" I tried to contain my amusement.

And that was that. The little angel drew up the finals and I approved without hesitation. I invited him to stay for dinner since we were ordering pizza, but Elliott said he had to get back to the House of Council to get started.

Hayden came into the living room to observe the work that was done while the techie packed up his things. He grinned. "I should have known you were going to put your own spin on these castors," he said to me.

"As if that surprises you," I replied.

"Looks like you've got your work cut out for you this time, little man," Hayden patted Elliott on his shoulder.

Elliott laughed and turned to me with a thumb pointing to

Hayden. "See what I mean?"

I giggled, watching him place the last of his belongings into his book bag. The thought occurred to me of the one thing I forgot to ask him. "Hey, Elliott?"

He looked up. "Yeah?"

"Your wings, what color are they?"

"Oh." He simpered. "Well, if you've seen Mister Hayden's wings, then you've already seen mine." He bounced his shoulders playfully.

I smiled. "Yours are black, too?"

"Yup," he bobbed his head and slung his over-packed book bag onto his shoulders. "See you guys soon." And then he was out of sight, right from his stance in the living room. I smiled as I kept staring at the place he had once been standing, still amazed with the means of travel for angels.

"Earth to the rainmaker," Hayden said through his fists like a megaphone.

"Huh?" I turned to him. "Sorry, what did you say?"

"Just wondered if you want your usual on the pizza."

"Oh?" I turned to him and smirked. "And what is my usual, Angel-man?"

His brow cocked. "Are you testing me?"

"Would seem that way." I poked with a laugh. He gave me his best you-have-got-to-be-kidding-me look. I really don't know what I was thinking. I knew he knew.

"So, here's the deal," Hayden started, "I'll order the pizza...with pepperoni and mushrooms, while you go and grab that leather for me that you have hidden amongst your bags of secrets."

"Are you sure we won't have any more interruptions today?" I was doubtful.

"Other than Luka coming back over this evening, we are free and clear of any more angel visits. Although, I can't speak for the potentially nosy neighbors. They may drop by with welcoming Jell-o salads for all we know." He laughed.

"Speaking of food, when are we going grocery shopping?"

He smirked at me. "I was thinking *I* could do the shopping in the morning. Luka can stay here to look after you. But...." here it came, "I'll need the keys to the pony."

I folded my arms and cocked an eyebrow. "I don't know, Darkwing. Are you sure you're ready for Aurora?"

Hayden looked at me incredulously. "Aurora? Oh, please don't tell me you've fallen into the world of the people who name their cars."

"No, Hayden. I fell off of a nine-story building straight into the world amongst the living and the dead. Hardee-har-har. But, yes, I did name the car Aurora." I grinned at him. "Get it? A-*roar*-a?" I couldn't contain my laughter. "She's got a mean engine."

He shook his head at me, but finally gave in and joined in with my laughter. "You've completely lost it, haven't you?"

I stuck out my tongue and headed upstairs. "Hey, naming my car is just about the most normal thing about me anymore. And anyway, you better watch it, or I'll make it rain on you," I called down the stairwell. But after saying that last part aloud, I wasn't so sure how funny it really was. It was more of a disturbing fact, that I could actually make it rain.

Hayden absolutely loved his new leather, and my heart swelled when I saw the huge smile on his face once he put it on. You would have thought he'd never been given a gift in his entire life. But, on second thought, I guess that didn't seem so unrealistic since he'd never had a childhood, or actual parents or family other than the Council. He checked himself out in the hallway mirror, admiring that jacket. I'd actually gotten him something that suited him perfectly. Once I saw Hayden give me that five-hundred watter and rip those tags off, it was one more thing that added to the list my heart was making; the list of reasons why I was falling in love with him. And when he said, "you did good, Pony-girl. It's perfect," I melted into a puddle of giddy moosh.

Dusk was finally approaching by the time our pizza came. I brought up my shock over Elka's pink wings again because, of course, I still couldn't get over the fact that it was even a possibility. But even though black was still the most shocking color I'd seen thus far, I was still holding on to meeting a gray-winged angel.

Just about the time we were finished eating, Hayden's head perked up as if he sensed something. A mild grin grew on his face.

"What?" I inquired.

"Luka's here with your present." That grin grew wider.

"You must know what it is, I'm assuming?" I pried.

"You assume right, Pony-girl." He grabbed my hand. "Come

on. We need to go outside."

We walked out to the front of the house. The sky was coated with the most amazing oranges and yellows along the tree line and above. I noticed the grass was still a bit damp from my rainstorm; I rolled my eyes at what a pain the new gift was going to be until I learned to control it. Then I saw Luka approaching and all I could do was smile. He was, yet again, appearing out of nowhere and sporting another new t-shirt; light gray with black print: "After I saw the seven wonders of the world, I started looking for the eighth. I stopped looking when I found a mirror."

"Charming," Hayden muttered.

I just laughed. Luka was obviously embracing his trial time with no human to guard. "Lukster, you're back!" I exclaimed.

"Yeah, the little man came back to the H.O.C. A few hours ago, so I figured you were done with dinner and ready for my visit," Luka said.

Little man, I thought. "Jeez, between the two of you, that kid probably has a complex," I said.

"He's a hundred and forty-two years old," Luka said defensively.

"So I've heard," I shook my head and smirked. "So, why are we outside, anyway?"

A grin grew on Luka's face when I asked the question. He looked at Hayden, who mirrored the same expression.

"Well," Luka started, "remember when I said I had a housewarming gift for you?"

"Yeeaaaahhh." My curiosity grew.

"It's more like a life-warming gift, per se," Luka explained.

"Life-warming?" I was baffled.

"He worked really hard to get this done for you," Hayden stole my attention. "And kinda had to break some rules."

I sucked air and my head jerked to Luka. "You broke rules?"

"Hey," Luka put his hands up and pointed to Hayden, "he is just as much a culprit as I am, I swear."

"Right," I played along. "Is that a pig flying up there above your head? Oh yeah, I think it is." Luka laughed at me. Rules are rules, according to Hayden, and he followed them to a "T."

Hayden folded his arms and gave me a smug look. "Okay, Luka, I think we better show her now. Her doubt in this is rather hurtful," he said tauntingly.

I sighed, awaiting what those boys had planned for me. I watched Luka put his fingers to his mouth and whistle one of those cool, loud ones that I could never, ever do. I saw that his eyes focused on the side of the house, so I turned to see what was coming. I heard the familiar bark of a dog and discovered the animal from which it came. A collie-shepherd mix dog stopped and wagged its tail, not even ten feet from me, cocking its head with ears perked. That was when my knees slammed hard to the ground. I felt my jaw drop, and I tried to focus better. It just couldn't be.

"Is th-th-that....?" I wasn't sure how to ask what I wanted to know.

"Beau! Come here, boy," Luka called to the dog, hunched over, clapping his knees. The dog trotted over to him, happily jumping up onto him and wagging that fan of a tail, being the same playful canine I always remembered.

I gasped as I observed the dog's every detail. Everything was identical. *Everything.* How could it be? There was just no way it was possible. No way. It wasn't him. It wasn't the same dog. It just couldn't be.

I hadn't noticed Hayden walk over, but he was right next to me, kneeling just as I was in that damp grass. "The nature harmon is a very powerful angel, Evika," he said to me. I kept staring at the dog, who was now rolling around on his back, panting, as Luka scratched his hairy belly.

I could hardly find my voice. "Is it really him?" I asked in disbelief.

"Bona fide and certified, down to the last collie-shepherd hair on his tail," Luka answered me. He got the dog to stand on all fours and tapped his behind. "Beau, go see Evika. Go on," he waved the dog my way.

With those ears perked up, dark brown eyes wide open, tail wagging, my dog darted over to greet me with one-hundred licks of his tongue. He kissed my face as if I'd just come home from school, just like he used to do. I smelled him, inhaling and exhaling slowly. It was that doggie-shampoo smell – like the one they smell like after a day at the pet-spa – mixed with the scent of rain. And that was when I broke down.

I threw my arms around him and squeezed his thick, hairy

neck. My tears fell hard when I realized he was actually there. It was unfathomable. I was touching him again. I could feel him, smell him, nuzzle my face into his soft, brown and golden hair. He was my dog, my Beau.

"How can this be? How is this even possible?" I cried as a list of questions kept recoiling through my mind and shooting from my lips. I didn't even know which ones to ask first.

Luka smiled proudly at me and Beau. "Let's just say this is a one-time deal and I probably couldn't get away with it again." He laughed.

I looked over my dog in amazement, feeling the shape of his body while he sat patiently, letting me poke and prod. I gazed into his big, brown eyes as he panted. "It's really you, isn't it, boy?" I whispered to him. He brought his nose to my face and started sniffing, then dove down into my lap playfully, nibbling at my hands to get me to move them. Then he lifted his head to get me to notice something. I finally saw it dangling around his neck. It was a dark blue collar with a silver dog bone tag catching the light of the porch. My hands raised to the tag. It had Beau's name engraved on it, with our new home address underneath.

"Omigod," I choked out, looking up at Luka in amazement.

Luka shrugged. "It's only to make it official, really. You won't need it for him. He'll never run off," he said.

"I don't get it, Luka," I said. "How did you do it?"

"Evigreen, every animal is part of nature. Their souls belong to the World of Light. Always. They don't have a choice like we do. They just *are*. There is no dark realm for them. They are innocents, pure spirits produced by the Creator, Himself," Luka explained. "Beau is not exactly...." he paused briefly to decipher his next word, "*alive*. I've just relocated him, pulled him out of the other world and put him in ours."

"You mean, he's like a ghost-dog now?" I inquired as I watched Beau skip over to Hayden. He covered every inch of Hayden's face with licks of his tongue. I smiled and cried at the same time when I saw Hayden let him continue, rustling my dog's hair and squeezing his face, talking to him in that silly voice people use when they tell an animal how cute they are. It made me melt all over again.

"Well," Luka thought for a moment, "yeah. When he's here with you, he'll be a constant, like Hayden. Constant, as in, everyone can see him, but I'm sort of his Guardian-slash-caretaker-slash-trainer now," Luka explained, "so as long as he's with me, he can go where I go. I've sort of been working with him, training him on the ins and outs of this lifestyle. He's the same Beau, just new and improved." Luka laughed.

I stood slowly to my feet, looking at Luka admiringly. "Luka, you didn't have to do this for me."

He took a deep breath. "Evika," he said, tucking his hands into his jeans' front pockets and walking over to me, "ever since this whole new life started, I know that you've been losing a lot of the past that you'd like to keep." He shrugged. "This was the one thing I could do to bring some of it back for you."

I saw that seriousness in those sky blue eyes again, the same kind I saw in them when we'd gone out the last time, the same kind I saw in them when he stood guard during my first save. I stepped forward and wound my arms around his neck, letting his new shirt catch my tears of joy.

"Thank you, Luka," I choked out.

Chapter Four *Line 'Em Up. Knock 'Em Down*

The dreams came, the bad ones, the kind that only the most creative mind could conjure. Or, maybe I mean the kind that only my mind could conjure. The kind from which you wake up in a cold sweat in the middle of the night, clutching your chest to get your heart to stop trying to break through your sternum. Then you gather up the sheets and blankets on the bed, holding them close as you assess your room to convince yourself that it was, in fact, only a dream. I knew those kinds of dreams all too well and the fact that the reality from which they originated was enough while I was awake, it was really killing me to have to go to sleep and see the same things, the replay of all of the messes I had to see after saving the Seekers.

One of the worst dreams I had was of the last Seeker I saved for the week, Edgar Peyton. He'd raped, kidnapped and killed seventeen women. And the murders were brutal. At first, his technique was just breaking their necks or drugging them, then weighing them down to let the corpses sink to the bottom of some random lake. But later, he became more creative in taking their lives. He'd choke them with fishing line, gag them, bind them, and drown them in his laundry tub. And things got messy after a while. He started to become careless and reckless. He buried one of them alive before the drugs wore off. He even went as far as skinning one of the girls' legs and letting her bleed to death in his basement. It was the most horrifying thing I'd ever seen. What do you do when you can't shut your eyes to stop from seeing the images? But, even then, how do you train your mind never to see the images again? How is it possible to rid these things from your mind once they've been etched in there indefinitely?

The worst part about all of it: he died of a heart attack in his prison cell two days before his death sentence. It was an easy death for me, fortunately, but his infamous legacy was something I could never forget.

The most horrifying dream I had was of Edgar chasing me down. It was late at night while I ran through the woods and, after a short effort of pursuit, he finally caught up with me and attempted every one of his tactics. But the worst thing was, I wouldn't die. He was getting frustrated with me, consistently beating me across the head with anything he could find on the ground. During this entire time of torture, I couldn't speak. I couldn't even move. I just kept heaving breaths, trying to scream, terrified out of my mind.

Soon, Edgar vanished, but I was still incapacitated on the ground, in a pile of mud and soggy leaves. I looked at my surroundings, all the same, but the sun was rising. It was no longer night. The ball of fire rose above the horizon and turned completely white. The light illuminated the forest and should have been blinding to the naked eye, but I stared at it, unscathed. As I kept my eye on this strange ball of light, a figure started to form, one that I'd already seen once before. The dark form approached me slowly, spreading its wings and cocking its head. It was close enough that I could see its arms stretched out to me, its yellow eyes looking into mine so desperately. Up until then, I thought it was a Drone, but after seeing its gray face and eyes turning black, I knew it was the Watcher I'd met.

I lay there, paralyzed, as he reached out to me, the endless, white light still blazing behind him. What did it mean? Why was it coming from a source of light? It was supposed to be a dark creature. I became confused and anxious when its claws finally reached near my face. Then, his eyes were completely black.

"Tenebrae," its voice hissed out. It was clearer than the first time it spoke to me in the streets the night Hayden was fighting the Drone.

All I could do was wonder where my angel was, like I did in every one of the nightmares that became my world after dark. Where was he? I'd ached for him whenever he was gone, and this dream was no different. Except, this time, the moment I wondered so desperately where Hayden was, he appeared behind the Watcher, beautiful black wings spread as he stood seething with wrath. He wrapped his arms around the creature and squeezed tightly, screaming with such rage, power. His booming vocals echoed through the trees and made the ground rumble. The Watcher burst into a massive cloud of smoke and dust, the delicate remains falling to the ground at Hayden's feet. The enemy was gone, and so was the blinding light. It was dark once again.

My angel's breathing was heavy as he placed his arms back to his sides and slowly looked over at me with an expression of hurt and anger. I stared back into his eyes, feeling safe again, waiting for him to come lift me into his arms and carry me home. But he didn't. He disappeared into thin air and left me there, wounded and lying on the ground.

That was when I awoke, panting and immediately feeling around my face, my chest, anything, checking for the damages that felt so real. I panned my eyes around the dark room, and sat up, finally realizing it was all another nightmare. I felt around in the drawer of my nightstand for the pack of Marlboro Lights I'd purchased at the beginning of the week. There were only a few left. Yes, the dreams came, and the habit was back. Smoking was a vice that helped me through the rationalizing phase that I had to do after each nightmare.

I popped a cigarette in my mouth and lit the end. The smell of the sulfur from the lit match was soothing. I took a drag and inhaled deeply, blowing the smoke out slowly as I looked around the room once again, my eyes finally adjusting to the darkness.

It was a good ten seconds before I saw him sitting at the edge of the bed, his back to me, head down. There was no time to put out the cigarette then. What was the point? I'd been caught red-handed. I tried to compose myself as I leaned over to see his face, his sullen eyes gazing at the floor.

"Why haven't you told me?" he asked in a soft, disappointed tone.

I was confused. He could have meant anything. "Told you what?" I said nonchalantly as I took one last drag and regretfully tossed the cigarette in the cup of water next to the lamp. "So, I started smoking again. Big deal. At least it's not Yager, right?"

He turned and looked at me with such scrutiny, but the sadness behind his eyes was even more prominent. "These dreams, Evika," he said, frustrated. "I've been entering into them for days now and, every night, you've been enduring these nightmares. Why wouldn't you tell me about these dreams?"

I narrowed my eyes, realizing that the last part of my dream *was* really him saving me from the dangerous figments I'd created just before I woke. I lay back down and rolled away from him, angry that he'd done it, meddled in my head. But honestly, I'd been warned. I knew he was capable of it and I should have known better. Nonetheless, I felt stripped of all of my privacy, weak and tired from the loss of sleep. I was straight up miserable.

Beau rose to all fours and brought his head to the edge of the bed by my hand. He looked at me with those big, round eyes with concern as I stroked the fur on his head and became relaxed, thinking about how lucky I was to have him back, how lucky I was to have a lot of things. "Because I know you'll call yet another, angel to come to my rescue, Hayden. You've all done enough favors for me to last a lifetime," I said. "I don't want any more favors from angels."

I heard him sigh. "So, that's what this is about? Your damn pride?"

I knew it wasn't going to be easy getting out of this. "I just don't want any more favors," I mumbled.

"They aren't favors, Evika," he argued. "They are talents, gifts that the angels have been granted that are meant to benefit you. They *will* be utilized. Keeping you safe and happy is a huge priority for all of us. Don't you get that?"

I lay silent, petting my dog, afraid to turn and look at my angel. I was so afraid anymore, afraid of the madness that started to consume my mind. My head was a melee. Crazy; that was where I was going. That dismal feeling started to override me again as soon as Elliott delivered those castors to the house only one week prior. I'd wondered how many times I'd have to send them out before those Seekers would just stop coming. Of course, I knew the answer; it was endless. My job would never end until my life did. I knew it in my heart, but part of me held onto that thread of hope that maybe inundating myself with the job would make me numb. Maybe I'd get used to it. Maybe.

I recalled the moment when Elliott left the house after dropping off the castors, and Hayden and I stood in the kitchen, staring at the delivery.

*   *   *   *

"He did an excellent job," Hayden said from behind me as he observed the opened boxes.

I nodded slowly in agreement as I stared at them. Orange, red, black and silver; they were all there. Despite the beauty of them, I saw the castors as the tools of my own destruction. It hurt me inside to feel that way and I didn't want to let it on, but I'm sure my thoughts on the matter were quite apparent. Finally, I started to pull each of the four castors from the box to set them out on the table.

"What are you doing?" he asked me.

"Setting them up," I said mechanically.

"Now?" Hayden sounded shocked.

I sighed heavily as I took the red and black castors in each hand. "Why hold off the inevitable, Hayden?" I could hear defeat in my own voice.

His eyes narrowed and he snatched the metal orbs from my hands, placing them back into the boxes. "You don't have to do this right now just because they're here," he said sternly. "We can wait until tomorrow."

"For what, Hayden? Huh?" I snapped. "To put this off even longer? You can't protect me from this." I could see the shock in his expression. "Whether I do it now, later, tomorrow, next week, next month, it's what I'm *supposed* to do. This is my life now, right?" My words came out more spiteful than I'd intended. "What are you trying to hold this off for?"

"Because of *you*, Evika! You're pissed...and closed off. I know how you get. This is one of your meltdowns, and I'm not letting you do this right now."

"No," I argued, pulling the red and black castors back out of the box, "what I'm doing is getting this started now. I'm not going to be any less pissed or closed off tomorrow, Hayden. So, let's just get this going."

He looked at me in disbelief, shaking his head and gaping, as if not sure of what he wanted to say to me. "What has gotten into you?" His quiet voice and concerned expression made me uneasy. He looked at me like I was so foreign to him.

I sat down in the chair closest to the window and looked out blankly. "Acceptance," I simply said. "That should make you happy. In fact, it should make all of you happy."

I heard the sound of a chair slowly gliding across the kitchen tile. Hayden slid it next to me and sat down cautiously. I could feel him looking at me, studying me. His momentary silence was indicative of his reluctance to comment. I could see his head turn toward the window in my peripheral. A slight drizzle of rain pattered on the window sill. I wondered if it was my doing or just nature.

"You know," he said quietly, "we haven't even talked about that first Seeker since before we moved here."

I shook my head. "I just want to forget about it."

"Forget about it," he repeated with a nod. "Will that make it go away?" Hayden asked condescendingly.

I shot him a piercing glare. "I don't know, Hayden, but

reminding me of it sure doesn't help."

He sighed, folding his arms and leaning back in the chair as he observed me minutely. "I saw and heard how much anger you had in you, Evika. Hell, I could almost feel it. I'm not sure what's been going on, but I need to be certain that you communicate with me on the things about which I don't know are happening."

"Like what?" I asked exasperatedly. *Ugh.* Why was I acting like this?

"In your head, Evika" He freed his hands and started ticking things off on his fingers. "Like your feelings, your fears, your confusions, your---"

"Jeez! What, are you my therapist now?"

Hayden ran his fingers through his hair and took a deep breath, exhaling it slowly, steadily. He was doing that thing again, biting his tongue, something I should have learned to do by that point in time. "Evika," his tone was stern, "don't close me off. I just want to be sure that you talk to me. That's all." He leaned forward in his seat, lifting my chin so our eyes would meet. I was taken aback when he looked down at my hands and brought his to mine, intertwining our fingers. Then his eyes looked pleadingly into mine, almost desperate. "Can you do that for me?"

How could I deny him what he was asking of me? How could I not tell him that the one thing I feared the most anymore...was myself? How could I keep anything from him, other than my true feelings for him while they could be tamed? I felt certainty, hopelessness and confusion all at once. How was that even possible?

Absolute Zero

Can you do that for me? His question played over and over in my head as we stared at each other. I finally looked away from his eyes and down at our hands. Mine were so small inside of his, but they looked protected, safe.

"Okay," I said quietly. Did I really mean it? No. Did I *want* to mean it? Yes. But Hayden had already seen how I could lose control. He'd known I'd physically tried to hurt the first Seeker before I saved her. It was almost embarrassing to me. What were the next Seekers going to be like? Would I have the self-control? I'd hoped to God.

"I know this is going to be much harder for you than it ever was for any of the previous Soldiers of Light," he said, "but I will do everything I can to get you through this. I promise."

I kept my gaze on our hands. Maybe that was all I needed, to think about him while I was in the middle of a "save." It worked the first time; knowing that I'd be back in his arms again got me through the event.

I sighed. "Hayden," I finally looked up at him again, trying to show him my determination. "I really need to do this now while I have the guts to do it."

He looked back at me wearily, but finally relented. Soon after that was when I started to lose my mind. After setting up four of the castors and sending them out, it took less than five minutes for all of them to be inhabited by new Seekers. I conducted saves for three men and one woman, all of which had murdered innocent people. I remember the silver castor the most. It was Roger Stoneman, who had apparently not meant to hurt anyone in the process of his robbing a

67

low-security bank, but inevitably did. It was unavoidable. He'd trapped nine civilians, wired them all up with TNT and threatened to blow the entire building up along with himself. Roger came outside with one of the hostages, but was gunned down shortly after he released the woman. Little did the cops realize, the detonator was in the criminal's hand, and the civilians and the building were blown to pieces in a matter of seconds.

I was not fond of the gunshots. The sounds of the shots ripped through my ears. *Crack!* It was a familiar sound, one that was not easily forgotten, and I was immediately reminded of my mother's death. All of these factors put me into a worse state of mind, reminding me of the past.

I felt the pressure of the bullets as they hit my body, going through and out the other side. The death was instant after the last one hit me in the head. That white light came, and then I was back in Hayden's arms.

I assessed myself, physically and mentally, to determine if I was okay, and then pushed myself to go in again. I was breathing hard and didn't want to give time to let the shock move in. I wanted to open the next castor – red – before Hayden had the chance to tell me not to. This was how the first four went; I was lining them up and knocking them down, so to speak. It was the only thing I could think of that would get me numb to the whole process. I tried to just do it and not think about it. It was the only way it was going to work. No one could block these images from me. My "gift" would succeed no matter what Hayden did to change anything. I would always see the terrible things the Seekers had done when they were alive.

"Again," I stated to Hayden, grabbing two more castors off of the bed and starting to reset them.

He narrowed his eyes at me. "No. Way," he said sternly. "You've had enough."

"That was only four," I argued. "We're doing more."

"No," he said sharply, "we're not." He took the orbs off of the bed and placed them in his duffel bag; I hadn't realized he brought it into the bedroom with us.

"You're making this worse for me." I spoke through my teeth as I felt my anger rising. "I need to do this now."

"Evika, I don't get it. Why are you trying to push yourself?"

"Because it's the only way this will work, Hayden. I just want to get them out of the way," I said as I hastily grabbed the bag from him and threw it on the bed.

"You will never get them out of the way, Evika," he assured me. "There will always be more and more. Every, single day. Always! This will *never* end!" He raised his voice to me, but I could see that he had a look of worry hidden behind his angry eyes.

"Don't you think I know that already?" I snapped. My eyes started to sting. God! Of course, I knew it would never end. I did. I was past that. A surge of guilt ran through me after barking at Hayden so harshly. I made effort to soften my tone. "I know this, Hayden." I sighed. "But I need to get used to this. Maybe if I just do this enough, all at once, I'll become jaded, numb to it. I need to get to that point."

He looked at me incredulously. "And you honestly think this is making it better?" I could tell he was concerned and finally stopped trying to hide it. "Look at yourself in the mirror and then, you tell me if this is, at all, a healthy approach."

He lifted his hand gently to my face, turning it toward the mirror as we sat on the bed. I saw myself, sunken-in eyes, worn expression, pale, ashen. I didn't recognize that girl, but not just due to those reasons. I saw the face of a sad and merciless being, an idle soul that had been touched by a darker force that was brewing inside her. A malevolence that lay dormant, just waiting, inescapable.

I turned and stared at him, awaiting his ever-wise words, but he just shook his head. Maybe it was a test. Maybe he was waiting for me to ask for his thoughts on the matter, luring me in by his silence. But it didn't work, I wouldn't buy into it.

He let me set up another round of castors. The rest of that day consisted of even more brutal murders and beatings and deaths for me to endure. I tried telling myself that I was getting used to it, but I knew it was a lie. A total lie. If I wasn't allowed to "judge" these people and choose their eternal fate, then what else was I supposed to do? Endure it. That was the only choice I had.

By the time the day was done, I'd argued with Hayden enough to save twelve Seekers. I'd done it, I'd begun my journey of saturating myself with the horror that was to be my daily life and kept my cool with every one of them, despite the fact that I was sending them to the undeserved bliss of their next life.

And...I hate them all. Every one of them.

I took a hot shower, trying to wash away the things I'd seen. I stared at the drain and imagined all the water that cascaded down my skin was a piece of the horrid things I'd witnessed; it would all leave me and get washed away to another place. I wanted so badly to believe that was what happened, that I could just forget.

When I got out of the bathroom, Beau was loyally sitting on his hind legs, waiting for me to open the door and head to my bedroom. I could feel Hayden staring after me from his room's threshold as I walked. I knew he knew something was wrong. It wasn't going to be something I would be able to hide, and that was obvious. He knew me too well.

I thought about who I really needed the most, and that was my mother. I longed for that familiar voice, that familiar touch and familiar hope with which she could fill me in just one of her winning smiles. I looked at my dog as he sat on the floor next to the bed, laying his ears back as he stared at me, those sad, brown eyes watching me curiously.

"You miss her too, don't you, boy?" I asked him.

Beau let out a slight whimper and placed his head in my lap, looking up at me. He let me play with his ears and twirl his fur around my fingers as I stared at the floor in a daze.

Hayden left me alone for the rest of that night. Part of me was relieved, but I mostly felt saddened by his choice to let me be. And that, in itself, got me even more frustrated. As if my emotions weren't running high enough already, I felt even more confused and desperate in how to handle the one thing I knew for sure; my feelings for Hayden. Those were always there, no matter how mad he made me, no matter how scared I was, and no matter how deep I fell into the despair that lingered within.

I went to sleep that night, exhausted and spent. That was when the dreams started. I saw their faces. I died all over again. I watched their offenses over and over again, unable to turn it off. And the most horrifying thing was, the brewing hatred in me just kept filling, readying itself to spill over at the imminent moment. The first official day, reluctantly embracing the new life set before me and my dream world wasn't even something in which I could find peace anymore.

*   *   *   *

"It's already been decided, Evika," Hayden said to me sternly, breaking my trance. "Jericho will be here tomorrow." He rose from the bed.

I turned in the bed to look at him. "So, that's it? I don't even get a say in this at all?"

"No," he snapped, "you don't. You opted out of that when you kept this from me. I'm not going to let this go on anymore."

My brow furrowed. I just wanted to avoid it all together, asking for help. Poor, helpless Evika again. I don't know what made me more mad, Hayden's meddling or the fact that I was clearly the most helpless and stubborn human being the Council ever had to deal with.

I said nothing, but managed to huff a loud breath as I turned away from him again. I lay there, petting Beau's fur until I fell back to sleep, letting the nightmares continue.

Chapter Five *Enter, Sandman*

I woke to the sounds of the birds chirping in the tree closest to my window. I leaned over to find my dog lying awake on the floor, patiently waiting for my awakening. I smiled at him and slid down to the floor, giving him one of the huge bear-hugs I was so used to giving him.

I thought about the previous night's events and immediately felt myself fill up with guilt. Letting the night come to an end the way it did with Hayden gnawed at me. I nudged Beau to his feet, and we tiptoed down the stairs to the kitchen. I peeked my head around the corner to see the angel eating a bowl of cereal. He didn't notice me until Beau rushed to his side to greet him. Hayden looked up at me and smiled weakly. I gave him one in return. He turned in his chair to nuzzle his face with Beau's, talking to him in that funny voice again.

I made myself a bowl of the same cereal and sat across from the angel, slightly afraid to make eye contact again. I knew in my heart that I wanted to apologize to him for the torment I'd been putting him through, shutting him out.

"Listen," I started, "I'm sorry I haven't talked to you about those dreams. The main reason I didn't is because I knew you'd bug another one of the angels to help." Hayden looked up at me from his playtime with Beau. "I'm really stubborn and I know that. *Believe* me," I rolled my eyes at myself, "I'm fully aware that I can be a pain in the ass." There. Progress.

Hayden smirked and looked up. "At least you can admit it." It amazed me how forgiving he was through all of the problems I'd created for us, the outbursts I'd perform."Nonetheless," he continued, "that's a trait that you're stuck with, which means I'm stuck with it too, and I've accepted that." He winked at me.

I studied him for a moment, mesmerized by his emeralds as the light of the morning sun shined upon his face making his eyes sparkle as if they were actual stones, gently highlighting his perfect lips which were turned into a little grin while he resumed eating. God, how I wanted life to be different, for life to be simpler, to have more moments like that one where I didn't have a care in the world except to savor the beautiful grace of my angel across from me at the breakfast table.

I suddenly became aware of the expression on my face and looked back to my breakfast before Hayden could look at me again.

"This will be good for you," he assured me. "Jericho has been asking about you. He's not normally so concerned about someone."

I looked at him inquisitively. "What do you mean?"

"I've never seen him so eager before. Even Luka is taken aback by Jericho's willingness to help." Hayden looked at me for a brief moment. I could tell he was editing his thoughts before speaking. "He keeps to himself a lot. He's not as....*extrovert* as the angels you've already met."

"So, what's his problem?"

"There is no problem. He is just one of the eldest next to Costello and has always been one of the serious ones. You know, for lack of a better word, uptight."

I cocked a brow at him. "I'm gathering that one of the things he is lacking is a sense of humor?"

Hayden half-smiled. "That's good gathering."

Great. I did sense that Jericho would not be as friendly as the others, either. I was hoping I was wrong.

No sooner were we done with breakfast than we had a visitor knocking at the door. Beau ran to the door and sat there waiting in the foyer. It would be the first guest in our house since his, well, second-coming. After that thought, I sucked air.

"Hayden?" I called as I grabbed Beau's collar, trying to pull him back into the kitchen. "Does Jericho know about you-know-who?"

"Calm down. Luka cleared everything up. We're not in trouble for the dog anymore." He winked. I felt relief set in and loosened my grip on Beau's collar.

I stayed in the hallway and watched Hayden open the door, and a tall figure walking over the threshold. He was easily a foot taller than Hayden with the build meant for a line-backer. He was an angelic tower with long, shiny, black hair tied back into a low pony tail, tan skin and dark eyes that seemed as if losing yourself in them may be the only option, and a mature face, one that seemed a bit more aged than the angels I'd already met.

I took in his attire. He was dressed in a light gray, silk button-up and ivory slacks with a pair of charcoal-black dress shoes, like he'd just come from church. Go figure.

"Welcome, Jericho," Hayden greeted him.

Jericho held a smug look as he nodded once at Hayden, an expression that relayed the extensive pride he had for himself. It was a look of superiority, as if he felt as tall as he was and loved every minute of it. His place in the Council, I'm sure, was one that made that possible. It was then that I knew he was different from the others. I could sense it immediately. I remained timid in the hallway before the inevitable introduction.

"Jericho," Hayden turned around, "this is...." He stretched his neck to find me. "Evika?"

A heavy foot stepped forward. "I understand the nightmares are rather taxing on you, Miss Stormer?" Jericho's deep, patronizing tone lured my head to peek out from around the corner again. I saw both angels looking at me expectantly. Jericho pulled something out of his pants pocket and held it while waiting for my answer.

I stepped into the foyer and nodded. "Yes, they have," was all I could say.

"I see," the giant angel said. "Well, I can take care of that problem for you, but I'm going to need a strand of your hair." He said it in such a no-nonsense way. There was no "good to meet you" or a simple "hello." The angel obviously made it known he wasn't into small talk and was only there to get the job done and get out.

My face contorted. I could feel it. *A lock of my hair? What the hell?* I looked over at Hayden for reassurance. My angel gave me a smile and a nod, giving me only a slight sense of relief since I was definitely not getting it from our guest.

"Uh, okay," I said to the giant. "Any particular spot I need to pluck it from?" I laughed inside after hearing myself. The conversation was weird enough as it was, and now I was asking from which spot on my head I needed to pluck my hair? Word of the day: Awkward.

"Any one of them will suffice, my dear," Jericho's voice was partially condescending as he took graceful steps toward me. I was amazed that someone so large could be so docile and light on their feet. I kept an eye on the hand that held the contents from his pocket, and saw a round circular object with a wooden frame, much like a typical dreamcatcher. It fit in the giant's palm perfectly. In his other hand, he held two, grayish colored feathers.

I pulled out a strand of hair from the top of my head where the hair parted, then handed it to Jericho. He reached out for it with the hand that held the feathers.

"Are those yours?" I blurted out to him. You know, a small conversation was all I needed out of him. He could redeem himself for being such a prick at first impressions.

The giant angel smiled at me, not smugly, but genuinely. It was the first attempt at warmth I'd felt from him since he'd entered through my door. "Yes, they are. I'll need to bind them with the strand of your hair in order for the object to work efficiently. I will then weave these through the netting in the center of this," he held up the dreamcatcher, "and as long as you keep this near you while you sleep, the nightmares should subside."

We all sat down in the living room. Hayden and I sat across from Jericho, watching him tie the necessary pieces together. I felt Hayden's arm slide around my shoulders, his attempt to comfort me in the situation, I guess. It didn't take long before the giant was complete with his craft, but it was enough time for me to recall the dangers it caused for Jericho. And despite his not being the most friendly angel, I still felt a natural concern in me about what we were doing and the effects it would have on him.

"Jericho?" I interrupted his concentration.

"Yes, dear?" he said without looking up. There was that pompous tone again.

"The dreams that this will rid me of....I was told that you will suffer from them. Is that true?" I really was concerned. The nightmares were awful and I didn't wish them on anyone, well, not anyone I loved or potentially liked, anyway.

A deep laugh came bellowing from the pit of the giant's stomach as he looked at me, finally smiling genuinely. "You need not worry about my well being, young Warrior. For it is not my choice to become human, nor will it ever be."

He said "human" as if it were a plague of some sort, an inferior race that he dared never become or lower himself to. I tried not to furrow my brow at him, but I did feel my eyes narrow as I over-thought the meaning behind his words. Okay, so I gave him that chance, and he blew it. Ugh, why was I so narrow-minded about this one?

"Hmm," was all I let escape my mouth.

If he was so much better than us *humans*, then why the hell was he even helping me? I wondered what he thought of my real angel mother when she Faded for Jack. I wondered if he perceived the entire Guardian-human set-up as a joke. I'd wondered if he'd ever guarded a human before. I felt indifferent toward the angel, and it was clear to me that he *was* different. I looked at Hayden, wondering if he'd possessed the same spite for Jericho, but it seemed as though it was just a normal conversation and nothing was out of the ordinary. My angel's expression was not at all changed. It was obvious that Hayden had more of a tolerance, or maybe he'd come to terms with the fact that it was just the way Jericho was. At any rate, he'd had much more time to get used to the antics than I'd had.

"There we are," Jericho smiled as he held up his work of art, admiring it as it dangled from his finger by the thread attached at the top. It spun in the air at first. I saw that he'd weaved the tied feathers around the outside border of the netted thread inside of the circled frame. It was actually a really nice creation and something I would have purchased at a store had I been into the whole dream-catching thing.

"Great work as always, Jericho." Hayden said.

Jericho bobbed his head with pride. "Thank you, son." He turned to me and placed the dreamcatcher in my palm. "You will need to hang this above the bed, place it on the nightstand, etcetera. As I advised earlier, anywhere in the room will do, as long as that is where you are sleeping."

I nodded as I took the object. It was light in weight and felt so delicate. I was extremely surprised that the giant angel's hands hadn't destroyed it before it was complete.

As I suspected, Jericho was the business-only type. He stood to depart only minutes after the completion of the dreamcatcher.

"I must be going. There is a Council meeting in an hour," he said with a hint of urgency.

I held my hand out to him. "It was nice to meet you, Jericho. Thank you," I said as I waited for his hand to wrap around my mine. His hand was massive and made mine look like a doll's. I felt so small next to him, but I knew that the harder I squeezed, the more of an impression I could make on him. So I stood my ground, so-to-speak, shaking firmly. I didn't want him to think he could look down upon me or Hayden without it going unnoticed.

"A pleasure, dear one," Jericho said with a smirk.

We soon unlinked our hands and stared at each other for a

moment. Those deep eyes of his were so endless. I wondered what thoughts his mind had composed behind them as he looked back at me.

Hayden shook his hand and thanked him as well, and then the giant was gone, vanishing into thin air right from the living room.

As soon as I felt it was safe, I folded my arms and scrunched up my nose, furrowing my brow while I turned to Hayden. Naturally, he laughed at me.

"Hmm. Do I sense an aversion to the dream harmon?" Hayden continued with his chuckling.

I shook my head. "Unbelievable. That guy is an angel? And here, I thought it was next to impossible to find someone more stuck on themselves than you are," I jeered. I really did want to keep the mood light between us, despite the fact that I felt invaded and belittled in so many ways.

"Come on, he's not *that* bad."

I cocked an eyebrow. Was he serious? "Not that bad? He's *awful*," I retorted. "You can see it in his eyes, how righteous he thinks he is over me, and over you."

"That is just the way he is and the way he's always been, Evika. And would you listen to yourself? What's with your being so judgmental? It's not like you," he said with a look of bewilderment.

Although Hayden was defending the giant, he was right. My perspective on other people, beings, had changed dramatically....and noticeably.

I shook my head and sighed. "I know that you are all different, with personalities, fun quirks, talents, but I expected all *good* differences. Every angel I've met up to this point has been sweet, caring, happy. Jericho just doesn't seem to fit the bill, that's all."

"Well, first of all, aside from me, you've only met a handful of angels. And second, you have to remember Jericho is one of the elite on the Council. He is the right hand of Costello and takes great pride in his placement," Hayden explained.

I rolled my eyes. "He's a pompous kill-buzz."

"Okay," Hayden said, palms up in defeat. "That's fine. Think what you want about him. But it won't change the fact that *that*," he pointed to the dreamcatcher in my hand, "will be what gives you sleep at night from here on out." I could tell he was getting frustrated with me.

"Gooooood morning!" Luka appeared at the front screen door. The first thing I saw was his short hair spiked up into a mohawk. Honestly, it made Luka cuter than he already was.

"Charmin?" I heard Hayden guffaw from behind me. "Please tell me that someone at the House at least attempted to stop you from doing that."

Luka shrugged. "I was bored this morning."

I grinned at him as I waved for him to come in and instantly looked at his t-shirt as the curiosity got the best of me. It was powder blue, with the green, female M & M in a cute pose, crossing her legs. Right below the character were the words: Go Green. I walked over to him and my dismal mood was suddenly lifted.

"Nice shirt, Lukster," I giggled as I lightly ran my palm across the short row of spikes on his head. "And I'm diggin' the hair, too."

"Thanks, Evigreen." Luka beamed with his best smile. "So, what did I miss?"

"Nothing much." I shrugged, holding up the catcher in front of his face. "Just a giant ego on legs, but he's gone now," I said.

"Oh." Luka laughed. "Are you sure he's gone?" he asked me as he patted Hayden on the shoulder. "Looks like he's still hanging around."

"Keep it up, Charmin," Hayden playfully punched Luka in the gut, making him laugh harder and doubling over with an ache. Beau jumped up, placing his front paws on Hayden's chest in a non-threatening way.

"Well, look who's come to my rescue." Luka chortled. "Come here, boy." He crouched down to embrace the dog. Beau bounced over to the angel, wagging his bushy tail.

I dangled the dreamcatcher from my finger as I headed up the stairs to my room. "I'll be right down. Gotta put this thing somewhere." I looked at it with disappointment. As much as I didn't want to accept it, I knew it was my only chance of getting any real sleep. Unfortunately, I was at the mercy of an angel of whom I wasn't too particularly fond, but it was obvious that I had no choice in the matter. I grabbed the tool kit from the closet and pulled out a nail and the hammer. It hung nicely against the clover green wall above my bed's headboard.

I turned to leave my room and saw Hayden leaning against the door frame with his arms folded. I hadn't even heard him come up the stairs.

"So, are you okay?" Hayden asked me.

I looked at him curiously. "I'm fine. Why?"

He dropped his arms and walked over to me. "It just feels like there's something going on with you. Despite the fact that you said you would talk to me now, I still feel like you're holding something back."

I sighed. It sounded more like a frustrating huff than anything else, so I tried to soften my expression as I looked back at him. Should I have told him about the hate that festered in me for all of the Seekers? Yes. Should I have told him about the fear that had been brewing inside of me for the past month? Yes. But the only thing I wanted to do was forget about it.

I looked over at the new ornament above my bed. I just wanted things to be back to normal, at least to the normal that it was supposed to be with exception to the oddities of my new life.

"I just want to be able to sleep again," I said to him, hoping it would suffice. I looked back at him again and decided that I'd admit something and let him gloat. "You were right. I should have told you about the dreams when they first started." There. I finally confessed.

A smirk grew on his face. I kept my eyes on his emeralds. "Wow," he said. That huge smile couldn't wait to come out.

"What?"

"I've really broken you down, haven't I?"

I gave him a confused expression. "How so?"

He tugged lightly on my pony tail, holding a smug expression. "You're not one to admit fault very often, if at all, and you're finally doing it quite a bit, lately." He chuckled.

I rolled my eyes. "Don't scare it away, Hayden. It's liable to stop."

His laughter filled the room and, as I watched his face brighten, I felt mine do the same. I knew it did because I couldn't stop laughing along with him. I was overwhelmed with so many emotions. Some feelings I was having were new. Well, who was I kidding? All of them were new to me. I'd felt more free than I ever had before and I knew it was because of Hayden. Despite the new, perilous life ahead of me, I wanted to believe that I would be happy living it. I wanted to prove that I could handle whatever this life meant, and the funny thing was, I based it all on the motivation of keeping Hayden close to me. He was like this drug, this antidote that my sad life needed to make it better. I guess it was funny to see it that way, but I felt that was the whole reason I was given a second chance at life. That's how I wanted to see it, even if I was wrong.

But even though I wanted our relationship to flourish, I knew it wouldn't as long as I felt like I was getting babysat my entire life. I knew his "mission" called for my constant protection, but there had to be some kind of boundary, and I was about to make one. The only thing I had left to myself were the feelings I wasn't ready to confess to him, because most of them were for him, and those were the ones he made me promise to tell him.

"Can I ask you a favor?" I inquired.

"Anything," he paused, "within reason." That sounded familiar.

I took a deep breath, hoping it wouldn't come out as harshly as I sometimes delivered my words. "Well, if this thing works," I nodded to the dreamcatcher, "there's no reason for you to poke around in my head, right?"

He looked at me incredulously. "I think I can see where this is going." He folded his arms again. "What are you hiding?"

"I'm not hiding anything, Hayden," I growled, then consciously softened my tone again. "I just...I just don't get much to myself anymore, and it would be nice to know that I can have a bit of privacy once in a while, even if it's only in my dreams."

His eyes narrowed for a moment as he studied me. Then I saw his expression change into one of concern, as if another thought had obstructed the original. "Is that how things feel to you, Evika? That nothing is your own anymore?"

I saw hurt in his eyes then, and I knew I had to convey to him what I wanted for him to understand. "No, Angel-man. That's not it. I'm just asking that you give me a chance to feel normal, to just trust me that if anything should go wrong that I'll come to you about it," I said. "That's all."

He breathed deeply as he hooked his thumbs in his front pockets, looking into my eyes with a penetrating stare. "Okay," he finally said. "Deal." I could tell he didn't like it.

I smiled at him with admiration. "Looks like you're not the only one who can break someone down," I poked to lighten the mood again.

"However," he ignored my comment and raised his hand to bring my boasting to a stop. "If anything weird happens and I feel the need to intervene, the deal is off." Of course there would be a stipulation like that. "So you better talk, Evika. I mean it."

I sighed. Honestly I felt more pacified than I thought I would with how the brief conversation went. "Deal," I relented.

He took my hand and led me down the stairs. "Come on, Pony-girl. We've got to entertain the mohawk in our living room." I let out a hearty laugh, comforted by his touch.

Luka's head turned to me once my foot hit the tile floor at the bottom of the steps. "So, Rainmaker, what's the haps?" I cocked a brow at him and smirked. "Oh, yeah," he boasted. "We didn't get to discuss that during my last visit since Beau-Beau was the hot topic, but word gets around. I know *all* about it."

Hayden bellowed a laugh and turned to look at me, giving a proud smile.

"Elka." We both said it aloud in unison, then became amused by our idiosyncrasy.

"The haps, huh?" I poked at Luka. "Well, Elka seems to think I need training in order to master the art of....whatever this is." I rolled my eyes as I plopped down next to him on the couch.

Luka nodded. "Blondie's right, kiddo. And who better to know that than the angel who can foresee natural disaster?" He laughed heartily.

I sighed. "So, what do you think about it?"

"My thoughts?" Luka grinned at me. "I think it's a bad-ass gift, Evigreen, and I can't wait to see what becomes of it," his grin turned devious, "other than your getting everything wet."

We all laughed at that comment.

"Listen, Luka," Hayden said as he sat down. "Speaking of hot topics, I was wondering if you heard of any changes as far as the dark minions go?"

"Drones?" Luka inquired. "Not that I know of. Why?"

"Because they haven't shown up anywhere since we left Ohio. It's like they don't even exist anymore. Those things should be coming at us left and right, and they're nowhere."

"And you're complaining?" Luka challenged.

"Not at all. But don't you find it odd? Like there is some ulterior motive behind it?" Hayden sounded concerned. "It's unnerving, to say the least."

There was silence for a few seconds as Luka was digesting Hayden's words. "I can see if the Council has any word on the matter, but for now, we should just enjoy the peace we're getting at the moment," Luka said. "Embrace it. Maybe we've just slid under the radar."

Silence again. I considered Luka's suggestion.

"Has this ever happened before?" I asked him.

"Nope." His lips popped on the P. "I don't recall it ever happening before."

Hayden looked over at me, as if reluctant to say what he wanted to say, but he gave in, knowing that I hated the secrets anymore. "Well, I don't like it," he admitted, "and I wish we knew what this was about."

That was all that was said about the subject. I looked back at Hayden and felt a worry in me, the worry that grew into a fear, which only added to the mounds of it that I already had. He was right. We hadn't seen a Drone in Georgia at all. Surely, they would have found us by now. Something was up. And even though I was happy not to have to deal with any of those monsters around, it seemed more bothersome that they weren't around at all. It was obvious that Hayden saw a danger in that fact.

"So!" Hayden broke the silence. "How about we go bowling?"

"Great!" Luka jumped up. "Let's get this soldier out for a while."

"And before you even wonder about it, yes, Evika, you can have a beer or two."

Luka and I exchanged a glance at each other and mouthed the word "wow."

I stood and prowled up to Hayden, holding a smile from ear to ear. "Hey, what was that cracking noise?" I asked him.

"Cracking noise?" he looked confused.

"Oh," I tapped his nose lightly, "never mind. That was the sound of you breaking," I said facetiously.

Luka doubled over in laughter. "You two are the epitome of entertainment. Hands down."

Hayden cocked an eyebrow at me, but I could see that smile breaking through.

Chapter Six *Outlet*

"Again," Elka demanded.

I dropped my shoulders dramatically and let my head fall forward. "Elka, I'm tired," I whined. "We've been at this for two hours already. I don't need anymore practice."

She and I had gone down to the shoreline to practice my "rain skills." It wouldn't have been so bad except we had to do it in the middle of the night when no one would be around and we had to be sure it was done over the ocean so it would go somewhat unnoticed. Hayden had invested in a used speedboat for me to use so my practicing could be done far from shore.

"Just once more?" she persuaded me, batting her perfect lashes.

I stood still and huffed, muttering, "That's what you said last time." But, nonetheless, I endured it. For her, for him, and maybe a little for me. By the end of the week, I'd managed to control the rain I'd produced, starting and stopping the rainfall, and I didn't even need Elka all over Hayden in order to get me to make it happen. I guess what kept me going was thinking of my mother. I could feel her there, watching me. At least, I'd hoped she was. I sensed her presence as I closed my eyes and listened to the waves crashing. As long as Elka wasn't talking, and I could concentrate. I learned to use the memories of my mother, good and bad, to control it. And when I couldn't search for that one memory that I needed to get me to stop the rain and to calm down, I thought of my angel's arms embracing me, just like he had the first time I was able to make it stop willingly.

Between the memories and the reality of my life, the practice with Elka was paying off. She'd instruct me when to start and when to stop, how hard to make the rain fall, and where to make it happen. The hardest part in all of it was the boundaries. I was able to expand the diameter of the rain circle once I realized I was using clouds to change their shapes and positions in the sky. Once I'd discovered I had control over those, I knew where to direct my focus. I became a bit more confident once the elements of the sky were listening to me, to my thoughts. And for more effect, I'd raise my arms, directing, commanding.

Control, it seemed to be what I needed to feel the most, and that was what I had over the rain on Earth, to an extent, anyway. The weather still did what it wanted to do, so the rain wasn't always mine. But, like Hayden said, rain was so "me." Most people ran away to take cover, but I'd be out dancing in it. There was a certain security I felt when I let the rain fall upon me. Exposure to it was liberating for me. And to have control of it, I guess I was starting to see the positive side. I didn't know what the hell it meant as to why I had the gift of cloud and rain control, but I managed to see the bright side, which was rather hard for me to do anymore.

"Evika, you're really doing great." Elka smiled as she swam toward me in the ocean water; she'd often jump into the water for a late night swim while I stayed in the boat. Sometimes, she'd spread her pink wings and use them as a raft.

"I *better* be doing great after all of this practice," I stated, unable to contain a yawn.

She hurled herself into the boat. "Come on, Rainmaker," she said, pointing toward the shore. "Let's get you home."

I let out the biggest sigh of relief once she finally said that. I was so ready for bed. Sleeping was something I actually looked forward to once the dreams became pleasant after Jericho's visit.

After the boat ride back to the dock, the walk was definitely not far back to the house, but I always insisted that we take my vehicle since I was thoroughly exhausted after practicing. The first day was brutal for me. Physically, emotionally, and mentally. It took more than just thoughts to get things to happen. Granted, I'd made it rain harder than rocks prior to that, but the anger always brought it on. After exerting energy into controlling the elements of the sky, it took more out of me than just the normal amounts of force. Elka assured me it was just like exercising, and that once you do it for a while, your body gets used to it. How she knew this, I did not know. I just tried to believe her.

Elka plopped into the passenger side of the pony, still wrapped in her towel. "Hey Ev, can I ask you something?" she inquired in a serious tone.

I looked over at her curiously as I started the engine. "Sure, Elka. You can ask me anything."

She took a deep breath, which sort of made me nervous. I'd wondered what she could possibly be so nervous to ask me.

Elka turned in her seat to look me straight in the eye. "If you had the choice to put things back to normal, like before your First Death, or to keep things the way they are now, which would you choose?"

She asked the question as if she'd been planning on asking me that very question for quite some time. I looked at her inquisitively for a few seconds and wondered why she'd inquire about something like that. Some thoughts ran through my mind as to the reason. First, I thought maybe she was fishing to get me to spill my guts about how I felt about Hayden, or even maybe that he could have put her up to it. But then I thought a little harder and realized that I hadn't really been myself all week. I'd gone through the motions of my new life, along with the nightly practices with Elka. She may not have known me long, but I was beginning to see that I wasn't the hardest person to read. I concluded that she was just concerned, but also a little curious.

To have the chance to change my life back to what it was should have been appealing to me. But, the reality was, my prior life was missing something huge. That something, or someone rather, was Hayden. Even though I hated the people I was saving, hated that I had been cursed for the remainder of my life to see the actions that placed them in their own, little hell....I would endure it over and over again, just for him, just to know him.

I looked at Elka confidently to give her an answer. "If I had the choice? I would keep things as they are."

Elka studied me for a moment, a peaceful moment. "For him," she finally said, as if she'd heard my final thought on the matter.

I knew that I didn't need to confirm it for her, but I did anyway. I nodded slightly. "Yes, for him." Her perfect, pink lips curled into a genuine smile. "The heart sure knows what it wants, doesn't it?" she asked me solemnly.

I breathed a laugh, looking down intently, as if waiting for my heart to jump out of my chest to agree with her. "It's been known to steer me wrong here and there," I said.

"But not this time," Elka assured me. "You'll see." She winked at me.

I just smiled at her as I put the pony into gear to drive back to the house, hoping she was right.

After getting home, I tiptoed past Hayden's room to pick up

Beau to come stay with me in my room for the rest of the night. I always liked his company after returning home from a practice. I recalled the harmless argument that Hayden and Elka had the first night she took me out to practice my skills. She figured it would be good to have "girl time" and that he didn't need to be there. She'd convinced him that I was safe with her, which he, of course, already knew. I could tell he was getting used to the idea that he didn't always have to be there with me as long as another Guardian was with me when he'd finally started to go to bed before Elka brought me home.

As I entered Hayden's room, my dog was laying on the floor next to the angel's bed. He'd been waiting for me. As I watched him rise to all fours and waited for him to leave the room, my eyes glanced to the face of my angel lit by the ray of light from the hallway. I smiled at the object of my affection, who was lying on his stomach, an arm draped over the side of the bed. Even in his sleep he was perfect, with his dark hair all messy and the smooth curvatures of his bare back and arms. I watched him lift his arm up and under his pillow, and my breathing shallowed. I shook my head wildly, as if to knock out the impure thoughts that were starting to invade.

Though I was exhausted and spent after practice with Elka, I'd felt the urge to get some things off of my chest, things that I just wanted to write down. An outlet. It was the first time I'd picked up a pen since my birthday when I wrote the prose for my mother. However, it felt like home when the pen was in my hand, and I lay on the bed with my journal and the light of my neon-green lava lamp while my loyal dog lay next to me. It still felt surreal to have Beau back again, but it felt right. Everything was in its place.

I thought about all of the things I'd taken for granted and about all of the things that I cherished the most. I thought about all of the things that I'd lost and wanted back again, things I never got the chance to do and wanted to, just to say I did them. I wondered if I was going to be okay, if life would ever get a little easier, happier. It was then that I realized that the only thing that was truly keeping me content and grounded was him, my angel. I guess I was looking for something to make me bawl my eyes out. I needed a good cry. I'd spent so much time shedding tears over losing my mother that I really didn't know how to cry about anything else.

Then it hit me; Elka had asked me if I'd want to go back to the way things were. I imagined a life without Hayden in it at all, a life that was mine where I'd known him, and then he was suddenly gone forever. My chest tightened and my head ached. Tears fell as I imagined a life without him; it killed me inside.

The pen hit the paper, and I wrote the words to a new melody:

Save Me

I can't face this world for one day without you
When you walked away, you left me here in the dark
I keep searching for the light around me
But when I close my eyes, the nightmares begin

Save me. Save me. Save me

Absolute Zero

From this darkness
A world without you isn't worth living in
Save me. Save me. Save me
From this darkness
I'm afraid of what I'll become
Without you...now that you're gone.

I hear your voice
But I can't find you
I see your face
But only in my dreams
You promised the pain
Would fade away
But I lie here
Breaking into pieces
Look at me
I'm breaking
Can't you see?
I'm fading
The darkness is waiting to devour me
There's no mending me now
Unless you come back to me

When will this stop?
When will this end?
My sadness falls deeper

Ireland Gill

My heart grows weaker
No one can take my pain away
It's killing me slowly; not having you here
The darkness is folding
Without you near
Make this hurt go away
Just come back to me now
I keep telling myself just to breath
But the moment won't pass.

Come back, so I can dream again
Come back, so I can breath again
Come back, so I can live again
My heart is breaking
Each moment that you're gone
Save me. Please, save me.

    I read the written words once more after finishing and wondered if I'd ever have the guts to show it to Hayden one day. I knew he wouldn't think I was crazy for writing something like that, a written nightmare where he was gone, but *I* thought I was going crazy. My head hurt with so many thoughts. All I wanted to do was run to him for comfort so I could feel okay again, but I didn't want him worrying for no good reason. It was my own damn fault for working myself up the way I did. I knew I was just being irrational, which seemed to be more of common thing for me anymore. I felt like I was losing the ground beneath me sometimes, and it was more than just my strong aversion to the Seekers. It was that thing inside me that came around when I wasn't near Hayden, the force of something that didn't feel good to me at all. It was a darkness I'd never invited. I was still too afraid to talk to him about it, even though I'd made a promise to him that I wouldn't shut him out anymore.

I breathed deep, wiping the tears away from my face and curling up next to Beau. He looked at me curiously and offered a few licks to my cheeks to rid them of the salty tears,

"I have to stop being so afraid, Beau," I whispered to my dog.

My arms wrapped around his furry neck as he laid his head over my shoulder. We slept like that until morning.

Chapter Seven *Masquerade*

"So, are you ready yet?" I heard Hayden call to me from downstairs. "Dinner is supposed to start in fifteen minutes and we still have to *drive* there, Pony-girl."

I grunted, tying the last bow on the back of my dress. "Please, Hayden," I called out of the bathroom, half-laughing and half-huffing, "haven't you learned by now that I'm never on time?"

"That's impossible to forget." I could hear him mutter with a low laugh.

I checked myself in the mirror, touching up my eye liner and neutral eyeshadow before adding a dark red gloss to my lips. I'd found a local seamstress to fix an old bridesmaid dress I found on sale to wear for my Halloween costume. It was an apple-red, strapless dress out of which I had her remove the zipper in the back to put eyelets all the way down and replace it with a black ribbon that laced all the way down.

The black angel wings I'd gotten with Elka at the mall were my own project. I'd gotten white, battery-operated mini-lights to string along the top of them and covered the wire up with more black feathers. They were complimented well by the black lacing down the back of the dress.

The final touch was the elegant, black, beaded choker that I put on last. I hooked it in the back, bringing my arms to my sides and observing my hair one last time. I'd curled it and put it completely up with a few twists in the front, and left a couple of curls to hang by my ears, bobby-pinning my silver halo to the top. I'd sprayed it all stiff with hairspray, something of which I despised, but this night called for perfection as I knew I wanted to look flawless and I would nothing to come out of place. I needed to have a good time and to worry about nothing but the fun I would have with my angel.

I slid on my black, silk gloves that came to the elbow and released a nervous sigh. "Here it goes," I whispered to myself as I left the bathroom, flicking off the light and heading to the stairs. I scanned the lengthy stairwell all the way down, lifting up the bottom of my dress and happy that I'd decided to wear my black combat boots. My pace slowed when my eyes stopped at the sight of Hayden at the landing.

He stood proud in a black silk, long-sleeved button-up tucked into his white dress pants and black dress shoes. I saw him remove his hands from his pockets and drop his jaw as I descended the stairs. His reaction was clear, and I was relieved.

"*Wow,*" he said, hardly audibly. I blushed at the sight of his awestruck expression. "Evika, you...look...." he paused, and my mind wouldn't stop wondering what he was trying to say. *Great? Beautiful? Overdressed for the occasion? WHAT!?* "You look absolutely breathtaking."

His words brought a smile to my face and stole a beat of my heart. I couldn't have expected him to say anything better than that. I was jovial.

"Thank you, Angel-man. You're looking sharp, yourself," I commented, "but I thought you had a costume."

He smirked, grabbing my hand as I stepped onto the floor, then he picked something up from the foyer table. It was a white mask. He slid it over his head, placing it over his face correctly, and I finally realized what it was.

"Phantom of the Opera!" I exclaimed. *God, he looked beautiful as a mysterious phantom.*

"I went for simple," he shrugged.

I laughed, still admiring his attire. "My art teacher always used to tell me, 'less is more.' *Now* I get it. You look perfect, Hayden." And he did.

He grinned and blushed a bit in the open skin of his left cheek. That was enough 'thanks' for me. "And if I didn't know any better, I'd mistake you for one of *my* kind," he said somberly, extending his arm for me to hold as we left the house.

I blushed. Again.

We took the Mustang to the restaurant. I let him drive. Bon Appetit was a place that I'd been dying to try and I was extremely excited when Hayden told me they were throwing a Halloween social. He'd made reservations for us a while back, and those came with tickets to get into the event down the street, which was a huge warehouse they fixed up into a dance club. They only opened it up for special events where production companies would rent it out for holidays like Halloween, Christmas, Mardi Gras, etcetera.

When we got to the restaurant, there was not one person without a costume. I felt relieved as it had struck me as odd that a restaurant as nice as theirs would throw an event, but Hayden assured me that wearing our costumes was expected.

We were directed to a table next to a window overlooking the main street. It was dusk, and I knew soon it would be dark. My heart sank. I hadn't really left the house at night at all since we'd moved, and the fact that it was Halloween made me question as to why Hayden was so relaxed, other than the fact that the Drones seemed to have been leaving us alone lately.

"Hayden," I inquired, "is tonight going to be....dangerous at all? I mean, I know that we haven't seen the Drones lately, but what about the Seekers? Are they going to be following me everywhere tonight after dark?"

"Oh," Hayden smiled wryly, "I sort of forgot to mention that Halloween is the one night of the year that any creatures or residents from the dark realm are unable to appear. You won't see any of them, even if you tried. The doorway to our world is impermeable."

"Uh....okay," I wasn't quite sure what to say. It was another small curtain, hiding another tiny secret. "Isn't that a little backwards?"

"What do you mean?"

"Well, usually everyone makes Halloween out to be some sort of evil day, a portal for the dead to walk the earth and for evil to lurk."

Hayden laughed heartily. "You have definitely watched too many movies, you know that?"

I shrugged. "Just ironic, that's all."

A young, male waiter with a Zorro mask came up to our table in a crisp, white shirt and black pants and apron, holding two glasses and a pitcher of ice water. "Good evening, guests." He smiled as he poured, "and Happy Halloween. Our specials tonight are..." and then he rattled off things I wasn't interested in until I heard lasagna. "May I start you off with something to drink tonight?"

I took one breath, ready to say I'd stick with the ice water, but Hayden immediately responded before I could utter a noise.

"May we each have a glass of your finest Riesling, please?" he inquired.

The waiter nodded once with a bright smile. "Right away, sir."

And he was off with the pitcher in hand.

I looked at Hayden incredulously. He took a sip of his water as he tried hiding the cutest smirk. "What?" he finally acknowledged my stare.

I plastered a devious, little grin on my face. "Hayden Crow, did you just order us alcohol...*willingly?*"

"I believe I did," he answered casually.

The most girlie giggle left my throat and, yet again, I was blushing. *Tonight is going to be a good night*, I thought. I knew it. I felt it. Hayden not fussing over my having a drink was a great sign, considering the habit was something he wanted me to break.

Dinner was absolutely divine. Everything was perfect; from the first sip of Riesling down to the last bite of our delectable dishes. Our conversation was non-stop, as if we could never run out of things to talk about. It was a much-needed night between Hayden and me, and I savored every minute of it, anticipating the rest of the evening.

We stood to leave after paying the bill when a little girl, no older than two or three years, ran astray from her father from the other side of the room. Her head was full of light brown ringlets, and she was wearing a light pink tutu with a set of mesh butterfly wings on her back. Her little feet, wrapped in cloth ballerina shoes, pattered over to our table and came to a halt. Her curious, hazel eyes looked up at Hayden as she smiled brightly.

Hayden removed his mask and crouched down in front of her on the floor.

The toddler smiled even brighter. "Wins!" she exclaimed with her little voice.

I watched Hayden smile widely at her. "Well, hello there, Chelsea," he said to her quietly. Her tiny hands rose to each side of his face and held it for a moment as her happy expression beamed.

Amazement. That's what I felt when I watched them. It was a moment in time that was so beautiful that it hurt, a moment that no artist would have wanted to have missed and I witnessed it. It was the exchange between a beautiful child and a handsome angel.

"Wins," she repeated to Hayden with a giggle.

The serene moment was broken by a frantic voice. "Chelsea!" A man in a pirate costume came running over to us. He removed the patch from his right eye. "I'm so sorry. I knew wearing this patch was a bad idea. Can't see a darn thing." He laughed as he picked her up and held her securely in his arms. Her eyes were still locked on Hayden.

Hayden stood once again. "No need to apologize. She's just a curious child." He kept his eyes on her, smiling and adjusting part of her little wing that got caught in her dress. "They all are."

"Daddy! Wins!" she clapped, then pointed to Hayden.

"Yes, sweet pea, you have wings on today, just like this young lady over here," the man acknowledged me standing next to Hayden. "Can you say *angel*?"

She giggled in her father's arms, still beaming at Hayden. "Wins."

The man chuckled and tapped her nose. "We'll work on that one. Time to trick or treat." He turned to us again. "Thank you for understanding," he said graciously as he started back to his table.

"Have a great evening."

"Not a problem. Happy Halloween," Hayden said sincerely.

The curly-haired toddler turned in her father's arms to look over his shoulder as he took her away and kept her eyes on my angel. It brought me the biggest sense of warmth as she muttered a faint "bye" from her lips and waved her tiny hand at us. Both Hayden and I watched the two of them leave the restaurant. Hayden just smiled after her while I stood in awe.

Hayden turned to me and grinned, taking in my moment of silence. "Ready?"

"Ready? You mean we're not going to talk about what just happened there?" I asked.

He chuckled. "You mean you have *questions?*" he said facetiously.

I nudged him playfully. "Hayden, she was pointing to *you*. She knew what you are. And you knew her name."

"Yes." He nodded. "Children are the purest of beings; innocent lives that have no fear, no filter and no mask, no guard to keep up. I already knew her name because she is still so young. I can sense her purity and simplicity, just as she can sense what I am. It's completely natural for us both," he explained. "But she'll have no recollection of this moment due to her youth. That is why it is not unsafe to reveal ourselves to children as young as she is," he paused to grab his mask, "regardless of whether or not we're in constant flesh form."

I stared at him, not moving a muscle. I'm quite sure I looked ridiculous.

"What?" he laughed lightly.

I searched his eyes for a moment, catching this hint of glee in them. "Did I ever see you when I was that young?"

He grinned and shrugged. "Maybe."

"Maybe," I repeated with a nod, crossing my arms.

"A few times," he added.

"Care to enlighten me?"

He looked back at the door where the man and little girl exited. "Aside from her curly hair, she reminds me of you when you were that age." He paused for a moment. "Jack and Nora would sometimes have trouble getting you to sleep at night, so I used to hold you and walk you around in your room while we listened to Coltrane. You'd lay your head on my shoulder and always put your hand on my cheek. It would get you right to sleep."

I beckoned the forming tears to retreat. "You're kidding me," I said to him in disbelief.

Hayden raised his right hand. "Angel's honor, I swear." He looked away for just a moment as he recalled something and smiled at the thought. "You used to call me Hush-bug." He chuckled. "It was something your mother came up with, and the nickname just stuck."

I gazed into his eyes solemnly and smiled. God, I wanted to embrace him right then. My heart was ready to burst for him, and I just didn't know how to tell him anything when it came to my feelings. I didn't even know if I should have even had them in the first place. I just knew that I loved him, so much that it was getting more and more difficult to hide it anymore.

How simple it was, for a child to just know something and share how they feel, having no remorse or idea of consequence. They just know what they feel and feel it, know what they want and try to grab it. No fear, just like Hayden said. I wanted to be just like that again, fearless. That was the trait that I envied in children, what I envied about Chelsea.

"Why haven't you ever told me this before?" I asked him, still staring in adoration.

Shrugging seemed to be his favorite body movement that night, because he shrugged again. "I guess it's just something I kept for myself." He paused and looked at me so radiantly. "Moments like those were what made me proud to be yours."

Right then, that first tear disobeyed and trickled down my cheek. I felt it roll from the corner of my eye and tickle my face.

"Tonight is not a night for tears, Evika," Hayden said softly as he lifted his thumb to my cheek, wiping gently. "Come on," he grabbed my hand, "we've got a party to go to."

Hayden escorted me to the passenger side of the pony and shut the door like a gentleman. It took less than five minutes to get to the warehouse. The brick building was at a busy intersection of the street and, after taking in its size, I'd realized why it was such a fabulous place to throw a huge fiesta.

"Why don't you get out here. I'm going to find a place to park *Aurora*." He rolled his eyes with a smirk.

I giggled and grabbed my phone, I.D. and bank card from my purse, the bare essentials I needed for the club. "Don't take too long, phantom." I winked and closed the door.

Hayden drove down the street, searching for a parking spot while I wandered about three feet toward the building when my cell rang. The grin on my face grew when I saw it was Joel.

"Happy Halloween, Jo Jo!"

"Ev-bear! Did I catch you at a bad time? I wasn't sure."

"Of course not. I'm just waiting for Hayden to park the car before we head into this huge Halloween party in downtown Savannah."

"No kidding? Us too! Evan and I are walking to one right now, but I just wanted to give you a quick call before things got loud."

"Really?" I was shocked, thinking of the time. "Isn't it like two in the morning there?"

"Gotcha. Well, we got a late start and nothing ever closes around here." He forced a laugh.

"Huh. Okay, just be sure to take lots of pics and send them to me later, okay?"

"I will, Ev-bear. Miss you mucho. Behave tonight!"

I laughed. "You too, Jo Jo Coleman. Love you lots, all the way from Georgia."

"Love you, too Evi, all the way from....behind you."

"Bye Jo---," I paused. "Wait. Jo Jo, what do you mean 'behind you?' You're messin' up our lines." I laughed.

He giggled his girliest of giggles, then I heard the click that ended the call. "Joel?" I fiddled with my phone, trying to call him back.

"You silly, imaginative girl," I heard a well-known voice carry across the light traffic behind me. "Hasn't anyone ever told you angels have white wings?" A familiar laugh followed.

I turned and gasped, practically dropping my phone when I saw him. Swaggering across the street with his hands on his hips, wearing a David Bowie costume - identical to the Goblin King in Labyrinth - was my best friend in the whole world.

"OMIGOD!" I exclaimed as I leapt across the curb. "JOEL! OMIGOD! OMIGOD!" I jumped up onto his skinny frame in the middle of the street, squeezing him, making him squeal like a girl and causing angry car horns to blow. I shut my eyes tight as I clung to him, hoping that what I felt was real, that it was my Jo Jo.

"Wow! If only you'd have been this lively the last time I visited." He chortled as he managed to drag me back onto the sidewalk to safety, hugging me all the while.

I jumped off of Joel and took a step back to look at him more closely. "Joel, I can't believe you're here! I can't believe it!"

Joel sighed, taking me in from head to toe and shaking his head, smirking, his blond Bowie wig all disheveled. "Jeez, girl, you look beautiful tonight." I could see the tears forming in his eyes. "Ugh. But *please*, no more running into the middle of busy streets," he scolded with a laugh.

"I'm thinking the phone call probably should have waited until we were *inside* the building," I heard Luka joke. I looked past Joel's shoulder to see the angel in all white, his ivory wings laying closely against his back and his head topped with a wire halo that lay crooked across that new mohawk I adored. He grinned at me.

"Luka!" I jumped. I was so overwhelmed with joy that I almost neglected to notice a tall figure at Joel's left flank. He was wearing a Superman costume, his dark hair slicked back with the exception of a perfectly plastered curl on his forehead. He smiled at me radiantly, confidently. I sucked air. "You must be Evan?"

His smile widened as he held out his hand. "Pleased to finally meet you, Evika," he said.

I shook his hand and grinned. His dark brown eyes were as sincere as his smile, and I knew instantly that I would like him. "It's great to finally meet you, Evan. I've heard so many great things about you."

"Oh, come here." He tugged me toward him and bear-hugged me against his chest.

I laughed. "Approved, Jo Jo," I said as Evan released me from his deadly hold.

"Well, he better be, Miss Stormer. We've been going strong for seven months now," Joel reminded me.

Everyone laughed.

I thought about the agony I'd put Joel through for most of those months and looked at Evan solemnly. "You're a great person for sticking with my Jo Jo through all that mess, Evan. I'm truly glad that Joel had you around when I wasn't." Evan and Joel smiled at each other, giving each other loving glances.

"He's my Superman," Joel joked, then looked at me seriously. "You've got some great, new friends, too, Evika. It's the only way this would have worked out."

I looked at Joel, then at Luka, who nodded toward someone behind me. I made the connection and smiled, and turned to see my angel leaning against the wall, smirking with his mask still in place. It was difficult to keep my lovestruck, beating heart at bay. It wanted to scream Hayden's name, even more so after having a hunch that he was the master-mind behind Joel's visit. He finally walked over to us, removing his mask, showing off that bright and cocky smile.

"I told you that you'd thank me later, didn't I?" he said to me smugly. I shook my head and laughed as I remembered when he spoke to Joel for the first time over the phone and had shut me out into the hallway during their entire conversation. I was, of course, livid.

"*This* is the roommate?" Joel's jaw dropped. A semi-jealous Evan smacked him playfully in the arm.

I giggled. "What, you haven't met yet after orchestrating this whole scheme behind my back?"

"Well, no. Not...*physically,*" Joel guffawed. Evan smacked him in the arm again, but a little harder this time. "Uh, I mean, you know, in person."

"Pleased to officially meet you, Joel, Evan." Hayden shook both of their hands. "I trust that Luka was on time at the airport and got you to the house okay?" he asked.

Both Joel and Evan nodded with smiles. I could see they were both a bit smitten.

"With plenty of time to spare, I might add." Luka declared proudly.

"The house is absolutely gorgeous, you guys!" Evan said.

"It is," Joel nudged me with a grin. "My little Ev-bear is living large now," he joked, but still had a curious look in his eyes. I could tell it bothered him that I wasn't able to tell him much of anything about, well, anything.

"So, how long are you guys here for?" I asked excitedly.

"We could only do three days, Ev," Joel answered with his famous pouting lip. "I'm already in a lot of trouble from my last little hiatus." He laughed nervously. "But, you know, since your actual birthday was royally sucky, Hayden and I thought it would be a cool thing to plan a visit for your half-birthday. So, here we are!"

I laughed loudly, looking between Joel and Hayden. "My half-birthday," I repeated the phrase. "Well, this is the best half-birthday present I've ever received in my life, you guys." I clung to Joel's neck and felt a squeeze in return.

He struck a dramatic pose. I knew instantly what would be next. "You remind me of the babe!"

Not missing a beat, I said my line, "What babe?"

"The babe with the power."

"What power?"

"The power of voo-doo,"

"Who do?"

"You do! You remind me of the babe!"

We were cracking up, doubling over by the time we'd recited our favorite lines from the movie, Labyrinth.

Joel planted a hard kiss on my cheek. "God, Ev, I've missed

you. I don't care how tired I am from this poopy jet-lag, tonight is going to be a night to remember."

"It already is, Jo Jo," I said somberly as I adjusted his Bowie wig a little. "How could it *not* be when you are dressed as our favorite character in our favorite movie of all time?"

Evan clapped. "I totally put the costume together for him! Jo didn't think we'd be able to pull it off, but," he sighed dramatically, "ye of little faith." He tapped Joel's nose lovingly.

"Yeah, yeah." Joel chuckled.

"Evan, you did a fantastic job. The resemblance is impeccable," I assured him as I looked over the tight, black leather pants and white renaissance shirt Joel was sporting. Evan's bright expression was so appreciative.

"What do ya say we go and get this party started?" Joel asked as he tried fixing his crazy wig again.

I looked at all of my boys surrounding me on the sidewalk and just didn't know what to say. I wanted to scream and jump around, laugh and cry, and just dance. I was elated.

"Whoo! Hoo!" Evan exclaimed. "Dark beer and dancing awaits!"

I smiled at Joel. "Dark beer, huh? The boy speaks my language."

"You have no idea," he said to me under his breath, jokingly.

"First round is on me!" Evan exclaimed as he grabbed Joel's hand and tugged him through the door, handing their tickets to the "gatekeeper."

I giggled as I watched Joel and Evan file in and felt each of my arms become linked with my other two boys, Hayden on my left and Luka on my right.

"By the way, Evigreen," Luka leaned in, "you look amazing this evening."

"Thanks, Lukster." I grinned at him. "Quite dashing, yourself."

We all found a good place to stand inside, close to the bar, to order our drinks. While Luka, Evan and Joel started in on a conversation about how "life-like" Luka's wings looked (ha ha). I turned to Hayden, who'd been standing right behind me. He had such a satisfied look in his eyes, as if this moment had been one he'd been anticipating for weeks and it was finally here, everything going perfectly.

"So, this was all you," I declared.

His arrogance was at a high. "Ohhhh, what can I say, other than....of course it was?"

I giggled. "You seem proud."

"Am I that obvious?" he asked sardonically.

"A little," I poked, then just stared into his emeralds, something I could never get tired of.

"What?" he laughed innocently, removing his phantom mask.

I sighed, still staring. "I don't deserve you," I said solemnly as I stood on my tip-toes to kiss his cheek. And for the first time since knowing him, I caught a blush in his cheeks. I kept that to myself.

Joel strutted over to us. "Happy Halloween and happy half-birthday, my Ev-bear!" He handed me a mug of Guinness and Hayden a Coors Light, keeping one for himself.

Luka was in tow with his beer. Evan clanked his mug to mine and said "cheers," before throwing it back.

A familiar song started playing and Joel and I shot each other wide-eyed glances.

"Poker Face!" We exclaimed simultaneously as we handed our beers to our significant others, then grabbed each others hands and darted to the dance floor.

Joel was literally the *only* person who could get me to dance to the song in front of everyone while I was still sober. We had a whole choreographed routine to the song and it had been a long time since we'd gotten to perform together.

As if never missing a beat in the months we'd been apart, Joel and I danced our moves on the floor, laughing all the while lip-syncing the words to our favorite Lady Gaga song.

I glanced over at Evan, Hayden, and Luka a few times, and they seemed to be amused by our performance. It made me feel higher than I already was. There was no other place in the world I would rather have been than where I was.

The rest of the evening consisted of Joel's and my goofy dances and more drinking. I was surprised at how well I controlled my habit, given that the environment we were in made it almost impossible, but I was proud of myself. And I could tell Hayden was too. However, Evan soon bought a round of shots, which consisted of none other than my poison, Yager.

I knew that Joel had gotten the idea that I had been working on cutting the habit after my fiasco months back because he gave Evan one of those we-will-discuss-this-later looks, but it was extremely hard to ignore the offer.

"Just one," I promised Hayden and Joel as I took the shot from Evan.

"Yeah," Hayden looked at me sternly, "I *know* it will only be one." I'm sure it was a friendly threat.

"I'll stick to beer the rest of the night, I swear." I offered him a reassuring smile. And honestly, he could. But I couldn't promise that my tolerance would hold up, because I was quite sure I didn't have one anymore. One shot of my poison, and it seemed as though I'd consumed ten of them.

Joel and Evan took their shots and headed back to the dance floor, but I felt the sweat starting to protrude from my skin. After about five minutes, I was hanging all over Hayden, and was becoming much braver with my actions than I'd ever been before. There were words that hung on my tongue like melting icicles, things I wanted to say to him that were ready to come out, and alcohol seemed to be the catalyst that would get them voiced. Well, I thought they would.

I felt giddy, high, and most of all, so beyond in love with him that I wanted to tell the world. But I kept rationalizing with myself that it was too loud to talk and, alcohol or not, the bravery in me shied away whenever I looked into his eyes.

"Evika, did you want to go dance?" Hayden gestured, pointing to our group. Joel and Evan were together, jumping around to the techno beat that started playing, and Luka had two girls bobbing around him, encircling him like sharks in a frenzy. I rolled my eyes and laughed.

"Umm....." I stalled for a moment, leaning into him as I felt myself teeter.

"Whoa." He caught me, then lifted me onto the empty stool at the end of the bar. "Or not," he decided.

My head sank. "I'm sorry. I only had the one shot, I swear to God." I frantically started to explain. "Well, and the beers, but beer is just beer. I didn't really--- "

"Evika," Hayden grabbed my shoulders and looked into my eyes. I stared back. "It's okay. I'm not mad at you, if that's what you think."

"Oh," I said with a sigh of relief.

"I do want you to remember this night," Hayden continued, "and, I'm quite sure, that you'd like to remember it too." He smiled, fixing one of my curls that blew into my mouth after a passerby.

The music was pumping beats that made everyone move. I looked to my right and saw my best friend and his boyfriend dancing with the happiest of faces. I saw my other angel laughing while a girl in a nurse's costume stole the crooked halo off of his head to twirl it on her finger, taunting him to come and get it. It made me smile. I finally turned back to Hayden, who hadn't removed his eyes from mine. I tried to focus on his eyes as well as I could; he was the only thing that kept me from feeling like I was spinning, the bad kind of spinning, the drunk kind. He was so close to me that I could smell him over everything else surrounding me, that natural rain scent that I couldn't stop breathing in.

"Funny that I'm wearing wings tonight, because I feel like I could fly," I said, consciously leaning into him.

He chuckled and shook his head at me. "Let's leave flying to the professionals though, okay?"

I nodded and half smiled at him. "Thank you for tonight. You have no clue how much I needed this, or how much this means to me."

His expression turned somewhat serious. "I do know, Ev. Since you've met me, your world has been turned upside down."

Oh, God. Did he feel guilty? Did he think I blamed him for all of my life's turmoil? Ugh. If only he knew how my heart felt. If only he knew that all the good parts of me were brought out when he was around. His emeralds were driving me crazy, that sexy mask, and oh, God, that shirt on him should have been outlawed. It was looking better and better by the second.

And those words I wanted to say, those melting icicles I kept trapped on my tongue were dripping like crazy, begging to be thawed and spilled, but I still couldn't bring myself to say them.

The bravery in speech never came, but my arms did raise to his face, slowly sliding off his mask, revealing his beautiful face. "Upside down's not so bad, Hayden." I gently pulled his face to mine and leaned in, closing my eyes and waiting for our lips to touch. I could feel his hesitation, then finally felt contact, but not with his lips. His hand cupped my cheek as his thumb rubbed my lips, lightly. My eyes flipped open as he leaned into my ear.

"Ev," he said, "you don't want to do this. Not like this."

"You don't know what I want, Hayden," I answered collectedly.

"I know you well enough to know that you're drunk and that you wouldn't want this to happen like this. Your head isn't clear right now."

"It's clear enough." I tried pulling his lips to mine again.

"No." He pulled away. "Evika, not like this. Please."

I dropped my hands and laid them in my lap, looking away from him as I huffed. All I could do was relent and realize he was right. I *was* drunk. The sober Evika wouldn't have the balls to grab him and make out with him from a bar stool. The sober Evika wouldn't have wanted a first kiss to be like that. The sober Evika wouldn't have tried to kiss him at all, in fear of rejection.

And that's exactly what happened.

Rejection.

Surprisingly, that was the moment I started sobering up. "I'm sorry," I said shamefully and hopped down from the stool. "I didn't mean to make you uncomfortable." God, I was heartbroken. I pushed my last beer away, leaving it for the bartender to take away. I was hoping Hayden would see and understand that I was done drinking for the night. A horrible feeling started to build from the pit of my stomach as my heart sank. Not only did I feel shameful, humiliated, and rejected, but I also felt sick. My embarrassment was the catalyst to that pivotal moment of the night, and it was obvious that consuming that shot was the worst thing I could have done.

"I need some air," I blurted as I frantically looked for the direction to the door.

"Okay," Hayden grabbed my arm, ready to escort me, "we'll go outside."

"No!" I said harshly, pulling my arm away. My pride had been maimed, and the hurt bled through my words. "Can you please just send Luka out? I'll be out front," I said quickly as I rushed away from him and headed toward the front entrance. I didn't have time to check his expression to see if he was hurt or angry, confused or relieved. All I knew was I didn't want to be near him if I threw up, and I certainly didn't want to be near him just after he refused me.

I darted outside to the sidewalk and leaned against the wall, holding my head between my legs as best as I could in the dress I was in. I took deep breaths, trying to tame the threats from my stomach. I shut my eyes tight and inhaled the somewhat-cool night air. It was warm, but there was a certain crispness to it that calmed my nerves. Soon, I let my stomach reveal it's inner-workings all over the sidewalk of Savannah, and before long, I heard the voice of the white angel.

"So, Evigreen, I hear I've been summoned--- Oh, shit!" Luka rushed to my side, and I felt his gentle touch, rubbing small circles onto my back while I remained hunched over.

That was the moment that I let it all come out; my tears fell like they had been plugged inside me for years, screaming to escape. I hadn't lifted my head yet, and so many thoughts ran through my mind. I hated myself for trying to make an advance toward Hayden. The reality of it all was sinking in even more as each moment passed. I was then in panic mode. I felt confused and broken, humiliated to a certain degree. And, of course, it was my fault.

I felt guilty that I'd asked Luka to come to my rescue rather than my best friend. Joel was the one who was always the one that saw my best and my worst, and he was always the one who would have the right words to fix the bad things, or at least, the right words to make things seem not as bad. And here, I'd called upon Luka, the one who I knew would understand me the most when it came to my most confusing emotion of all: Hayden. For some reason, I wasn't sure I was ready to even touch that subject with Joel yet. I wasn't sure why.

"Luka," I mumbled into my dress after spitting out the last of my stomach's assortment, "I'm an idiot. A total idiot."

He laughed, kneeling down next to me. "Now, why would you say something like that?"

I looked up at him. "I'm totally sloshed and I tried to kiss him, and he didn't want me. I'm such a flippin' moron, Luka! I thought that maybe, just maybe....I don't know. I thought maybe he wanted me, too. We always get so close, and then it doesn't happen. God, I can't even tell him anything about how I feel, and here, I get drunk and try to suck his fucking face!" I cried. "What the hell is wrong with me?"

"Wrong with *you*?" Luka broke my rant. "Evika, there is absolutely nothing wrong with you. You're a bit on the drunk side, and I have a feeling he's just being careful." He sighed. "Maybe he's just as reluctant as you are."

I shook my head. "Ugh!" I grunted and slammed my head back into my knees again. "I'm being so stupid. I don't need to dwell on this." I looked up at him again. "Why am I worried about this at all?"

Luka took the bottom his shirt and raised it to my cheeks,

123

tenderly wiping the mess of black smudges and tears from my skin. "Because you're in love with him and you don't wanna screw it up." He said it, plain and simple, no hesitation.

I gasped at his remark. He tended to know the feelings I had, regardless of what I was trying to say. I opened and closed my mouth a few times, trying to retort, but I had nothing to say. I couldn't disagree with him, for obvious reasons, and I certainly didn't want to admit it.

"It's okay, Evigreen, you don't have to say anything. Your secret's safe with me." He shrugged with a light laugh. "Here," he pulled something from his back pocket and handed it to me, "I knew this would come in handy tonight."

I looked down at the stick of wrapped gum and smiled. "Always looking out for me, aren't you?"

"Always."

I chewed the gum, breathing in the minty freshness and closing my eyes while I leaned back into the wall again. Luka did the same. We listened to the bass of the music coming from the inside of the warehouse. Blasts of it would escape as clubbers would make their way in and out of the door for smoke breaks or just to get some air. We were silent for a long time, enjoying the soundtrack of the ending evening when the door swung open again.

"Everything okay out here?" Joel walked over and towered over us, his blond wig dangling. "The hottie said you were feeling sick. You okay?"

I giggled at his comment and smiled at him lovingly. "I'm better now, Jo Jo."

Joel raised an eyebrow, averting his gaze to the mess I made beside me, then looked back at me incredulously. "Well, I'm sure you're better now that all of *that's* out of you."

I gave him a chagrined smile.

"Little Evigreen will be okay," Luka assured Joel and patted my shoulder. "Let's go back inside and get some water, then we'll head home."

With that, we three stood. I'd grabbed both of their hands to help me up. I wrapped my arm around Joel's waist and laid my head on his bony shoulder as we walked in. I still couldn't believe he was there. The doors opened as we followed the white-winged angel, and we were blasted with another wave of dance music. I looked up to focus on the first thing in my view and saw none other than the face of my angel as he stood holding a smile and full bottle of water. Still troubled by the evening's events and my deplorable conduct, I still wanted to let him know everything was okay, so I forced a smile. I didn't want any hiccups between us to ruin anything.

But it was that moment that I'd decided, I would never try to claim those lips of his again. It was he who would have to be responsible for that first move.

And I so desperately wanted him to make it.

Chapter Eight *Porch Swing*

"So, things are pretty good with you, huh?" Joel inquired while he scratched Beau's belly. Joel and I hadn't known each other during the early years of my life when Beau was around, so I was grateful that I didn't have to explain my dog's ghost story. To Joel, Beau was just a dog that looked a lot like the one in some old childhood photos with me.

We were sitting out on the front porch swing in our pajamas

after having been the first ones to awaken. Joel had come into my room really early in the morning to bring me a cup of extremely strong French coffee that he'd brought with him and couldn't wait have let me try it. After the first sip, I felt pretty good and surprisingly, didn't have the hangover that I was expecting.

"Things are good, Jo Jo." I smiled at him.

"You're liking this new S.P.A. gig?" he asked.

"Yeah." I nodded, not quite looking him in the eye as I remembered the time I'd told him I was joining the Seekers Protection Agency, a job with the government. It was hard not to roll my eyes at myself, but even harder to ignore the knot of guilt in my stomach. "The gig's okay. I'm still in training right now, but I think I'll like it." The bullshit poured from my mouth.

"That's good." Joel offered me a forced smile. I could tell that, behind it, he was aching to know more, ask me more. Normally, he would have found a way to pry the details out of me, just as he'd done on the phone a few months back, but for some reason, his questions stopped there. I felt more uneasy about not having to talk more about my fake job than I did about the idea of coming up with more fabricated stories.

It was quiet for a moment. An extremely *long* moment.

"So," Joel mused as he stared out into the distance, "this is Georgia."

"Yup," I bobbed my head to concur, "this is Georgia." I looked out at the tree line, searching desperately for something else to say. "What about Paris? Everything been okay there?"

Joel nodded. "Yup," was all he said, still petting my dog.

We both sighed, as if we were trying to fill in the silence with a miscellaneous noise. It was awkward and unsettling. I hated it. For the first time in the history of our friendship, Joel and I were at a loss for words. How could two people as close as we were, knowing everything about each other, be so damn tongue-tied? I soon found out that the awkwardness didn't go unnoticed on his end.

"What's with us, Ev?" Joel asked, looking at me pleadingly. "Seriously, what is this shit? We're not even talking. Why do I feel like we're coming apart?"

"What?" I was actually shocked that he put it that way. I'd figured it could have been said a bit more subtly. "Jo Jo, we're not coming apart. I guess...I guess we just have a lot to catch up on and we don't know where to start, you know?" I watched him nod and I rolled my eyes at myself. Was that the best I could come up with? Where was my creativity?

"I should never have moved." Joel shook his head. "That ruined everything." I pursed my lips, frustrated that he was going to start blaming himself again. He turned to me. "Are you really okay? I mean I *see* that everything is okay, but....*are* you?"

I looked at those expectant eyes, full of concern and love for me. "I'm great, Jo," I embellished a bit. "I really am." I wanted to sound convincing and I didn't want him blaming himself for anything that had happened. I knew he still had reservations about the huge changes in our lives taking us in such dramatically different directions, but I didn't want our bond to break. Not now. Not after all the years we'd been friends. I didn't want another reason to be angry at God. "This new life is really working out," I said to him assuringly, and I knew I'd pulled it off when I saw him smirk at me, but he didn't look into my eyes. He kept his stare on my dog. "What's with that look?" I asked with a giggle.

Joel shrugged. "Maybe the new life has a lot to do with...the roommate?"

I laughed. "You're just saying that because you have a crush on him," I joked, relieved that we'd gotten past our moment of tension.

Joel sucked air. "That is *so* not true! I'm totally taken. I find him attractive, that's all."

"Well, I knew that already," I razzed him, taking a sip of the strong coffee.

"Although," he tapped his chin, "the other one is a cutie, too." I laughed at him. "But, seriously, I haven't really seen you smile the way you smiled last night in a long time, and I don't think it was all because of my showing up," he said. I gave him an incredulous look, and he sighed. "I mean, I know you are completely jovial about my visiting and all, but I saw you with him, Evika. Hayden pulls out this face in you that I can't even describe. You're like *glowing* when you're around him."

I raised an eyebrow. "You can see all that just from last night, huh?"

He looked at me with one of his are-you-kidding-me looks. "Please, girl. Don't insult me. How long have I known you now?"

I grinned. "Okay, okay. You're right. You know me like the

back of your hand," I admitted. I recalled the moment that I'd tried to kiss Hayden and wondered Joel had seen that part.

Joel kept his eyes locked on me and threw his hands up. "*And?*" he tried to get me to continue.

"And....you're right." I looked around to be sure no one else was there to hear my admission. "I totally have a thing for the roommate."

He smiled smugly and sighed. "I know."

"And that doesn't make you mad?"

"Ev, why would that make me mad?"

"Because you didn't want me to fall into something bad when I moved in with him."

"Yeah, but that was before I talked to him and before I met him."

I looked at him curiously. "So, that's all it took? One phone call and one night out at some Halloween party to conclude all of this?"

"Pretty much," Joel said blithely.

"Wow."

Joel laughed. "Why is that surprising to you?"

I looked at him seriously. "Because you have always been the one that's been protective of me. I didn't think it would be that easy." I was sort of disappointed.

He shrugged. "You said it yourself, Ev-bear. He's a twenty-twenty person. Maybe I see the same thing that you do." He smiled. "And honestly, it's not just what I see in you. I see something in him, too. The fact that he brought me and Evan here to surprise you, he really cares about you, Ev. A lot. And the way the guy looks at you, I mean, *wow*." If only Joel knew it was Hayden's job to watch over me as a Guardian angel.

I blushed as I thought about what Joel said, but I couldn't help wondering if he saw something that I didn't. I tried to kiss Hayden that previous night and got pushed away. Not to mention, all of the other times there were chances of our lips touching, it just never happened. I wondered if what Joel thought was based off of Hayden's angel charm, or if he really saw these things in Hayden. Nonetheless, it felt good that I had Joel's approval on the current situation. It made things a bit easier.

"So, does he know?" Joel inquired, breaking my train of thought.

"Know what?"

He gave me a puckish grin and leaned into me to whisper. "That you're in love with him, Ev-bear," he said.

I breathed a laugh. "Seriously?" I shook my head, slightly annoyed.

Joel looked at me inquisitively, then laughed heartily. "Ooohh, I get it." He grinned and leaned back in the porch swing.

"You get what, Joel?" I was slightly frustrated.

"You're not ready to admit the obvious yet, are you?"

I studied him while I thought. He was right. I didn't want to admit it, that I was in love with Hayden. Even though I'd admitted it to myself, there was no way, after the previous night's events, anyone would get me to admit it aloud.

"It could change the entire dynamic of our relationship," I said. "I'm not ready for that type of change yet." Joel's eyebrow raised as he gave me a hard, incredulous stare. "What?" I asked defensively.

"Right." He rolled his eyes. "And did you realize that before or after you tried to kiss him last night?" he asked bluntly. My eyes widened as I looked over at him in shock. "Yeah," he said, "I saw that too." It sort of stung finding out there had been an audience to my embarrassment. "Knowing you, you're never going to try again, are you?" He said it as if he were disappointed in me. I looked away, but I could see him shaking his head in my peripheral. "You are relentless in every, other way, and yet, you let something like this stop you."

Joel didn't really need me to answer, because I knew he already knew. It was the one thing about me; it took a lot for me to get to the point I was at in order to even try with Hayden, and I'd failed miserably. Luka, and I'm sure, Joel, both shared the same opinion, that it was just the wrong time and place for my advance. But it didn't matter. I was still turned down, and it hurt like hell.

"Well, it was a mistake. Shouldn't have even happened. Besides, we work together," I said, trying to deflect the topic of the conversation. "Bad idea, all around."

He nodded, then started playing with Beau's fur again. He still held an expression that told me he wanted to ask more. My stomach knotted again when I saw the look on his face. I wished so badly I could tell him everything that was going on with me, but then he would know too much. And I knew in my heart if I told him, he would uproot his life in an instant to move back home. I knew Joel, and I knew he would feel it necessary, that is, unless he thought I'd gone crazy... Then again, my alleged insanity would probably only further accelerate his need to come home to take care of me. I needed him to see that I was okay, no matter how much internal turmoil I had going on. I didn't want him to feel so segregated from my personal life.

"Believe it or not, I talked to Brittonia last week," Joel said.

"Did you really? You were nice to her, weren't you?" I pried. Joel was never a complete fan of Brittonia being in our friendship circle, but he still made efforts to tolerate her.

"Of course I was nice to her," he guffawed. "I'm not an ass, Ev-bear. She *did* impress me quite a bit ever since you were in coma-land, you know."

I'd forgotten that Joel and Brit had kept in touch while I was comatose for those few months. Brittonia had done a lot to help me out, and even offered help to Joel, but he was too proud to let Brit's dad pay some of his bills. Joel had let a lot of things go unpaid so he could use the money for his flight to come visit me in the hospital.

"I think her heart's finally thawing a little." I giggled. "I haven't talked to her since right before we moved, but she seemed really happy with some new guy she started dating a few months ago."

Joel nodded. "Yeah. Some dude named Christian?"

"Yup, that's it," I said.

"She seemed really smitten with this one," he said. "And it's got to be some new record for her, no doubt. She's never with anyone longer than a few weeks." That was true.

"I'm happy for her. He sounds like a keeper from what she told me."

Joel shook his head. "Oh, the poor boy."

I laughed. "Don't be mean." I nudged him and smiled. "So, how about you and Evan?" I changed the subject. "You two were meant for each other. That's pretty clear."

Joel let out a dramatic, girlie, I'm-in-love sigh, "I know." I could see him melting. "I'm gonna marry that boy one day."

I giggled. "I swear, you should have been a girl, Jo Jo."

"This is true," he agreed with my joke. "But, like I said before, he's my Superman. Enough man for the both of us." He chuckled.

I looked at him solemnly. "I like him a lot, Jo. He's good for you."

Joel gave me a genuine smile. "Just as Hayden is good for you, Ev-bear."

I looked at my best friend with admiration, so happy that he hadn't seen Hayden as a threat to our friendship or my life, but as a reason for him to let go of his constant worry. Maybe Hayden knew all along that, not only did *I* need that visit, Joel needed it even more. He needed to witness, for himself, just how good things really were on the surface, so he didn't have to carry that guilt so much like he always did since the day he left for Paris. It was honestly the perfect solution in order to heal the both of us.

I could feel the smile on my face as I sipped my pungent coffee and I laid my head on my best friend's bony shoulder. The both of us swayed in the porch swing along with the light wind and watched the sun finally peek out from behind a cloud.

Chapter Nine *Airplanes and Angel Dust*

Driving Joel and Evan back to the airport was bittersweet. It felt like the beginning and the end of something. A certain clarity fell upon me during those three days while having my best friend visit. It was as if he brought the feeling of home with him, but in some ways, the feeling felt a bit foreign as well. A huge change had taken place in my life, and I'd somehow managed to accept that. Part of that change, other than my whole lifestyle, was in me. I felt more grown up in some ways, like a certain level of maturity had fallen over me. In a way, I was relieved and felt silently proud of myself.

Toward the evening of the second day of the visit, Hayden and Joel teamed up and made a full course dinner. They marinated chicken and steak all day long for the grilled shish kabobs. Joel made his famous au gratin potatoes as a side, and they even made carrot cupcakes with cream cheese filling and topping.

"The man can cook," Joel wiggled his eyebrows at me as we all started eating.

Hayden laughed. "Funny, those are almost the exact words Evika said when I cooked her breakfast a few weeks ago." I looked over at him to see his smug expression. Always one for tooting his own horn. I had to laugh along with him. We all did.

On the last day, we'd decided to have a movie marathon, just like Joel and I used to do. Comedy, horror, action, chick-flicks; you name it, we had it. It was funny how we'd all melded into our positions in the living room to watch the movies, Luka on the recliner with Beau's huge body spilling over his lap, Joel and Evan huddled together in a blanket with a constantly-filled bowl of cheese puffs, and me, comfortable with my head in a pillow on Hayden's lap while he played with my hair.

We were like this happy family. We didn't need to go out and drink or party to amuse ourselves. We didn't need to be out shopping and spending money. All we needed was one room, one television, a pizza delivery, and each other. During moments when my attention was elsewhere, I'd steal a glance at Jo and Evan. I saw those content faces, those smiles they wore, and once in a while, I'd catch them feeding each other a cheese puff. I imagined them in Joel's little apartment in Paris, together. I felt satisfied to know they felt comfortable enough to be who they were around me, around Hayden and Luka.

Memories of the first time I took Joel to the airport, months before, played through my head. I tried to pinpoint the emotion I was feeling when we walked into the lobby. I took a deep breath, watching Evan and Joel walking side by side with their luggage as Luka and I trailed behind. I realized it was a little easier to let Joel go this time. I wondered why that was. I loved him with all my heart, but I guess I just felt better that the void that used to be my place was now filled with someone who could be with him all of the time since I couldn't. Evan had this awesome sense of humor that could get Joel out of his worst mood. He possessed this patience that was remarkable. It was all the things that I couldn't really be for Joel anymore. In theory, it was all the criteria to make me jealous, but not an ounce of jealousy ran though me. I felt content and relieved because I was placing my best friend in the hands of someone that was, essentially, better for him than I was.

"Why is it always me going on the airplanes, Ev?" Joel nudged me with a forced smile.

I smirked and shook my head at him. "You're not the one with an aversion, silly boy."

Joel's face stiffened once we got up to security, as if he were holding those tears in, but it only made it harder for me to control my own. "We're doing it again, Ev. We're making this seem like a final 'goodbye.'" I knew he was referring to the time he left for Paris. Airports always meant 'goodbye' for us.

I stepped up and wrapped my arms around him, squeezing him hard, trying to focus my energy into the hug and not into the tears. "It's not 'goodbye,' Jo Jo. It's only 'see ya later.' Remember?" I said in a shaky voice.

Joel sniffled as his gripping hold around me tightened. "I'm gonna miss you all over again, Ev-bear," he said quietly. "It feels like something is missing when I don't have you with me."

I breathed deep and squeezed my eyes shut tightly to get the last of the tears out, but that hit home. And it hit hard. Why were those words coming out right when he was ready to board a plane again? Why wasn't it something we'd talked about when we were alone that first morning? And why was I having to be the strong one all of the sudden?

I slowly broke our hug so I could look at my best friend's drooping face, wet with tears. "I've been feeling that way too, Jo," I admitted, wiping my own tears, "but you know that, no matter what, we'll always have each other. Even when you become the next Iron Chef," I teased, and he chuckled. "I'll be there to witness it." I glanced at Evan, who was standing a few feet from us with his hands in his tattered jeans' pockets, rocking back and forth on his feet, trying not to let his wet eyes pour. I gave him a sympathetic smile. "And so will Evan." I nodded at the boy, and he took that as his cue to dart over, arms wide open, hugged Joel and me into him.

"Oh, you guys make my heart melt. I can't stand it," Evan bellowed theatrically. I think he was trying to lighten things up, but I could sense that we really were getting to him. I trusted that he would console my best friend on the flight home, and he was strong enough to do it, just as he had been once before.

We stood there hugging for at least a minute before all three of us turned our curiosity to the silent Luka a few steps away. He was picking at a hanging thread at the end of his t-shirt, oblivious for a moment, then finally looked up to see each of us staring at him and waiting.

He put his hands up. "Oh, no. I draw the line at group hugs." He chuckled.

"Oh, come on. You know you wanna melt too," Evan teased.

We three huffed a laugh as Luka blushed and shook his head. It was worth a shot.

I gave Evan and Joel kisses on their cheeks. "You better call me as soon as you guys land." I pointed my finger at them.

"Promise," Joel nodded and took a deep breath before lifting his luggage. "Come on, E-Zone."

I chuckled at the nickname and smiled at Joel with adoration. "You finally came up with a good one for him, huh?"

Joel grinned. "It wasn't hard after he started calling me Jo-Zone."

"I see." I smiled wryly at Evan. "So you're the creative one in the relationship now, eh?"

Evan leaned in, but spoke loud enough for all of us to hear. "Girl, you have no idea."

I gasped at his admission and laughed, shaking my head at the endless meanings of that comment.

"Love you, Jo," I said.

"Love you back, Ev." Joel forced a small smile.

Luka walked up for a final handshake and fist bump with the boys, then put his arm around my shoulder as we watched them walk away.

"You gonna be okay?" Luka asked.

"Sure," I answered unconvincingly. "I'm fine."

He tilted his head at me. "You do know what *fine* means, don't you?" My eyebrows raised, waiting for him to enlighten me. "It's an acronym for...feeling intensely neurotic and edgy."

I burst out laughing. "Where do you come up with this stuff?"

"No idea. It's a gift." He spun around on his heels, locked my arm in his and directed us to the way out.

Luka and I returned back to the house after taking Joel and Evan to the airport, and he decided to take Beau out for a walk. I swear he was getting more attached to that dog than I was the second time around.

I sighed and took in the quiet that fell upon the house once again, somewhat sad and somewhat relieved. But it was also an unnerving feeling, knowing that I didn't have the distraction of Joel and Evan to get me out of awkward moments with Hayden since Halloween night. I knew I'd have to get it over with, that first alone-with-Hayden-after-I-attempted-to-kiss-him-but-failed-miserably moment.

I took a deep breath and ascended the stairs, passing by Hayden's room. I crept up to the door and leaned against the frame as I watched him fan and re-fan out the top sheet to his bed. The laundry basket was sitting next to him. I smiled, taking in the moment as the sunlight shined into the room and casted light around his shadow. He looked over at me and smiled in mid lift of the next attempt of getting the bed sheet over the mattress.

"Hey," he said.

I walked into the room. "Hey."

"Send the boys off?" he asked, shaking the sheet out again.

I nodded. "Yup."

He studied me for a moment before lifting the sheet again. "You okay?"

"Yeah, I'm good," I said nonchalantly. "Need some help there?"

"Nah, I got it." He shook the sheet out again and it floated further to the right this time. "Dammit," he muttered.

I rolled my eyes as I saw him lift that damned sheet into the air again and jumped up onto the head of the bed to grab the other end before he tried fluffing it a fiftieth time.

I chuckled. "I thought you were good at everything," I teased.

"Ha!" he guffawed. "So did I."

I shook my head at him and laughed as I placed my end of the sheet down and smoothed it out evenly over the corners of the mattress, giving him a smug look.

He tossed the second sheet up into the air and I caught my end, but I was awestruck by the particles floating in the air and smiled at the memory of which I was reminded.

"My mom always used to tell me that the fuzzies in the air were angel dust," I recalled. "She said the angels would come down and sprinkle your laundry to give you good dreams." I breathed a laugh at the thought, shaking my head.

"You believed her for a long time," Hayden added. It didn't surprise me that he had a comment. There were hardly any memories I had that he hadn't already witnessed. "Even after the whole Santa Claus thing," he added.

We placed the down comforter over the top of the bed and threw the pillows up toward the headboard.

I looked at him and shrugged. "I never really had the bad dreams to ever prove her wrong."

He looked over at me with a solemn expression. But, as if he were editing words in his head and deciding not to say them, he looked down at the bed and put his hands in his pockets. "Thanks," he said with a simper, nodding at the bed.

"No problem." I walked over to the empty laundry basket and picked it up. I grunted inside my head. I wanted to say something else. Anything. "You know," I turned around with the basket on my hip, "maybe she was right."

"About what?"

"Angel dust," I answered. It may have sounded strange, but I knew that he would understand what I meant; my subtle way of telling him that I was okay.

He studied me for a moment, then finally grinned. "Maybe," he humored me.

I carried the hamper and a coy smile with me as I walked out of the room.

Chapter Ten *The World Is Darkest At Midnight*

Another dream. A new feeling of tranquility. Sleep had become my sanctuary, a way to escape my new reality, and as far as I knew, Hayden had kept his promise of leaving my dreams private. That fact alone was another reason to love him even more than I thought was possible. We'd finally had an understanding, he and I. That felt good.

It was the end of the second week with the dreamcatcher when the dream occurred. I'd had the pleasant dreams, as expected. Some consisted of my mother, Joel, Ms. Makerov, other acquaintances throughout my life that my mind had chosen to remember for some reason, and even some floating moments of Hayden that I was easily able to distinguish as indelible memories. But this one night, this one dream, a new presence became apparent. It was the dream in which I'd lost control again, unable to place myself where I wanted to be.

I'd been playing the piano alongside my mother when the scenery had changed. I was standing on the shore, barefoot in the sand. I felt the wind lightly graze my skin and I looked down. I was wearing a light gray, cotton sun dress with some tiny, purple flowers embroidered around the waist line. In reality, it was a dress I'd shoved to the back of the closet and hardly ever wore unless there was an occasion that called for it. I looked up again, recognizing my surroundings as the beach closest to my home, and was going to shrug it off until I saw a figure walking toward me from only a few yards away. It wasn't someone I knew, but something inside of me told me I should.

A black dress shirt, completely unbuttoned and draped over his perfect chest muscles as he walked toward me with a swagger, his hands in the pockets of his loose-fitted khakis. The sunset highlighted his mocha skin and hairless head with a golden tint. I felt myself staring, taking in this new character. My first instinct told me that, due to his beauty he had to be an angel, one I hadn't met yet. It was during that thought that his grin grew from ear to ear, revealing his flawless, white teeth. It was a winning smile that only an angel could have possessed. I was sure of it.

He finally strolled up to me, putting his swaggering to a stop. I gazed at the man's handsome, ageless face and into his eyes. They were like the guilty gray that painted the sky after a devastating storm, the aftermath of destruction, defeat that followed a perilous battle. They were mysterious, with a slight sparkle I hadn't missed, an assurance to me that I had nothing to fear.

I giggled lightly in his presence, an uncontrollable release on my behalf. "Hello," I simply said smiling with embarrassment.

He nodded once, holding his grin. "Good evening," his liquid voice said as he lifted my hand gently to his warm lips to give it a tender kiss. He returned it to me so delicately. A gentleman, to say the least.

"Do I know you?" I inquired.

"I'm afraid that you do not, my dear, at least, not in this manner," he said disappointedly. "But," he perked, "I'm quite sure that you will....in due time."

I looked at him curiously, slightly baffled that his identity was to remain a mystery, but it was an impossibility to argue with him – a skill of mine that was most prominent and I couldn't even bring myself to do it.

I heard an acoustic guitar echoing throughout the atmosphere, a hazy sound with no origin, but clear enough that I could recall the familiarity of the song titled "A Stranger." Then his hand reached out for mine.

"May I ask you to dance, fair one?" His alluring grin held my gaze and my hand floated up to his involuntarily as I placed the other on his broad shoulder. He was warm to the touch. He placed his other arm around me, lightly pressing against the small of my back and pulling me toward him, but not too close.

I did as my body wanted and felt my feet step in time along with his. The sand under our feet became a small, wooden, dance floor, big enough only for us. The sun was still setting upon us and, in that moment when the words to the song were sung, I felt as if we were the only two left on the entire planet. An isolation of two strangers, together. And yet still, I felt no fear.

Our steps were slow, but even if they were faster, my feet surely would have been able to keep up. My body moved without my knowing. I put no thought to the motions as I stared into his eyes, thousands of questions pinging against the walls of my mind, aching to be asked.

The handsome stranger lifted my arm into the air with such grace, beckoning my body to twirl on its feet. And I twirled. My light dress flowed along with the turn and we were back in our original position, his hand on my back once again, pulling me closer. I didn't retreat. I let it happen, still captivated by this stranger of my dreams.

I felt an urge trembling inside of me, an eagerness, the one that I'd had to hush lately. I didn't know what was going on with me and I was afraid to ask questions and was especially too afraid to know the true answers to them. What was it about this stranger that was doing this to me?

His expression was undaunted and he held me with such confidence, which also showed in his stature. His stare into my eyes was penetrating, and it was then that I started to falter. I begged my eyes to turn away from him, and they finally relented, looking down at the sand around the shiny floor upon which we were dancing.

I froze, hitching my breath and locking my eyes on them, the shadows. Our shadows. I felt my stomach drop at the sight. They were dancing together, but they were not alike. His body casted something of another world on the sand. I traced the outline of the shadow with my eyes; first, the large wings that spread from its back, and then to the head that towered over mine, an inhuman silhouette. He was not from my world, nor was he the angel I so ignorantly mistook him for.

The music continued to play, but was drawing to a close as I slowly leveled my eyes with his once again. "Who are you?" I demanded, pushing against his chest in a panic. I gulped as my heart sped, searching deep in his eyes for an answer.

He stopped swaying and curled his lips into a wicked grin, lifting his smooth hand to my cheek; this time his touch was as hot as sunbathed asphalt, yet cold as ice. I couldn't decipher which I was experiencing.

"This, somehow, gives new meaning to the phrase 'dancing with the devil,' does it not?" He asked.

I sucked air, backing away from his touch. *Alysto!* I screamed in my head. That's when the sun was gone and the night had come. He'd disappeared. It was black all around me, and the silence was deafening, frightening. My heart sped, and my body's trembling began.

"Is it not true that you know yourself better in the darkness?" his liquid voice asked all around me.

I stood rigid, not knowing where to turn, but I was able to answer. "No," I shook my head. "I'm lost in the darkness."

"Oh, but I disagree, Fortis, Brave One. For, in darkness, you are home."

My breath hitched again at his words. I couldn't breath, and I was afraid to even twitch. I wanted to wake up. This place was not becoming what was promised, my dream world had been infiltrated by an intruder. I had to wake up.

I looked around and into the black of night, took a deep breath and shut my eyes. I listened to my surroundings and heard only the wind softly blowing and heard what sounded like tall palm leaves and a creaking porch swing. I felt no change, but when I opened my eyes, the scene had become something else, entirely. I was in the yard behind the house. This time, it felt more real. It felt like that place between asleep and awake. I kept telling myself to run home, but my body was disobedient.

I felt a rumbling under my feet and the speeding increase of my heart. I wasn't alone, there was a presence unseen, but felt amidst the fusing heat that changed the air. A figure start forming in front of me in the tree line. I blinked hard and tried to keep an expressionless face. I didn't want it to know I was afraid, whatever it was. I didn't want it to feel the fear radiating from me.

But what I saw next was hard to fathom. Walking slowly toward me out of the night was a tall dark creature, much more majestic than the ones I'd encountered before. His wings were magnificent, putting a Drone's wings to shame. They spread out endlessly, filtering my view of the full moon light. The eyes of an ancient soul, that soft gray once again, this time like the calming clouds that would threaten an overcast, the kind under which I felt most content. It was hard to let my eyes wander to the rest of his features, but he stood close to seven feet tall with a gargoyle-like shape for his body. His dark gray skin was smooth, and every muscle on his chest and in his arms and legs was defined, in perfect proportion. I took in the gracefulness of his body movements. It was as if he were dancing slowly, so as not to make a wrong move that would startle me. In a sense, he was the beauty of the darkness.

"Alysto," I gasped his name in disbelief.

He bowed his head slightly, giving me confirmation. "Yes, Brave One," his seductive voice whispered down to me. "We finally meet." I was even more mesmerized by him after he spoke to me again. He seemed to have the same respectable disposition he'd had in his previous form on the beach.

I hardly knew what to say next. I went blank. "Is-is this your true form?" I stuttered.

He gracefully lowered his back end to the ground and sat rigid with his shoulders squared and his head cocked. "It is," he answered wryly. "However, you seem to have the ability to see my less monstrous appearance, what I used to be. This is apparent."

I swallowed hard. "You did not will yourself to appear that way?" I asked.

He shook his head slowly. "I did not. For, this is the form in which all perceive me, what I have become."

A chill crept down my spine. "And is this still a dream?" I asked.

His deep laugh was patronizing, "It is now very much reality,

Brave One."

I froze, unable to look at anything but his dark eyes until I was finally able to curl my bare toes, feeling the ground beneath. The wet grass was cold and soft under my feet.

"Hmm. Dreams," he said distantly. "Any good slumber is a rarity on my list of activities. I am sure you can find relation to this statement, yes?" His mannerisms were that of a cat giving into its curiosity.

I looked deeper into his dark eyes and focused on the tiny sparkle I'd caught in them earlier, hoping that this meeting was meant to be non-threatening. "Yes," I nodded slowly. "I, too, do not see much sleep anymore." I assessed his expression minutely, so eager to know why we were meeting. I forced myself to ask the question. "Alysto, why did you call upon me?"

His eyes narrowed. "Call to *you*?" His brow cocked as he lowered his head to mine. "Fortis, I've only answered to the your call upon *me*. Perhaps, a particular instrument has been beneficial in this matter?"

I looked at him curiously. "Instrument?" I inquired. I thought for a moment, but it didn't take me long to figure it out. "The dreamcatcher," I breathed out in awe. He gave me an expression of satisfaction which gave me my answer. The giant angel came to mind, and I cringed. "Jericho," I whispered, narrowing my eyes and flexing my jaw. I knew there was a reason that angel left a bad taste in my mouth. "He did this? Why?"

"Let us not cast blame just yet, Warrior. You've taken just as much a part in this encounter as my ally." He let out a musing sigh. "There are many riddles in life that will never be understood, Brave One. But know this; that which is dark is not always evil. And that which is light is not always good."

"But I don't understand. It was you who brought me here," I retorted.

"Was it?" he asked. His eyes lowered to my chest and he slowly rose one of his massive claws, touching it tenderly against my heart. "I believe your heart is following a different path, Fortis. It knows what it wants."

I shook my head, not wanting to believe him. "No."

"Then let us explore other theories, shall we?" he laced his long claws together and looked up in thought. "Do you not think it plausible that not only has your God abandoned you but that you have abandoned your faith in God?"

He was right. I'd lost faith years ago, all three of them if you wanted to get technical. I stopped trying to follow any sort of path or faith, but I didn't want to agree with him. I shook my head violently this time. "I don't want to believe that," I said unconvincingly.

"No?" he asked in a patronizing tone. "But deep down, and more recently I might add, your heart feels it. Does it not?"

I was afraid then. A new fear swept over me, and I'm sure that it emanated from me. Was he right? Oh, God, he was. I'd felt so many strange emotions after leading this new life and they were all dark, wrong. What if my heart really was trying to tell me something?

He continued. "Perhaps there is a reason that one of my

children saw something in you that night not too long ago? He saw something different in you, Fortis, something of which could never be found in the others."

I stiffened as he rose to pace around me, circling the ground on which I stood. He was waiting for an answer. I continued to argue.

"The only reason I would call to you would be in the hopes that I may better understand your reign over the Seekers, perhaps ask a request of you, to discontinue this imbalance and to reign over them as you were meant to. My destiny is to fight against you, but I don't want to if there is chance that you may have reason in you." I started to falter again, fumbling over my choice of words. "Th-that would be the only reason my heart would have had any desire to call to you."

"I see." He stopped pacing and planted himself in front of me, lifting his head. His eyes widened with enthusiasm. "That is a reasonable theory, Brave One. However, I hope you do not take offense to my lack of motivation in making any attempt at changing this *imbalance*, as you call it," he huffed with a small laugh, then slowly took in his wings and laid them into his body. His movements were soundless.. He studied me for a few seconds. "Optime," he said to himself. "Although....," he looked at me with his alluring eyes, "Be honest with me, Brave One. Do you see a light within them? When you save these wicked souls, do you truly find even the slightest bit of compassion within yourself to know you are really doing the right thing? I do find it intriguing that you would determine that your heart's desire to beg me to let these souls all move on is your only reason for calling to me."

I looked at him, confused. "Intrigued? Why is that? And why am I, what you call, Brave One?"

"Do you not know the history of the Soldiers of the past, before your time? Not one has called my name in good standing." He watched me, waiting for an answer.

"I wasn't told much about you," I answered honestly.

"Then, I believe that your Guardian has much on which to educate you," he said facetiously.

"Then it was due to fear? No one called to you due to fear?"

He shook his head slowly. "It was not fear of *me* that kept them from calling my name. It was, and is always, fear of Him." I thought about this statement, and it confused me even more. He continued. "You are the Brave One, as you may still fear me, but you do not fear changing the rules of this destiny, nor do you fear trying to alter the inevitability of your own fate in order to change the fate of others."

How could he even know these things? How was it possible? I searched his eyes with curiosity. Something told me there was more to this creature than just an evil darkness. I wanted to believe this so much. "Am I wrong to think that I am capable of such a thing?" I started pacing slowly as I spoke, never taking my eyes from his, but trembling all the while.

His head cocked, and as his brow furrowed as he lowered his neck, bringing himself closer to me. This kept me from pacing and I froze. "You are wrong to think *I* am capable of such a thing, Fortis." I stared at him with wide eyes and let him continue. His expression softened, which put me a little more at ease. "For, you must see something in me that the others never had?"

I thought for a moment, trying to examine my intuition, how my heart really felt about the devil. Finally, I felt myself slowly nodding. "Y-Yes. I feel this. I feel you must have some reason in you. Even an ounce of goodness inside you could make that possible. You were once full of light. That's the story I was told. You must still have some of that left, even after all this time." My heart had hoped with all its might that I was right. I wanted to crack him somehow, to get him to search inside himself to find that bit of light that I could see in him.

"Ah yes, the unavailing gift you possess, this ability to find the good in others." He rose a hand to his chin and started rubbing it as if he were pondering. "Can you honestly see a light within *me*?" His tone seemed condescending again.

"You're mocking me," I stated disappointedly.

He crouched on all fours to my level again. "It is only my curiosity, Fortis."

I nodded. "Yes, Alysto. I believe there is goodness and light in everything. Even in you. Some just get taken by the darkness. They let it embrace them and they lose themselves."

He let out a booming laugh. "Indeed. But it is quite needless to say that the darkness always wins. Yes?"

I shook my head. "No." I started pacing again while staring into his eyes. "The darkness doesn't always win. I know this."

He gave me an incredulous stare. "I find it amusing that you preach this to me, that all can overcome the darkness, yet it is *you* who forces yourself to release the Seekers from their doom and all the while you do not see that light within them. And you never have, not once." His stare was penetrating once again. "You struggle with this....because you can actually see what they've done to be placed in my realm."

My stomach dropped again. How could he know these things? I was an idiot to think I could keep my feelings from him. He seemed to know it all.

"There must be a light within them if the Creator has chosen them to move on," I argued as I lowered my head, becoming discomposed, "even if I do not."

"So, you do admit that you must battle with yourself to save them? Am I correct?"

I became agitated. "It's not my choice." I raised my voice and looked him in the eyes again. "God has mercy, something of which I never had, and something of which you've lost entirely."

"*Wrong!*" he seethed through his teeth, furrowing his brow. I jumped at the boom of his voice. "Remember this, Fortis, and heed my words. I am no different from the Creator." His face came closer to mine. I shivered. "If your God is so merciful, why it is that I even exist? Hmm?"

I couldn't help my short breaths, scared out of my mind. Alysto softened his expression, as if he felt regret in instilling me with the fear he could so easily raise in me. He looked at me with solemn eyes, and then as they narrowed. "And this tenebrae, this darkness within you? The darkness of which you have been repressing for a while now, will you have the strength in order not to let it destroy you?"

I froze again, realizing what he was referring to, the part of me that I feared. The part of me that I kept to myself. Alysto seemed to be the only one who could see it. I battled with myself, trying to tell myself that he was only using these things to make me waiver, to break me down. But I had no words for him. At that point, his uncanny knowledge about me was disconcerting and I felt sick to my stomach.

He let out a dramatic sigh. "It must be so frustrating, knowing that you are unable to avenge your mother now, is it not?" he asked me blithely.

I found my voice again as the subject sparked a new emotion. "What are you talking about?"

His smug look pierced my heart, as if he were proud that it was so easy to get to me. "Why, Mr. Carter is with me now, Brave One. And he will be for a very, very long time." My face must have turned ashen. He smirked at me, realizing I'd understood. "Is it possible, Fortis, that you come to me with an agenda that is only to mask the *real* reason you are here before me right now? Is it possible that this impressive dichotomy of which you've controlled in yourself has finally started to unravel?" His face moved slowly toward mine, and I could feel the heat of his breath in my hair. I did not dare look up, but trembled in my stance. "Tenebrae," he said as the back of his hand rose to softly graze my cheek. The heat was simultaneously icy and stifling as he touched me, but the pain I anticipated did not exist. "Is it possible," he purred, "that the reason you called to me tonight is because you feel the pull of that darkness within you?"

I panicked inside. Was this a trick? Was this really just a trap that I'd set up on my own in order to give in to him? What the hell was my *heart* doing to me that I didn't know about? Was my curiosity going to be the reason that this entire legend would fail?

I was breathing heavily, but composed myself before I spoke. "No," I shook my head as I looked up into his eyes once again. "If my heart's agenda was to meet you, then I've come to you in order to plead with you to let go of the Seekers that are supposed to move on as they were meant to move on." I gained some of myself back and tried to regroup my confidence. "Alysto, I plead with you to reign the underworld the way you were meant to reign it. I want that balance back for all of mankind and for all of the lost souls, but most of all, for me."

He looked at me inquisitively, then smiled wryly. "You *do* see the things they've done. I was told this."

"By a traitor to the Council!" I said angrily.

"And a rogue angel I no longer need," he added.

I ignored his remark. "If you do possess that light I see in you, then you will, at the very least, think about my request. We can achieve balance again as long as you agree to it, or else I'll just have to save a thousand times more Seekers than any Warrior before me."

He spoke through his teeth, frustrated, whispering into my ear. "What is it that makes you think any of them are even worth saving at all? You see the evil they've done. When you save them and you die for them, do you even shed an ounce of empathy after witnessing the horrid mess they've created for themselves and for others in your world? How is it that you would even come here in hopes to save those miserable mutants from the hell that they deserve?"

His discomposure was surely apparent then, and I could see that this subject had angered him, but I had to save myself. I wanted to say it aloud, not only for him, but for myself to hear. I needed to know I was there for the right reason, even though I had no recollection of calling to him. "Because that was the balance that was created and *meant* to be followed. You chose to break the balance in order to gain more power. All the Seekers who have served their time with you have been with you long enough. It is time to let them go."

He pulled himself away and sat rigidly again on his hind legs, huffing, his wings loosening. He was smirking at me again. "Why do you think it is, Brave One, that I gain more power from keeping them imprisoned with me?"

I shook my head and shrugged. "I don't know."

"Oh, come now," he said. "It is because the darkness within them has never subsided. I was meant to hold onto them and call them forth on their judgment day, and to release them to the Creator's World of Light. I, like you, still see a part of them that others do not, but I see that darkness is still within them. But even they do not see it, or feel it. I ask that you remit me for my paltering, but you must see that I have good reason of my own to deny you of your request. There will be no relinquishment of the reign that I have over these wicked wanderers."

Like you. The words sounded over and over inside my head. I was nothing like him. He was supposed to be the epitome of the evil I was to rise against and overcome, and he had the audacity to claim we were anything alike? I felt angry about what he'd said, but I wasn't sure if I was more perturbed that he would voice such a falsehood or if I had been angry with myself at the thought that he may be right, that we were alike in some way. Could this be? Our gifts in seeing a concealed truth in other beings, was it possible that we shared the same gift? I decided to argue.

"We are nothing alike," I said to him sternly as I tried to convince myself.

He narrowed his eyes, searching mine once again. "We are more alike than you wish to realize, Brave One. I only need to wait for your surrender to the calling. For, you cannot escape who you are or what you were meant to be." We stared into each other's eyes with intensity, and then he spoke again. "I do wish that you could see this my way." He sighed. "Nonetheless, we must continue with *this* balance." He rose above me and stood tall, unfurling his wings and raising his head high above me. "As I have once said, your Guardian has much on which to educate you." His smile grew wider. "And I do admit that even I feel rather anxious to know when certain things have come to light for you, Fortis."

I searched his dark eyes curiously. "Certain things?"

"Oh," the beast's eyes narrowed, and his lips curled into a wry smile, "there is much to be revealed to you, fair one." His head jerked away. "But you will find out in due time."

I swallowed hard, afraid to ask for specifics, and afraid to move, mesmerized by this creature.

"I do hope that you've been enjoying my gift to you," he said.

"G-gift to me?" I was confused. "What is that?"

"My children have been ordered not to harm you for the time being. I'm sure you've noticed things have been much...*quieter* since the last attack, yes?"

Favors again. I was getting them from every direction. "Yes, my Guardian has been worried about this."

"Ha," he guffawed. "There is no need to worry right now, Fortis. Things will be as they are meant to soon enough." He narrowed his eyes. "But I do suggest that you keep this encounter between us, as I am sure it would be devastating for you to witness the terrible things that I could inflict upon him, should your Guardian get involved," he threatened. I narrowed my eyes, feeling protective and helpless. He seemed pleased that his threat bothered me, and then continued. "After all," he continued, "it was your invite tonight. That fact alone would be something he could never bear to hear." Guilt pierced my heart at his words. "You and your Guardian have your faith and I, of course, have my own. I've had centuries to acquire the virtue of patience, something of which you do not have." He laughed lightly and continued. "I do not need to use force on you, Brave One, as I know if I wait long enough, you will surrender. Until then, I bid you adieu and shall gravel in my acquired virtue. Time is always on my side, unlike yours," he teased as he inched himself closer, towering over me. My eyes met his chest and I could feel his hot breath fall over me. "Unless of course, you should choose to surrender to my world now, to surrender to that *darkness* I see that you have within you?"

His taunting angered me, and despite his efforts to be civil, I felt a rage that took me over. I pushed against his chest to move him away, my right wrist pressing hard against his heart. A singing pain burned within my wrist as it touched his skin, and I heard him bellow a loud roar, backing away from me holding his chest, panting. I looked down at my burning wrist and saw that my birthmark had become darker as it throbbed. I held it against me to try to get the pain to go away as I looked back at Alysto. He was observing the mark left over his skin, the mirror image of my negative zero. It was a frightening site. *Backwards.* I gasped.

"So," he said between his panting breaths, "it is not the devil that marks the astray child, but the astray child that marks the devil." He looked at me in amazement for a moment, then curled his mouth into a smirk, caressing the new scar over his heart. "Such a team we would make, Fortis."

I stared deep into his dark, ancient eyes. "Never," I said, still holding my throbbing wrist.

"Numquam?" his thick brow rose. "Very well then." He bowed his head to me in a gentleman-like fashion. "Although, I'm not entirely convinced that you'll be able to keep that promise to yourself." He laughed again. "Bona fortuna, Fortis, dum conaris retinere lucem tecum." He flashed me a devious smile, then he slowly backed away into the tree line. I was still frowning at him as he prepared to leave. "Vale, Brave One." And then he was out of sight, darting off into the air with bullet speed. He may as well have just disappeared.

I was left alone in a heavy silence. The night around me felt cold and unwelcoming. The pale moon light brought me back to reality as I let my eyes get used to the darkness again. I concentrated on the ground below me, digging my toes into the grass. It all felt so real, and it was, just like the sick feeling in my stomach. It hadn't been a dream. I checked my surroundings once again and found the direction to run back to the house.

It was unexplainable. What was to become of this? Why would he want me in his world? I found the good in people. *Tried* to anyway.

I thought about the possibility of how much power he could be acquiring through keeping the lost souls within his realm. He was the Keeper of the Wicked, but somehow turned into this monster. I couldn't help thinking there was still a chance to reason with him, though. Something had to be enough to make him give in to my request, I just didn't know what.

I tiptoed back into the house, checking the clock.

It was a little past midnight.

I looked down at my soiled feet and gasped, mechanically walking to the bathroom. I needed a shower to clear my head and to cleanse myself entirely. It was too bad that the water couldn't erase that night's events. I couldn't fall back to sleep that night thinking about the intense visit with Alysto. It bothered me that he said he found a darkness inside of me. Had I not felt it myself recently, I would have thought it a trick on his part to throw me off course, so-to-speak. But I *did* feel it, I *was* trying to repress it. What did that mean?

As I thought about all of these things, heading back upstairs to my room, I saw my journal laying open on the bed. I grabbed the book and read the page to which it was opened. Something told me I'd already written about that encounter with the devil, but I had no recollection of it. The entry was undated.

Crash, Burn and Crumble

When we collapse
Adapt to the waiting
Crash, Burn and Crumble
We'll all stop breathing
The dreams I dream
The dreams I seek
Will make me fall
Will make me weak
Deep in your thoughts
Deep in your wake
I will take your place
For everyone's sake
Lost once again
Cannot be found
Taste nothing but fear
Hear only one sound
The last beats of my heart
Which split in two
As I end this life
That I once knew

I gasped after reading it. I stood from the bed, shaking as I read the poem over and over again, each time a little less cryptic. I paced the room, calculating what I was going to do next. I threw the journal into my nightstand drawer and pulled out my ash tray, staring at it, wondering if I really wanted to do what I was thinking I had to do. My eyes averted to the ornament above my bed, the one thing that was supposed to give me peace at night.

Alysto could threaten me all he wanted, but I wasn't going to give in. I would never let him or his pathetic, angel-ally bring me down, nor would I ever let them touch my angel. I felt fierce and protective as I ripped the dreamcatcher off of the nail in the wall and tossed it into the ashtray. A blast of thunder and pelting rain solidified that I was furious. If destroying the dreamcatcher was the one thing I had in my power to keep Alysto away, then I would do it, even if that meant sacrificing my nightly bliss. The responsibility was clear.

I turned out my light and lit the match, watching it burn for a few seconds before tossing it into the ashtray. The dreamcatcher caught flame in record time and singed into nothing but ash after a few minutes. I lay in my bed, staring at the flame until it went out completely and listened to the rain outside while I fantasized that Jericho could feel his wings burn.

It was dark then.

I sat motionless, reluctant. Any move I made, it all led to Hayden. I wanted to be near him. I needed to be with him. I finally walked down the hall to his room, and a new shiver sent itself up my spine, setting my feet at an urgent pace. I couldn't get to him quickly enough.

I stood in the light of the doorway, listening to the light rainfall and focused on his face as he slept so peacefully in the bed, the moonlight glazing his face with a soft, pale blue. As if something woke him, his eyes fluttered open and he looked at me, startling me instantly.

"Evika?" he said sleepily as he sat up. "Are you okay?"

At first, I couldn't move or speak when he asked me. I just shivered, holding my arms across my body. Finally, I found my voice, ready to answer. "I....I get it now."

"You get what, Ev?"

I took a deep breath, trying to will away the shivers. It only pacified the trembling for a few seconds. "I get why I am who I am, why I have to save them." I found his eyes in the dark. "Balance. There has to be a balance. I'm....I'm the only one who can maintain it."

He gave me a tired smile. "Come here," he beckoned me with a wave of his hand and lifted the sheets. I scurried over to his bed and curled up into it with him, laying my face in the crook of his neck and inhaling him as he wrapped his arms around me. That was when the trembling stopped. That was when I truly felt safe, in the warm embrace of my angel's arms.

Nighttime in Hayden's room was different than in my own. He didn't listen to music to get to sleep, so the extreme quiet made me pay more attention to the little things, like his breathing. I counted five of his breaths before he took a deeper one to speak again.

"Are the dreams back?" he asked softly, stroking my hair with his tender touch.

I held my breath for a moment. I was afraid it was going to come up, that question. But how was I to answer him? I didn't want to lie, but I would have to. I would have to protect him. I would handle the issue myself, and I already had.

"The bad ones are gone now, Hayden. I'm sure of it." It was true. I hoped I sounded convincing enough to satisfy his worry.

"Then, why were you just shivering in the threshold of my doorway, Evika?" he challenged.

Dammit. He knew me all too well. I inhaled him once again, this time taking in the scent of his freshly-laundered t-shirt along with his natural, angel-rain scent. "I just needed you, Angel-man," I answered with a whisper. "Just you."

I felt his arm pull me closer, as if it were possible, and then felt his perfect, warm lips touch the top of my head. He held them there for quite a long time, then turned his head to lay his cheek against my hair while he continued playing with it. God, I loved him more and more each moment we spent like that.

"Hayden?" I closed my eyes and whispered his name.

"Yeah?" he whispered back.

I contemplated the question I wanted to ask him – how I could phrase that I wanted to stay there in his arms all night long.

"Can I, umm, I mean, do you mind if I---?"

"You can stay as long as you like, Ev," he assured me.

"All night?" I inquired.

He let out a tired laugh. "Of course, Pony-girl. I wouldn't kick you out. That'd be rude." He tucked the sheets in around me once more, as if settling in for the rest of the night was the only option.

I laced my fingers through his and welcomed the arm that was wrapped around me. I breathed deep breaths, content.

I fell fast asleep in his arms, something I'd never done before, not like that. I entered into the dreamlike state once again, and it was the first time in a long time that I'd dreampt of nothing at all.

Chapter Eleven *An Invitation*

Things had been calm for months after my initial meeting with Alysto. The bad dreams subsided, thankfully. I'd come to terms with who I was and just did the job I had to do. The one thing that kept me from feeling that everything was perfect was the fact that I was keeping something so huge from Hayden. I was dying inside, holding the secret from him. I tried my best not to let the guilt eat away at me. The first and only time he ever questioned why I didn't have the dreamcatcher hanging above the bed anymore, I told him it was "tacky" and I "have it in my drawer." That lie was the easiest in comparison to the others. I tried burying the awful feeling in justifying that I was protecting my angel, which I was, but in turn, I was protecting an unknown traitor of the Council. Not only was I betraying Hayden, but I was betraying the entire Guardian Council. One would think that my white lie wasn't half as bad as what Jericho had done, but I managed to convince myself that I was doing the right thing in the long run. They would find out about that jerk sooner or later, at least, I'd hoped. It was only a matter of time before the rogue got caught, and I was sure that I would find a way. His day would come.

I'd wondered how long it had been that Jericho was an ally to Alysto. For as long as my life? During, or even before my father's reign as Soldier of Light? I'd wondered what his motive was. I'd wracked my brain trying to come up with the answer until I came so close to telling Hayden the truth. That was when I tried my hardest not to think about it anymore. I would have to find another way to rat Jericho out. Somehow, I just had to. But, despite the turmoil in my heart and mind, life had to go on or I was going to go even more crazy than I'd already let myself get. As usual, I needed a distraction, a change that would get my mind off of things enemy-related. And I was lucky to have gotten my wish sooner than I thought possible.

Hayden and I had made a trip to the grocery store to stock up on everything we'd needed to make meals for the next few weeks. Before he went back home, Joel wrote down a bunch of new recipes for us to try out. We'd been through a few of them and they seemed to have turned out really well, as long as Hayden was the one preparing them, of course. We came home with the new load of groceries and I grabbed the mail on the way into the house. My eyes blinked hard to re-read the envelope. The return address was Brittonia's. I looked at the lower, left-hand corner of the envelope and saw a drawing of two doves holding a red ribbon that was tied into a heart-shaped bow and my eyes widened.

"No. Way."

Hayden set the last grocery bag onto the floor and looked up. "What?"

I hastily opened up the envelope to find the inevitable contents. "Omigod," I breathed out with a smile.

"And again, I ask *what?*" Hayden grew impatient.

I looked over at him and held up the invitation.

A smile grew on his face as he read the card. "So, someone finally found a way to melt the Ice Queen," he declared. "I'm impressed."

I grinned at the light purple RSVP card for the reception: "We have two seats reserved in your honor." I had a wedding to travel to, and I couldn't wait to bring my "plus one."

Chapter Twelve *Wedding of the Year*

We were only an hour outside of Cleveland and it was about eight in the evening. I decided that driving would be best as I was still in love with my new Mustang and wanted to take her on a little road trip to break her in. Well, honestly, I just knew that some of the states had a speed limit of about seventy to seventy-five, so I was looking forward to pushing that a bit more since you can usually get away with going five to ten MPH's over the limit as long as you're careful. Oh yeah, and let's not forget my aversion to planes.

Despite the fact that I thought their marriage was a little too soon, I was happy that Brittonia had found the love of her life. The last time I saw her in person was when I was in the hospital and she seemed so happy, so different. I was looking forward to seeing her, and even the other bean pole friends. I was truly anticipating meeting her new soon-to-be-husband, Christian. I had to hand it to him for taking on such an Alpha-woman.

Mostly, I was anticipating how my initial introduction of Hayden would be to that crowd. I figured I would have to stick to the same story I told Joel, which really wasn't far from the truth anyway. Hayden was technically my roommate, and the only other classification for him was "friend." Although, there was this unspoken assumption about our relationship, like something more than just his guardianship over me. I'd felt it for a long time and was unsure as to how Hayden perceived the subject of "me and him." But I did get my first clue a few weeks prior to our trip back to Cleveland for that wedding, a hint that maybe, just maybe, Hayden felt he was more than just my protector.

*   *   *   *

I'd just finished folding the last load of laundry when Hayden came in to my room, waving the wedding invitation around and placing it on the dresser.

"So, who do you think you will take for your plus-one?" he asked me.

I shrugged. "Hmm. I don't know. I was thinking of taking

Luka," I said playfully.

Hayden nodded, but couldn't hide his boyish simper. "He'd probably like that."

"Yup. I think we'd have fun together." I started out of the room. "Oh, and since I'm on my driving-no-flying rule, we'd have to get a hotel room for a night or two. No *way* am I driving home right after that reception." I headed down the hall, waiting for his response.

Sure enough, Hayden came around the corner. "Although...."

I stopped in my tracks and smiled.

"I am, *by far*, a better dancer," he said.

I spun around on my heels and raised an eyebrow. "Mr. Crow, are you bribing me?"

"Oh, no. Not at all," he said playfully. "But don't come running to me when Luka stomps the crap out of your feet. I'll just say 'I told you so.'"

I sucked air dramatically. "I'm going to tell him you said that!"

Hayden laughed. "Believe me, it's no news to him. He knows he can't dance to save his life."

"Well," I said, "I guess I should probably go with the better dancer, huh? I mean, I *do* want to have a good time at the reception." I walked up to him, batting my eyelashes.

He shrugged. "That would be my advice. But, by all means, you should take who you want to take." He sighed and grabbed his pile of clothes from my bed.

I shook my head and laughed. Clearly, he wanted to go with me, and there was no one else I would rather have taken.

"Angel-man, would you please accompany me to Brittonia's wedding?" I asked.

Hayden was slick on his feet, turning on his heels and giving me the hugest grin. "I thought you'd never ask."

"Right," I gave him my best sarcasm. "So, do you have a suit?"

He shook his head. "Nope. Do you have a dress?"

"I will if we go shopping." I jumped in place.

He laughed. "Oh, now this will be an experience."

"I'm pretty picky," I assured him.

"Yes," he said. "That's exactly what I'm anticipating."

I puffed out my lower lip.

He patted me on the shoulder. "Cheer up, grasshopper. We have all day tomorrow to shop."

"I'll be sure to clear my schedule," I said.

"Great. We can start at the mall. They open at ten. I'll have Elka meet us there." He said it with such confidence, as if he'd already made the plans. I couldn't help but giggle at him as I watched him leave the room.

* * * *

We made it to the downtown Hyatt hotel before ten o'clock at night and grabbed our bags, making our way to the front desk. The desk clerk was a young guy with glasses too big for his face.

"Good evening, and welcome to the Hyatt. How may I help you today?" he asked with an eager smile.

Hayden quickly glanced at the clerk's name tag. "Good evening, Daniel. We are here for the Saunders-Vandelin wedding. Reservations were made under Crow. Hayden Crow."

I whispered to myself, "Bond. James Bond." Hayden smirked and rolled his eyes, obviously in earshot of my attempt at humor.

Daniel typed some information into the computer. His fingers moved faster than I could blink.

"Ah yes, Mr. Crow. We have you down for two nights, one room with two queen beds. Is that correct?"

"Yes, sir." Hayden smiled and placed the credit card on the desk. "I held it under this card."

Disappointment washed over me. My heart sank, just as my shoulders dropped. The reaction was involuntary, and it made me angry that I'd even thought we would have anything but two, separate beds. Honestly, why was I that surprised? Ugh. I could have just kicked myself for letting it bother me.

Daniel placed two key cards and the credit card onto the desk. "Okay, you are all set. The elevators are right around this corner." He pointed to his left. "Room 1409 is straight down the hall to the right after exiting the elevator. Our breakfast bar opens at seven A.M. every morning. A receipt will be printed and slid under your door of your final morning for the rapid check-out, and if you have any other questions, please feel free to call the front desk. Thank you for choosing the Hyatt and we hope you enjoy your stay here."

Yes, I thought, the Hyatt, where you reserve a room with two beds and get....two beds.

Hayden took the cards and grabbed our luggage. "Thank you, Daniel."

"Sir, would you like help with your luggage?" Daniel asked.

"Oh, no. We're quite fine. Thank you," Hayden answered, then turned to me. "Ready?"

"I can get mine." I bent down to grab my suitcase. "It's no big deal."

Hayden whipped it away from me and grinned. "I got it, Pony-girl. You can push the elevator buttons."

I held onto my purse and huffed over to the elevator with Hayden in tow with the luggage. I pushed the "up" button, folded my arms and tapped my foot, not saying a word.

"Something wrong, Evika?" he asked. My foot stopped. I hadn't realized I'd been so obvious.

I didn't know what to say. I had no reason to be upset about the two-beds thing. In fact, who knows how the heck I would have felt had Hayden really reserved a room with just *one* bed? I'm sure I would have just been upset about that too, angry with him for assuming it was okay for us to be in the same bed together. Then, I would have wondered what his intentions were, even though my intentions would have been the same. I'm sure I would have felt a bit undermined by him. Jeez, I was being ridiculous and I was such a hypocrite.

"Nothing's wrong," I finally answered him. "I'm just nervous about seeing everyone again. That's all." Lie.

We proceeded into the elevator and up to the fourth floor.

"I see." He smirked, obviously unconvinced, looking down at

the elevator floor. Ugh. What did that mean? Did he know why I was really acting that way? I decided I should just put on my happy face. I was crazy for thinking the weekend would be anything other than what we had at home - two beds. In fact, we had separate rooms. Why would a hotel stay be any different?

After a silent elevator ride up to our floor, we finally headed for the room. The room was huge and actually had decent décor. The bathroom was the most impressive, sporting a stand up shower with glass doors and a jacuzzi tub with massager jets. I made a mental note to add one of those to my own bathroom at home. I was looking forward to watching the flat-screen television after we got settled in. We often liked to find some low-budget horror film on the Sy-fy channel and make fun of it.

Hayden plopped our suitcases over by the desk at the far end of the room and hung our bagged wedding attire up in the closet. I darted into the bathroom to take a quick shower and get my pajamas on, and came out to find Hayden already in his. It was uncanny how we both slept in t-shirts and flannel pants. It felt disappointing that we were already "turning in" by ten o'clock, but we'd had a long drive, and my body felt like it had been put through the ringer.

We both crawled into our separate beds to watch television, and I thought of a great ploy to get Hayden to come to my bed.

"Hayden?" I sounded whiny.

"Yeah?"

"Can you pleeeeeease rub my shoulders? Please? Please?"

He cocked an eyebrow. "Okay, but you'll owe me."

"Owe you?" I looked at him. "Why?" He never played that card before.

He jumped out of his bed and walked over to mine. "Because I give something way better than just a shoulder rub."

I looked at him questioningly.

He laughed and shook his head. "Just lay down. You'll see what I mean"

I laid tummy-first on the bed, facing the TV. I felt him climb onto the bed and sit on my butt, careful not to put his total weight on me. He shimmied up my shirt - something I did not expect - then ran his fingers along the waist-line of my pants, pulling them down along with my underwear to just about the top of my ass-crack.

I gasped. "Omigod, Hayden!"

"Hey, I warned you. And need I remind you? You were the one whining over here." He chuckled. "Just relax." He placed his warm hands on my lower back, thumbing circles up and outward, pressing into my skin.

At that moment, I didn't care about what was on the television. I stared at it, but I couldn't even recall what I was watching. Hayden's hands roamed upward as his thumbs pressed along my spine. He massaged my shoulders and my upper arms for a few minutes, then he drifted to the sides of my torso, almost grazing my breasts with the tips of his fingers. It was invigorating, what I was feeling through his touch. And then, I had a thought.

"Hayden," I could hardly speak with any volume, "are you doing that thing you do?"

I felt myself and the bed vibrate as he chuckled. "Nope. It's all natural right now. Why?"

"Because....this feels....so...."

"Really, really good?" he gloated.

I took a deep breath, too relaxed to speak again, but still managed to answer him. "That's an understatement."

He continued massaging me for almost half an hour before I fell asleep, so I'm not sure when he stopped. But I remember waking up in the middle of the night to see that I was tucked in the bed, and with the illumination of the television, I could see Hayden sleeping peacefully in the other. I felt a smidgen of discouragement fall over me before falling back to sleep.

Our wake-up call was at nine, but we lay in our beds for half an hour to watch cartoons. I, again, just stared at the television, paying no attention to the channel. I lay there wondering why Hayden hadn't just stayed in the bed with me after that massage. Would that have been so wrong? I was getting so tired of myself for dwelling on that, thinking too much and wanting things that I probably shouldn't have.

The wedding was at noon. I wasn't too sure how long the ceremony was going to be, so I wanted to be sure that we ate beforehand.

"Hey, I saw a little coffee shop down there and the breakfast bar is still open. Do you want to go get something real quick?" I asked Hayden.

He ruffled his hair. "Nah. I think I'll get ready first. But if you're still going, could you grab me a bagel or something?"

"Sure." I grabbed one of the key cards from the desk. "I'll be back." I headed for the door, purse still on my shoulder and pulled out my iPod.

"Okay, but just remember we don't have much time." He tapped his wrist. "We need to leave here by eleven-thirty-five to get to the church on time and get our seats."

I rolled my eyes. "Golly gosh, Hayden. Where would I be without you to keep me organized?" I said sardonically.

"Definitely *not* on time. I can tell you that much." He snickered. He was so right, but I gave him a disapproving look before closing the door on my way out.

I put in my earbuds and turned on my iPod, scrolling through the music. Let's see. What did I want to listen to? Ah yes, perfect: "Playing With My Heart," by Kate Voegele. That song hit the spot. It was going to be my new favorite song for the weekend.

I hit pause as I reached the cafe and prepped two plain bagels with extra cream cheese. I figured we better not overdue it so we'd be hungry for reception food, but I couldn't leave without grabbing two sides of eggs, sausage and two orange juices. I bagged the food and loitered around the lobby looking at brochures of the attractions in Cleveland. It's funny how you live somewhere and don't really take advantage of the place until you're officially gone. When you come back as a tourist, it takes on this whole new light. I discovered there were so many attractions that I'd been oblivious to while I was living there. Cleveland would always be how I left it and it would always be there when I returned. I found comfort in that.

Ireland Gill

  I was still blaring the same song on repeat while I danced into the room. I looked around and saw the bathroom door was left slightly ajar, steam rising from under it. My curiosity got the best of me, so I crept up to the crack in the door. Hayden was in the shower, his backside facing me. I froze there like a deer in headlights right after pulling my earbuds out and letting them drop to my sides. My heart sped as I stared in awe. The shower curtain had not been completely pulled to the other side, leaving half of his naked body in my line of vision. I had no choice but to let my hungry eyes stare at the beautiful sight, this gorgeous work of art standing there naked in the shower. Water drenched him from head to toe, rolling down his skin in small cascades, layering every perfect curve of his shoulders, back and arms down to his buttocks. My eyes paused there, absentmindedly admiring the build of those cheeks that looked as if they could shatter a rock into a million pieces if brought to the challenge.

  I watched the water fall along his legs, washing over his toned thighs and calves. I glanced back up to his shoulders and saw the movement of his back muscles and arms as he washed his hair, and then felt my bottom jaw drop. Holy. Hell. He was so beautiful and flawless, it hurt. How could one thing in this entire world be so perfectly put together? His charm, his laugh, his smile, his eyes, his tenderness, his willingness to put up with me....and the body of a god! I imagined my hands against his skin as the water sprayed on his body. He started lathering the bar soap and washing his arms, still facing away from me. God, I wanted to be that bar of soap so badly. *Dear God, please, just let that water keep running so I can stand here and keep watching this beautiful man.*

"You know, Evika, I doubt I'd be this fascinating to you had you paid closer attention in your anatomy class."

I unfroze just enough to let my eyes widen and bug out of my head. *Omigod. Omigod. Omigod.* He knew I was there! I had to think of something quickly. What would I say? Of course, blame him for the issue at hand. "God, Hayden! Ever heard of locking a door?" I ran away from the bathroom and slammed the door shut behind me, panting heavily.

"Ever heard of knocking on one?" I heard his muffled voice retort.

Crap on a stick! This was bad. How could I have let that happen? Ugh! And why couldn't he have just locked that damn door? I was never going to live that one down. My palms and face were sweating profusely.

After a few minutes of pacing around the room, I heard the water shut off. My hands were sweating like a whore in church. I had to look busy, so I put the television on, and what was on? *"Dr. Phil: Teen Sex."* Oh, for the love of heavenly bodies! I flipped through the channels and found something officially boring and couldn't tell you what it was. I quickly pulled my dress from the closet and out of the bag, evaluating if I had time to get into it before he came out of the bathroom. I figured I did. I was quick. Ugh. But Hayden would have to zip it up for me. *Jeez!* I decided to get into the dress anyway and just act as if nothing happened. Maybe he didn't know how long I was really standing there. Maybe.

183

My dress was on and I zipped it up as far as I could, contorting my upper body as I tried to reach my arm around far enough to zip it up completely. It was no use. I stood frustrated and exhausted in front of the mirror. I sighed deeply and made one last attempt at the zipper, but he emerged from the bathroom, steam following behind him. He was in his black pin-striped suit, a dark green shirt that matched my dress, and a black and green striped tie to compliment. I could hardly make myself look him in the eyes, but I relented and caught his most cocky expression.

"Looks like you could use some help." He grinned at me.

I sighed. "Yes, please," I muttered and gave in. I only wanted to get the zipper up and dash for the bathroom to do my make-up to avoid the awkwardness. But no, I needed *him* to help me with my dress. He stood behind me, looking at my partially-naked skin.

"Wow, Evika, isn't it a little early to start celebrating Christmas?" he said as he looked at me in the mirror, bringing the zipper to the top.

"Huh?" I looked at him through the mirror, confused. Then I saw my beat-red face. Perfect. I was red and green all over. Well, it was obvious then; I looked guilty. I braced myself for anything he might say about the previous event, but he surprised me by ignoring it all together. It threw me off. Not that I didn't appreciate it, but it didn't make things any better for me either. I was sure the subject of my seeing him naked was bound to come up sooner than later.

"Oh, I almost forgot." Hayden walked over to his suitcase and pulled out a thin, black box. "Stay right there," he said as he proceeded to pull out a piece of jewelry. He walked it over to me and placed it on my neck. It was a thick, silver chain with an emerald square-cut stone as the charm. I lifted my hair up high and watched him close the clasp. It lay just a few inches below my throat and I swear, it couldn't have matched the dress more perfectly – not to mention, how closely the color resembled his gorgeous eyes.

He placed his warm hands on my shoulders, observing me through the mirror and smiling. "Perfect," he said.

I turned and looked at him in awe. "Hayden, where did this come from?"

He smirked. "Oh, you know, I had to find *something* to occupy my time while you were trying on dresses. I think it was between dress number thirty-eight and forty-two."

"But, how did you---"

"Oh, come on. Like I didn't know you were going to pick the clover green dress? This was dress number seven, if I remember correctly." His hands draped along the skirt of my dress, and his eyes looked it over with admiration.

I shook my head, astonished. "You take great pride in knowing me so well, don't you?"

He shrugged. "I'm also great at being on time, so don't ruin that for me, Pony-girl."

I smiled and squeezed the charm as I grabbed my make-up bag. "Thanks."

Hayden nodded with a proud grin. "Looks good on you," he said, grabbing his breakfast from the desk.

I skipped to the bathroom. Butterflies were forming, and I'm sure it was a cross between the ones I always had around him, along with my nerves about this wedding, *and* the fact that I knew that this "shower scene" was not going to dissipate quietly.

I was done putting on my face after about five minutes and I had just enough time to eat my food before we were out the door, right on time like Hayden wanted. I took pride in managing to be ready on time that day. We'd gotten to the church with ten minutes to warm up our seats for the ceremony. We, of course, sat on Brittonia's side of the church. After sitting, I looked around at the beautiful stained-glass windows, depicting stories of the bible. Testaments, Old and New. For a short moment, I felt as though I wanted to go back to knowing those stories as the only truth. But that thought quickly left my mind as I looked over at Hayden, who was smiling at the cross hanging above the alter. He looked so peaceful in that moment, as if he were "home," and I wondered what he was thinking. I thought that he might be praying or reflecting, something of the sort, so I didn't want to disturb whatever it is that angels do when they are in a church on a wedding day. I was content just watching him as we listened to the organ playing.

I glanced to the front of the church and saw Christian, a handsome, young blond with a crew cut standing with his groomsmen. He was in a white tux, sporting a violet-colored rose and holding the proudest smile. His best man patted him on his back assuringly as they stood. Then the sound of the music started the ceremony; Ave Maria. It was one of the most beautiful songs. I'd heard it a few times during my childhood, but never really listened as intently as I had in that moment. The flower girl walked by, her blond locks bobbing as she dropped violet petals onto the white runner down the aisle. The bridesmaids, Shelby, Demi and Clara, - aka, the bean poles - were all in their Victorian lilac dresses, holding a modest bouquet of white roses. Demi walked by and offered me a wide smile and I couldn't help but return one. I looked toward the door and saw the matron of honor, Brit's sister, Josie, coming down the aisle. I was eagerly awaiting the moment we'd get to stand to see Brittonia and sure enough, that moment came.

    We all stood and gasped as she came through the church entrance in her strapless, white dress, holding onto her father's arm with such a glowing, confident smile on her face. If she was nervous, you would have never known. She took her time walking down the aisle, holding her bouquet of white and violet-colored roses. She faced the front of the church, keeping her eyes on her future, her love. It was the same face of realness that I'd seen of her in the hospital when she'd visited me, a genuine happiness and innocence. It amazed me that she'd become so mature. You could just see the difference in her, at least, I could. She took my breath away as she walked past me, my eyes followed the train of the dress, admiring the sequence trails of flowers embroidered into it. It looked like it was made for her. It was all so perfect.

    The ceremony began once she reached the alter, her father gave her away and sat down. I listened to the whole thing curiously. I'd never been to a wedding in my life, and the only ones I'd experienced were the cliché ones on television. My curiosity spiked when the nuptials came up. "For better or for worse, for richer or poorer, in sickness and in health, till death do us part." I'd wondered where it all came from originally. I wondered if that was what it meant to be married. "Till death do you part;" then what? You move on? I guess that's what most people did, but if there was such a thing as a soul mate, then how could you truly be happy without them? Why did death have to end your love for that person? It created a longing, I'm sure, but why would death have to be the end at all?

    I looked over at Hayden, who was also watching just as eagerly as I was. But he spared me one second of his time and glanced my way to smile his five-hundred watter. I melted in place in that pew. God, he drove me crazy. Sometimes it took all I had not to belt out in song or poem about how he made me feel, but even then, I wouldn't even know what to say without being extremely abstract. My lips wanted to tell him, my hands wanted to tell him, hell, my whole body reacted to Hayden. I ached for a way to express to him how much I adored him, how much he meant to me.

    I was disappointed in myself for not taking a hold of one of his hands during the ceremony. However, I would have started thumbing circles into his palm, focusing on his skin, then thinking back on him in the shower at the hotel and, oh, I really wanted a drink. I really, really wanted a drink. Just a beer. One would be okay, and I knew Hayden would be fine with it. Or even a glass of wine, I'd settle for that. There I was, supposed to be witnessing a friend's wedding ceremony, and my ass was thinking about alcohol and Hayden's body.

I annoyed myself to no end.

The ceremony was over, and the priest pronounced them as "Mr. and Mrs. Christian Brian Vandelin." *Brittonia May Vandelin.* It had a ring to it.

I grabbed Hayden's arm, and we walked out the doors, grabbing our little container of bubbles.

"This is a really nice church," I said casually.

Hayden smiled at me. "Yes, it's beautiful."

And so are you, I thought.

I hadn't realized how many people had come to the church since we'd sat more towards the front. I had a feeling it was going to be an impossibility to greet Brittonia and Christian before the reception since they'd have to get back into the church for the photographs. They came out and we all blew the bubbles and cheered as the newly-weds emerged from the church doors. I thought Brittonia was beautiful in the church, but when the sunlight hit her, she was astonishing. Maybe it was also this new light I was seeing about her. I mean, she was always beautiful, but that day, she looked magnificent.

I hadn't met Christian yet, but I watched him watch his bride as she batted playfully at a few of the bubbles floating by her face. I felt my heart swell. You could easily see that he was undeniably in love with this girl. I would give almost anything for someone to see me the way he was looking at her. It was beautiful, that moment.

I looked to Hayden, who was next to me shaking his empty container of bubbles and puffing out his lower lip. I laughed at him.

"You want the rest of mine, Angel-man?"

"Nah. Save them for later. We'll have a bubble-blowing party back at the hotel." He winked at me.

A few light raindrops hit his nose. He looked up at the overcast sky and raised his hand out, then looked at me incredulously. "Evika, really?"

"What? Rain on your wedding day is good luck."

He shrugged. "No downpours, though. Keep it to a light sprinkle."

I rolled my eyes and grinned at him. "Don't piss me off today and I can fully commit to that."

The crowd dissipated and the wedding party ran back into the church. I looked around and saw the Hummer limo waiting across the street.

"Wow, talk about going all-out," I said.

Hayden laughed. "Says the girl with the sixty-thousand dollar Mustang."

I smacked his chest playfully. "Whatever. Let's get back the hotel and hang out at the swanky bar! We have some time to kill. Oh, and I think Joel's parents might be coming." I tugged on his arm.

He placed his hand on the small of my back as we walked slowly to the pony.

We reached the car and I dangled the keys from my index finger. "You wanna drive this time?"

Hayden clutched his chest and faked a mild seizure, adding some choking sounds. "You mean, you are actually going to hand those keys over...*willingly* today?"

"Yeah, unless you don't want to." I headed for the driver's side.

"Oh, no you don't. Hand them over." He came up behind me, placing his arm around my waist and lifting me off the ground gently. His other hand tugged at the keys.

I laughed uncontrollably. "Okay! Okay!" I managed to say through laughs, handing him the keys. He zipped over to the passenger side, holding the door open for me. I sat down and watched him close my door, then shoot over to the driver's side like a little kid. I found it hilarious, how happy he was.

He sat in the car and closed the door, sighing dramatically with a smile on his face. He started the engine and closed his eyes, grabbing the steering wheel. "Oh. Yeah," he said.

I laughed at him, shaking my head. "You are such a goober, you know that?"

"I hardly ever get to drive this thing." He flashed his teeth at me, holding his cheesy smile. "Hey, have you let Luka drive yet?"

"Nope," I said. "Not yet."

"Hmm. I should rub it in."

"You're terrible."

He wagged his eyebrows. "I know."

We headed back to the hotel, where the reception was held, and hung out at the bar. I decided to make Hayden happy and only ordered a glass of Riesling. He ordered the same. We sat there waiting for our wine and spun the chairs toward each other. I had a feeling it was the moment; he was going to say something about the "shower scene." Well, I was right.

"So," he looked down and grinned widely, playing with the buttons on his suit jacket, "you didn't think I was just going to let it go, did you?"

Great. Here we go. "Let what go?" I played dumb.

"Seems to me that you got quite an eye-full this morning, wouldn't you say?" His chin went up and our eyes met.

Oh, sweet, baby Jesus. We are going to talk about his naked body. I quickly composed myself. "Hey, forget about my eye-full. I learned that you don't know how to lock a door," I said defensively.

Hayden laughed. The bartender set our wine on the counter in front of us and I quickly grabbed my glass, sticking it up to my lips to sip.

"You know, Evika, this would be so much easier if you would just admit it. It's no big deal, really," he taunted.

For cripe's sake, is he proud about this? God, please just open a huge hole in the ground and swallow me up right now. I felt my face flush.

"Hmm." Hayden observed my face, "how strange that your face is the same shade of red as it was this morning. Is it all coming back to you now?"

My jaw flexed. "Hayden, why are you tormenting me about this? I'm sorry. Okay?"

"I'm only curious." He shrugged.

"Curious about what?" I snapped and took a another generous sip of my wine.

"About what you thought."

I choked in mid-swallow of my next swig. Oh. My. God. "What. I. Thought. You wanna know what I thought?" I was hoping I hadn't heard him right.

He sat straighter in the stool and gave me a smug expression. "Yeah, I wanna know."

The thought occurred to me that maybe it had been a set-up. He wanted me to walk in on him taking that shower, and strategically left that crack open in the door just to taunt me even more once I walked in on him. But I cleared the theory. Why would he do something like that?

I looked at him incredulously. "What is it that you want me to say, Hayden?"

He grinned, took a sip of wine, swallowed and looked me dead in the eyes. "The very first thing that came to your mind."

Oh, you mean like the fact that I wanted to become the water that was spraying all over your body and cascade down every part of you? That I wanted to run my hands all over you and lather you up with that soap? Oh God, Evika! Just answer him! Say something poetic! Say what you felt!

I looked him square in the eyes. "I thought you were the most beautiful thing I'd ever seen." And that was the God-honest truth.

Hayden gave me a surprised expression. I think it was the first time I'd seen him speechless. A smile grew on his face as he stared at me. I could tell it was genuine. No tricks.

"That's all I wanted to know," he lifted his glass to mine, "so, thank you."

I bobbed my head once in response and looked at him curiously. I waited for more on the discussion, but it never came. I was relieved, but still eager for more on the subject after I'd seen Hayden act that way. It was like he didn't expect me to say that to him, my honest answer. If he didn't expect me to compliment him, then he must have anticipated a disparaging remark from me, something I'd normally do just to get off of the subject and move on. But I was done with those games, and it was hard enough for me to express anything the way I wanted to.

I held up my glass. "A toast....to a fun evening."

"I'll toast to that," Hayden clanked his glass to mine.

We finished our wine and headed for the reception in the banquet room down the hall. The receiving line was already there, greeting the guests as they walked in. The bridesmaids were first.

"Hey, girls! Long time, no see." I was greeted by a group hug.

"Oh, Evika! We couldn't wait to see you!" Clara exclaimed.

"Yeah, Brit said you were coming." Shelby jumped.

"You look so great!" Demi gave me another squeeze.

"Thanks, guys." I smiled. Despite our fair-weathered friendships, it was still great to see them. "This is Hayden." I gestured by pulling him closer.

"Pleased to meet you, ladies." Hayden said.

Demi's, Shelby's, and Clara's bottom jaws dropped.

"Wow," Clara held out her hand to him. "Pleased to meet *you*!"

Next was Brittonia and Christian. "Hi, Brit." I beamed.

Brittonia turned to me after welcoming the guest before me and her face lit up like a holiday tree. "Oh. My. God! Evika!" She wrapped her arms around me and squeezed tightly. It made me laugh. "I'm so glad that you came!"

"Brit, we wouldn't miss it!"

"*We?*" Brit's eyes moved to Hayden and she smiled widely. "Ah, this must be the *roommate?*"

I giggled nervously. "You must have been talking to Joel."

"But of course!" *s*he teased me. "It's nice to meet you, Hayden, is it?"

"A pleasure, Brittonia." Hayden took her hand and kissed the top of it like an old-fashioned gentleman. "You look absolutely stunning this evening." Brit smiled and blushed.

Oh, the swooning. It was kind of cute and priceless.

"And this," Brittonia gestured to her new husband, "is my Christian." She said it so proudly.

"Evika, I've heard so much about you. It's great to finally put a face to the name." Christian said. He was an absolute gem. I could tell this right away.

"Christian, it's great to finally meet you. Now I can finally stop worrying about this girl." I thumbed over to Brittonia, who kiddingly stuck her tongue out at me.

"Christian, Hayden. Hayden, Christian," I said.

The two men shook hands and smiled.

"The wedding was magnificent, Christian. Thank you for having us." Hayden said.

"Our pleasure. Hey, you guys are staying at the hotel, aren't you? We tried to reserve enough rooms for the people coming out of town." Christian's concern was a trait I could see that I liked.

"Oh, yes. We got in yesterday and we're staying for one more night. Beautiful hotel." Hayden said.

We had to start moving, as the majority of the guests were filing in. I tugged on Hayden's arm.

"We'll talk to you guys later when we make our rounds after dinner!" Brit called to me. I gave her a thumbs-up.

The hall was gigantic. All the chairs and round tables were draped with white cloths and the centerpieces were large glass bowls filled with water and a floating candle with clear, white and violet rocks layered on the bottom. The dance floor was massive and looked of dark wood, clean enough for you to eat on. We looked for our table and found that we were seated with Joel's parents, Rick and Wendy. I saw them sitting there chatting with their wine glasses in hand and bounced over to them.

"Hi, Mr. and Mrs. Coleman!" I squealed.

They both turned to me and beamed. Wendy darted out of her chair and embraced me like the daughter she never had.

"Oh, my goodness, Evika. It's been so long." She held my face with her petite hands.

And from there, we talked until dinner was served. Hayden behaved in such a decorous manner, greeting new people, shaking their hands and making small-talk with all the guests to whom I introduced him. It amazed me how charming he was with everyone; not just the women, but even the men. Any subject thrown at him, he knew it from A to Z. He was genuine and compelling, and the others who spoke with him enjoyed their conversations.

After dinner, most of our table had gotten up to go mingle. Brittonia and Christian sat with us for a while and we talked about how all of us met, our "jobs," and the remainder of the exchange resorted to me and Brit talking about the good ol' days while Christian and Hayden looked debonair, discussing manly things amongst themselves. And that was the moment I saw it. Both of them stopped talking to watch Brittonia and me. Christian had that look on his face; the expression of admiration for Brittonia that I envied back at the church. Then my eyes moved to Hayden, and I melted as I found he held the same expression for me. I was awestruck by it. Even though it only lasted for a short moment, it was enough to tell me what I needed to know.

Shortly after that, our conversations came to a close and the newlyweds were to continue their table-hopping. The dancing had begun. The father-daughter dance was emotional for both of them. They danced to Rascal Flatts' "My Wish." It was the perfect song and I'm sure that Brittonia was more emotional than ever at that very moment since it was her mother's favorite song. The DJ happened to mention that little tidbit before calling Brittonia and Mr. Saunders to the dance floor. I couldn't help but feel sorry for myself, that I didn't have either parent to share the moment with whenever my wedding day came. It was a sore spot that I didn't want revealing itself so I stayed quiet and plastered a smile on my face until it was over.

Once the main dances concluded, Hayden leaned into me and

said he'd be right back. I watched him walk up to the DJ. *Oh, no. What is he up to?* I thought. He never ceased to amaze me, and I had a feeling this was going to be another one of those things. They had a quick discussion. I saw the DJ bobbing his head and saying something to Hayden, then the angel came back over to our table, grinning widely.

"You better get up there so you can get a front-row seat," he warned. "I'm about to perform."

"What?" I called after him as he sprinted back out to the dance floor. He turned and winked at me. God, he was hot when he did that.

The last song ended and, from what I could tell, the song Hayden requested was on because he made his way out to the middle of the floor. The new song started playing. Everybody Loves Me, by One Republic. I knew the beat right away, and then the song's lyrics started flooding my mind. Really? He requested this song? I was beginning to see that I'd possibly underestimated his ego. I started laughing when his body took on the rhythm. It was as if he'd already had a routine for the song.

Hayden started stomping his feet to the beat even harder, clapping to get the crowd going and taking up most of the dance floor as he mouthed the words as they were sung. The lights started working in his favor by dimming and the D.J flipped on his strobe light. It had to have been part of Hayden's request.

The crowd was engaged. Hayden directed his arms in choreographed movements and even did that fingers-through-the-hair thing that drove me wild. Hayden readied himself for the main chorus and dropped to the floor on his back.

The gathering crowd was now growing and shouting as he spun on his back, busting out moves like a professional break-dancer. It was unreal.

Guests grabbed their cameras and cell phones, and the photographer was already getting the best shots. Hayden jumped back onto his feet after kicking his legs into the air, arching and balancing back to a standing position. He loosened his tie and unbuttoned the top two buttons of his shirt as he strut along the inner circle of the crowd, which included myself. You would have thought Justin Timberlake busted in on the reception. The mass of women in the crowd were howling in delight. I was still dumbfounded, but I could attest that I was enjoying myself, to put it mildly.

I felt a few pairs of hands grabbing each of my arms. It was Clara and Demi mouthing their "oh-my-God" faces and fanning themselves. Okay, so the angel could dance. What *couldn't* he do?

He was on the floor once again, repeating the break-dancing moves, then switched into a hand stand "walking" along the floor and arching back to his feet for the rest of the song. Only this time, he added some pelvic thrusts to finish his number. I caught myself wishing I could drag him back the room by his loose-fit tie and make sweet, passionate love to his rhythmic body. *Oh, sweet, melodic church bells! What am I thinking?!*

During the climactic ending, Hayden spun around in multiple three-sixties and ran across the floor sliding on his knees, stopping dead on the last beat of the song. Everyone had witnessed this angel's performance and was ecstatic.

"Ladies and gentlemen, give it up for Hayden!" the DJ bellowed into the microphone.

The crowd cheered and patted Hayden on the back as he sprung to his feet. He gave a few bows as the cheering continued. The hollering slowly died down and a new song started playing. This time, it was a slow-paced song. Most people stayed on the dance floor and met up with their partners.

Hayden walked back to me from the other end of the dance floor. He wore quite a smug look on that angel-face of his. My heart started beating faster as I waited for the moment I would be touching him again, but I didn't let it show. I stood there staring at him with narrowed eyes and a cocked eyebrow.

"Hmm. Your thinking face, I think." He came close to me. "What's on your mind right now?"

I couldn't hide my smile. "I am just absolutely amazed that you were even able to fit through those doors with an ego of your size," I jeered. "It baffles me."

He looked over his shoulder at the entrance, then back to me while curling his lips into a devious grin that made me melt. "They were double doors," he whispered. "It was manageable." I giggled at his admission.

Hayden grabbed my hand and held my waist, pulling me close to him. We started swaying to the music. He leaned into my ear, and it sent happy tingles throughout my body. I enjoyed breathing him in, thinking how funny it was that, even after all that dancing, he still smelled like that wonderful scent of rain.

I looked him in the eyes once again. "You know, not only did you conquer the entrance through those doors, you've also managed to charm everyone in this room indefinitely," I razzed him.

He lifted my arm above my head and spun me during the rest of the main chorus. After a few spins, he brought me back into his arms again. I felt beautiful in my new dress, and being there on that dance floor with Hayden made me feel like I was on top of the world. It felt enchanting, how docile my body was when we danced. It was like I didn't even have to try, as if we'd rehearsed the moves our entire lives.

"What about you?" he asked me.

I looked at him curiously. "What about me?"

He smiled and leaned in slightly. "Have I managed to charm you?" For a moment, I thought he was toying with me, but his face couldn't have been more serious.

"Are you kidding me, Angel-man? You had me at 'get on'," I chuckled nervously as I thought about his rude first arrival on the Harley the first day we'd officially met, but when I offered an assuring smile, I'm quite positive that it would have given him his true answer.

I caught that solemn look in his eyes and realized the moment I'd been waiting for would probably never get any closer than it was right then. That song and that dance was the catalyst to what I truly wanted, his lips. My heart pounded. The confidence in me grew as I readied myself to stand on my tip-toes, to place my lips on his as I'd dreamed of doing. I was going to break my promise to myself. I was going to try one more time to claim that kiss.

I closed my eyes, but before I could even move, Hayden planted his angel lips on mine. The moment they touched, I could feel my body start to intoxicate. It was nothing like the thrilling charge I'd imagined it would be, it was a thousand times better than that. I became happily lost. The kiss was supernal, euphoric and serendipitous, and I didn't want it to end. Ever.

I'd forgotten all but who we were and what we were doing as I felt myself leaning backwards, only to have Hayden's strong embrace secure me in my tilted position. He pulled his lips from mine slowly. I opened my eyes to look up into his and saw the most radiant expression. I caught the luminescence of the soft, ceiling lighting shine behind him before he gracefully pulled me upright once again. I was captivated by him, more so than I already was. I loved him. I loved him. I loved him.

His lips turned into that confident smile that I adored, showing teeth and all. "I just had to be sure," he whispered to me.

Hayden took my hand in his, placed his arm around my waist and we resumed dancing to the song. I was spellbound. I looked deep into those emerald eyes of his, my heart still pounding. At that moment, I was certain that Hayden felt for me the same things I felt for him, and it was everything my heart ever wanted since the day I'd met him.

He chuckled as I gazed at him. "It's very rare to see you this speechless, Evika. Will you please say something?" he pleaded.

Why was it so hard for me to speak? "I-I-" *Oh, come on, Evika.*

Say something! I swallowed hard. "I've wanted that kiss since the day I met you." It was completely true and only a fraction of what I wanted to say to him.

He looked at me and smiled genuinely. "So have I."

I wanted him to do it again, kiss me just once more, but we finished out the song by dancing in our own, little world.

We spent the rest of the evening dancing and hardly spoke, but we were comfortable together. We definitely didn't kiss anymore. The one kiss just may have been enough, I guess. Even though I wanted that moment all over again, there were many distractions. The reception moved along for another couple of hours and mostly consisted of new "Hayden-fans." He had been dubbed "the hot guy who can dance." I found these things out while Hayden danced a few songs with the flower girl. The younger children at the reception flocked to him and reveled in the attention he was giving them. He was so sweet with the kids, teaching them a few of his dance moves and even help them in doing the limbo. I beamed at the sight, and it just made my heart grow even more fond of him.

The night came to a close and the mass of people dwindled. We said our goodbyes to Joel's parents and to Brittonia, Christian and the girls, promising to keep in touch. As we walked to our room, my nerves set in, reminding me of the possible awkwardness that awaited us, if not handled with care. As much as I thought I was ready for that kiss, I wasn't truly ready for what it inevitability led to. Although I trusted him, I wasn't sure what Hayden was thinking, and I was reluctant to ask. As we rode up to our floor in the elevator, you could hear a pin drop. I was even afraid to look at him.

Hayden sighed and lifted my chin. "Evika," he said, "I can tell you're nervous, but you don't need to be." He said it so assuringly. How did he know what was bothering me? *I* wasn't even sure of what was truly bothering me.

"I don't?" I asked him. I sounded so helpless.

He shook his head. "It was just a kiss. That's all."

My expression changed. "Oh." What, exactly, did *that* mean? Just a kiss? Really? *Really?* I felt my heart sink and my timidness start to evade.

We reached our floor and I was first into the room, grabbing my bag and heading for the bathroom. I hastily removed the necklace Hayden had given me and tossed it onto the bathroom counter, satisfied after hearing the hard knock it made against the granite. I was sure to lock the door, checking it twice before starting the shower. I needed one, and it was the only excuse I had to get out of the main room, away from him. I needed to think. Just a kiss? Was he crazy? I was rather perturbed that *that* was all he had to say about it. After all of our time together, he had the audacity to kiss me with those sweet, angelic lips at a wedding reception while we slow danced and tell me *"it was just a kiss?"* How in the hell was I supposed to carry on with him after that? I felt slighted, used and ignorant. Our "relationship" from that point on would be incurable and unmanageable as far as I was concerned.

After turning off the water and towel-drying my hair, I stepped into my pajamas with a slight haste and swung open the bathroom door, only to find Hayden standing there waiting for me with nothing but his naked chest and flannel pajama bottoms. *God! What did I do to deserve this?*

"Okay, look," he explained with his arms up in surrender, "Evika, that came out completely understated. I didn't mean it that way at all. I'm so sorry."

"*Really,* Hayden?" I gave him a disbelieving glare as I whipped past him. "Why would I care anyway? It was just as trivial to me as it was to you, you jerk." I slammed my bag onto the floor and smacked the power button to turn the TV on.

"Oh, now, who are *you* kidding?" he jabbed. I pursed my lips as he walked up to me. "Ev, I just meant that you didn't have to worry about any pressure after we got back to the room. I didn't want you to feel uncomfortable, as if I were expecting anything more than just that kiss."

My glare subsided, and the feeling of stupidity slowly started to wash over me, taking its form as the tomato-red hue that colored my entire face. My expression softened.

"Evika," Hayden said, "by all means, I had no intention of trivializing that kiss with what I said. I felt more in that kiss than I've ever felt in my entire existence, and I want you to know th---"

I grabbed his neck and pulled him to me, the impact of our lips harnessing a force more powerful than the first, something I thought would have been impossible. I gasped as his hands laced through my wet hair, sending those familiar, wonderful tingles down my spine that made my body quiver in delight. My hands caressed his neck and moved along the muscles of his back. Feeling his naked skin was sending my senses into a craze. I pulled him by his waist to have him against me completely, but he lifted me and placed me onto the bed. He hovered over me, giving soft, delicate kisses on my lips and neck. It was driving me crazy. I wanted him more than anything, but I knew I wasn't ready. Not yet. The hotel wasn't home. It wasn't the right moment to take it to that level. I concentrated on the patterns of our kisses. Just as he'd promised, we'd only kissed. Nothing more.

I could hear myself panting shallow breaths. Everything I was feeling was euphoric and intoxicating. Hayden pressed his lips once more to mine and lay next to me on his side, holding his hand to my cheek and smiling.

"You interrupted me, you know?" he poked.

I laughed. "Sorry," I said with a hint of sarcasm.

"So, now do you understand what I was trying to tell you?" Hayden asked.

I looked him in the eyes, and before I could get lost in them again, I answered. "I do."

He wrapped his arm around me, and I laid my head on his shoulder, holding him in return as we lay there together on that hotel bed. We fell asleep that way, and my contentment in that moment was absolutely unassailable. I wanted to keep it forever.

Chapter Thirteen *Intentions*

I woke the next morning to a peace I thought only existed in good dreams. I saw his angel face inches from mine, still sleeping. I smiled and couldn't help the butterflies that fluttered throughout my stomach. I was happy, and Hayden and I had finally broken through that barrier I'd always felt was there. It may not have been as apparent to him, but I always felt the unspoken tension when it came to us getting so physically close and never acting upon it. I wanted more from him. I wanted to know if he cared for me the same way I cared for him. I even wanted to know if he loved me the way I knew I loved him. I could admit it to myself, but to say it aloud? Ha!

Trust me, I wanted to tell him. I wanted him to know that I felt those three words, but saying them out loud was somewhat of a challenge for me. I couldn't see it happening without some sort of confirmation from him. His kissing me should have been enough for me, you'd think, but I was still reluctant. Where did we go from there?

I lay there, running my fingers through his thick, dark hair and inhaling that scent of rain he always carried with him. I caressed his cheek softly, then moved my fingers down along his arm, watching my fingers bob along the contour of his muscles. I relished the moment as I was so close to him, his naked chest and his peaceful expression as he slept next to me. From the moment I met Hayden, he was everything I wanted, needed. After we'd shared those two wonderful, memorable kisses, I started thinking about the next steps in this fantasy. Those kisses solidified everything I wanted, yet opened a whole new door to something else entirely. And it wasn't until that morning, as I watched the angel sleep, that I'd realized what that kiss meant.

This moment was everything I wanted. But on the flip side......it *wasn't* what I wanted. I knew what this meant. If Hayden cared enough for me he'd want to eventually Fade for me, and it wasn't something I would let happen if I could help it. I was fine with him staying the angel he was. We could make that work. I knew we could. There was no good reason for him to change anything.

The very thought of Hayden becoming human scared me out of my mind. Why hadn't I thought of all of that before letting that first kiss happen? I was so determined to touch him, kiss him, do *anything* with him to express how I felt, and here, it may have been the one thing that he was waiting for in order to make a decision - if he'd been contemplating Fading at all. That is, if he loved me back.

If he became human, that meant he would be just as vulnerable as my real mother was. Lavinia didn't even get to see my first year of life before she died. I didn't want to end up like my father, ruing the day that his love Faded for him.

I thought about how close Hayden and Luka were and I knew then, if Hayden ever decided to Fade, he would ask Luka to be the Guardian who broke his wings. I knew I would have to speak with Luka as soon as possible. I needed him to promise me that he would talk Hayden out of it. My mind was spinning all through the morning, and it was hard to concentrate on anything else but the meaning of the previous night. Hayden started stirring, and I put my thoughts to the back of my mind in order not to ruin the time I had.

"G' mornin', Angel-man." I kissed his cheek.

Hayden smiled, his eyes half open, and put his arms around me squeezing me into him and kissing my cheek in return. "Good morning, Pony-girl. You been up long?"

"Not too long," I answered.

Hayden rubbed his eyes and scooted up against the headboard, stretching his arms. He looked past me to check the clock on the night stand.

"Wow," his eyes widened. "It's almost eleven."

I gave him a playful, pouting lip. "I know. I kinda let you sleep longer. I'm a bad influence on you."

He made the bed vibrate with his hearty laugh. "Not entirely." I rolled my eyes and laughed at his lame attempt at arguing.

He leaned his head down to mine, closing in on my lips. I wanted them so badly and welcomed them as we touched, my brain losing focus of anything rational. I felt his strong arm wrap around me as he pulled me close to his skin, our bodies pressing against each other, making our temperatures rise. Unfortunately, reality brought me back to my senses when Hayden pulled away.

"Check out is soon. We better go before they kick us out," he said.

We had the car packed and ready to go after getting a quick bite to eat at the hotel cafe. We didn't really talk much. We just did some speed-eating to get onto the road by noon. Hayden insisted on driving, so I let him, of course. It was quiet for the beginning of the ride while I sorted through my thoughts. I thought about the changes that would occur, and it scared me to death. I wasn't sure what was going through Hayden's head. Was he planning for the weekend to go as it did? Was he expecting me to bring it up first in order to confirm something? Was he waiting for me to profess my love for him before we even talked about our kissing? I felt so strange, awkward. My brain felt like a melee, battling between my emotions and rational thoughts. I wanted Hayden for myself, to claim him as my own, but my biggest fear of all was losing him. His Fading would just personify the danger that was eating away at me that very moment. I thought of my father and Lavinia, wondering if my father would have asked her not to Fade if he could have seen her death coming. He had to lose the love of his life. And for what? What was so great about her becoming human? As an angel, she was practically invincible. Things could have been entirely different for Jack, happier. They could have lived happily ever after as "angel and human."

Then, I thought back on the moments of the wedding that weekend. Christian and Brittonia stating their vows "till death to us part." Why did that have to be the end at all? Why was it always death that ruined everything for the living, ruined life entirely? The ones left behind suffered the most and it was as if saying, upon death, your connection to that person was over. Who's genius idea was that? It sucked, and I hated that I was contemplating those things at all. It was starting to make me crazy.

"I know you have questions for me and you're afraid to ask them." Hayden broke my trance, keeping his eyes on the road.

I looked over at him, eyes wide and innocent, then my face tightened in frustration. Was I that transparent? Of course I was. Who was I kidding? To Hayden, I was nothing but see-through. I'd accepted that a long time ago, but it was still hard to get used to.

"How do you always know when I have questions for you?" I stalled.

He smirked, shifting the gear to get to a higher speed. "Because you give it away," he muttered.

"By doing what?" I asked pointedly.

He chuckled and shook his head. "*Oh*, no. I'm not telling you. You'll just make a conscious effort never to do it anymore."

"Ugh," I grunted. "That is so not fair."

"Not to you, maybe," he joked. I glared at him and huffed. He looked over at me and grinned, wagging his eyebrows, which just made me roll my eyes and look out the window. He laughed.

A few moments passed.

"Okay, okay. You really wanna know?" he finally asked.

I nodded, still looking out the window. I know it may have looked like I was mad at him, but I really was still trying to figure out how I would bring up what I really wanted to talk about.

He still kept his eyes on the road. "You do this thing with your hair."

"Huh?" I looked over at him.

"You twirl a section of it from behind your ear around your finger." He shot me a quick glance. "You're doing it right now, actually."

My attention went to my hands, one in my lap, and the other twirling that damned piece of hair behind my right ear. *Jeez.* "Figures," I muttered, consciously crossing my arms.

I could see Hayden give me a small smile. "So, what did you want to ask me?" he asked as he turned off the music.

I sighed, still wondering how I would bring up the subject, but ended up blurting out the first question that came to mind, and it was literally out of left field. "Are Christian and Brittonia going to hell?" I almost smacked my hands over my mouth. *Really?*

Hayden took a sip of his coffee and practically choked. "*What?*" he asked in shock, laughing.

"Uhh, I mean, well, you know what I mean. Not hell, but....ugh! I don't know. You know how Brittonia was never really all innocent and Virgin Mary, and all that? And I'm sure he wasn't either, you know?"

Hayden nodded, still laughing. "Yeah," he responded. I waited for the meaning of my question to possibly sink in so I wouldn't have to say any more before Hayden understood what I was asking. I kept my eyes on his expectantly while his chuckling came to a slow stop. Finally, he gave me a wry smile and a raise of his eyebrow. "You're assuming that Christian and Brittonia have had sex, well before their wedding, and wondering if the Creator will throw them into the deepest pits of darkness with Alysto because of that, right?"

God, did he seriously just say that so casually? My face instantly flushed. "Well, um......figuratively, I guess that's what I mean, yeah," I stumbled over my words. I thought about what I was really trying to ask and it wasn't even about Brittonia and Christian at all. I just didn't know how to get around to it.

"I see," he slowly nodded with a smirk, keeping his eyes on the road. *Ugh.* If only I could have known the things he thought when he made those faces. The mystery drove me insane. "Well, something you should know about that is the fact that it's not entirely wrong."

I looked at him, surprised. "It's not?"

Hayden shook his head. "Not if it's done as a result of love, or passion." He threw in that last word as if he knew that some people, like Brittonia, may have gotten those two words confused. "The act, as long as it is done for the right reasons, is not sinful unless it is done out of spite, anger or against one's will, anything of a negative nature or intention."

I turned my head slowly to look at the road ahead. "Huh," was all I muttered. I knew Brittonia had been pretty "passionate" about a lot of people in her life. It made me giggle, but then I sat quietly, thinking even more. I really didn't know what kind of "road" my mind was taking me on, other than the one on which my brain was starting to hurt more and more with the questions that were begging to be asked.

"But..." Hayden's hand reached over to mine, pulling my arms out of the tight criss-cross they'd made across my chest, "that wasn't entirely what you wanted to ask me, was it?"

I let out a long-winded breath, taking his hand in mine automatically and feeling the energy when we touched. "Nope. My head is sort of racing after last night. Believe it or not, I'm thinking a lot about my dad and my mom – Lavinia, I mean."

"And this is all stemming from Christian and Brittonia's wedding?"

"Sort of."

Hayden looked over at me and smiled, nodding to me as if to give me the floor to speak. I knew he wanted me to get everything out there, and I'd wondered if he'd hoped I'd want to talk about our kiss, and what it may lead to. The fact was, I wanted to know, but I didn't. I started out with a wedding-related question first.

"You once told me that Lavinia and my dad never had a chance to get to the House of Council for their binding ceremony," I started.

"Why wasn't the regular matrimony enough? Why was this binding thing so important to Jack?"

Hayden smiled somberly. "Marriage unites two people until death do them part. The House of Council can make a marriage binding even in death, but only once the angel has fully Faded. They both need to be human. It is a gift that can be bestowed upon only the most in-love of humans and Faded angels. It not only binds their hearts, but their souls. They become one. In this particular rite of passage, death is not the end for them, only a new chapter. In binding, there really is no loss to the one left behind because, after the death of one, they are still able to communicate." He looked over at me to see if I was following before he speaking. I nodded to prompt him to continue his explanation. "Some bindings between the souls are stronger than others. In some instances, the one still living is only able to hear the voice of their partner. In others, they are able to interact, even feel each other. Your mother was too sick and passed away before they got the chance to go and meet the Council for the ceremony." His face grew more somber then. "Your father was determined that, even though they were never officially bound, his and Lavinia's connection with each other was stronger than ever possible, and that they'd still be able to communicate after she died."

I looked down at my jeans and started picking at a loose thread at the hole in the knee as I thought about my father's pain. "Is that why my father became so angry?" I asked quietly. "Because he could never communicate with Lavinia after she died?"

"Not the way he thought he could. You see, binding is a green card between worlds. It guaranties the connection of those two souls, no matter what realm they are in, no matter if they are living or gone." He shrugged. "Your father felt extremely guilty for a lot of things he'd done, and not having gone through the binding ceremony before she passed away essentially killed him."

"So he felt like he'd lost her completely," I confirmed. "That's why he was so eager to end his life, to see her again."

"Not just that, Evika. Upon his Final Death, your father's priority was to save you. But yes, in turn, he was also saving himself. He wasn't the same anymore, after Lavinia was gone. For him, going on in life brought nothing but heartache, pain," he paused, "insanity." He said these things as if they were all examples of emotions that were more profound than what other people have experienced in their loss of another loved one. But then, I sat on that for a moment, thinking about how I'd feel if I'd lost Hayden and I could feel an ache in my chest already, just like the night I'd written about it one month prior. Just the thought of losing him to another world and still being left behind was excruciating. It was a different kind of pain that I could foresee, like something entirely more powerful than a normal feeling.

I furrowed my brow. "So that's all the help that the Council gives to one of their own? They conduct some binding ceremony to unite the souls of a human and one of their own, and that's it?" I'm not sure what made me angry about it, but it just seemed like the Faded angels got gypped, and so did the human. It didn't seem fair. Of course, when *did* I think anything in life was fair anymore?

Hayden looked over at me with a concerned expression. "It's

not just the marriage that binds them. The souls are bound in a way that, even after death, they find each other. The bond and the love is so strong that the one left behind can find their other half in dreams, but also in reality. Their souls are one and can never be separated again, no matter what. If one is lost, the other will find them, even in the darkest moments of the afterlife, if that is where one of them goes." He looked over at me briefly, keeping a serious tone. "*That* is a powerful gift from the Council, Evika, something of which only a handful of people have had the opportunity to experience."

I looked over at him to study him for a moment, wondering if he'd been angry that I'd even questioned the Council, as I usually did. But he wasn't phased at all. He was patient with me, as always. I leaned my head back against the head rest and smiled at him. I could tell he knew I was looking at him when he squeezed my hand a little tighter.

I fell asleep like that for the rest of the ride home, holding my angel's hand. But there was still something on my mind that would bother me, that festered. And talking to Luka was the only way I knew I'd feel better about it.

Chapter Fourteen *The Truth About Lying*

'We need to talk,' I texted to Luka's cell as soon as Hayden and I dragged our luggage into the house and I was alone in my bedroom. I didn't have to wait long for a response.

'K. Want me there? I can bring Beau back,' Luka's text read.

I knew we would need to speak face-to-face, but I didn't know when I could talk to Luka without Hayden around to hear and I couldn't convey my thoughts the right way through a bunch of texts.

"Hey, Ev?" I jumped at the sound of Hayden's voice after a light knock on my closed door.

"Yeah?" I answered him.

"I'm taking a quick shower before bed," his muffled voice said through the door. "Just wanted to let you know."

"Uh, okay." I didn't really know what else to say. Why would he give me the specifics of his where-abouts in the house? Was it some new thing we were supposed to be doing? And where was "bed" for him? His room? My room? Did "tandem" apply to sleeping arrangements after that kiss? God! Why did I have to complicate everything?

I looked at Luka's last text and replied. 'Yes. My room. NOW.'

It was literally four seconds after I'd hit "send" when Luka's voice whispered behind me. "Am I in trouble?"

I jumped again. "God, Luka!" I almost dropped my phone.

"Wow. Your nerves fried or something?" He laughed. But then he studied my face, and his expression grew solemn. "Hey, are you okay?"

I took in a deep breath and released, starting to pace the floor and ignoring his question. "Luka, you can't let him do it," I pleaded. "You just can't."

Luka cocked his head. "Can't let who do what?"

"Hayden. You can't let Hayden Fade," I continued as I paced. "This weekend at the wedding, everything was just perfect and...*omigod*." My true feeling of fear grew even worse as I'd said it all out loud. "What the hell was I thinking? Luka, you have to promise me you won't let him do it. Promise you won't break his wings if he comes to you."

Luka's expression was still one of cluelessness. "And why in the world would I promise *that?*"

"Because I'm asking you to."

Luka relaxed his body and folded his arms. "No way."

My pacing came to a halt. "What?" I asked in shock.

He shook his head. "No can do, Evigreen. You can't put me in the middle of this."

"But you already are in the middle of this!" I said in a loud whisper, frustrated. "Why can't you just talk him out of it if he asks you? I can't-I can't let this happen. I mean, maybe I'm jumping the gun a little on this, but I saw it in his eyes, Luka. We danced. We connected. We kissed. We held each other innocently in the bed all night and – Ugh! I woke up, realizing what this may lead to," I rambled, but finally stopped after I caught the angel's expression. He was smirking.

"So, he finally kissed you, huh?" He said it without surprise in his voice.

I looked at him, exasperated. It was as though he was not taking me seriously at all.

"Luka," I stared into his eyes penetratingly. "You don't get it. I didn't want this. At first, I did, but now..." I trailed off. "I didn't think this through." I sat on the bed. I felt my face tighten as I tried holding back the tears. "I know that he'll come to you," I said softly.

Luka sighed, sitting next to me bumping my shoulder with his. "And if he comes to me, I will be honored, Evika," he said confidently. "I'll do as he asks."

I squeezed the tears from my eyes. I was hurt by Luka's rigidity, by his lack of understanding what I was telling him. I wanted to say something that would make him think about what he'd really be doing to Hayden, to me. "You'll be killing him," I advised him in a blithe tone.

He came to his knees on the floor before me. The white-winged angel pulled my chin up until our eyes met, his narrowed and looked at me with concentration. "I'd be giving him life, Evika. Whether you want to see it that way or not, he'll get what he wants, from me, from Elka, or whichever Guardian he asks to do the break for him." I flinched when he said *break*. "If Hayden wants to Fade and to be human for you, he will do it no matter what, no matter who does it for him."

I shook my head at him in frustration. "No, Luka. You don't understand."

Luka looked at me, perplexed. "What is it that you are so afraid of?"

"Just---" I didn't know how to tell him, "it's way too dangerous for him."

Luka huffed a quiet laugh. "For him? You're worried about Hay---"

"*Yes,*" I cut him off.

The angel was quiet for a long moment as he searched my eyes, then held a look of clarity. "Something happened," he declared.

I nodded slowly, shamefully.

"Evika, what is it?"

I stayed silent, biting my lip, unable to speak.

The angel rose one of his eyebrows. "Evika, whatever this is sounds like more of a danger *not* being told to me. If you know something, anything, you need to tell me."

I shook my head at the angel. "I can't."

He studied me. "Were you threatened?"

I started to become irritated again. "Luka, I didn't even want to say anything at all. All I wanted to do was ask you to talk Hayden out of Fading if he was even thinking of it."

"And, like I said, I can't do that," he answered me bluntly. "Now, Evika, please tell me what is going on."

I narrowed my eyes, even more frustrated. I was starting to regret ever asking for Luka's help to begin with. But I looked into those patient, crystal-blue pools of his and felt trust. I didn't even need to wonder if I could trust Luka; I already knew I could.

I sighed. "You have to promise me that this stays between us, Luka."

The angel looked at me intensely for, what seemed like forever. I knew he was calculating the worth of knowing along with his, Hayden's and my friendships, and quite possibly his obedience to the Council. I'd almost chickened out before spilling my guts to him.

"Okay." He nodded. "It stays between us," he answered assuringly.

"Angel's honor?" I asked.

"Angel's honor," he agreed.

I took a deep breath and let it out. "Alysto visited me in a dream a few months ago."

Luka's eyes widened to the size of golf balls. "He *what?*"

"I didn't know who or what he was until I saw the shadow he'd cast of his true form. And then it just went dark and he showed me his true form as the devil." I felt my throat close and my eyes start to burn.

"Evika," Luka held my face in his warm hands, "how did this happen? How did he get into your dream? Do you even know?"

I narrowed my eyes as I thought of Jericho. "He was given a way in," I said blithely. "By one of your kind."

His face became ashen before he spoke. "How do you know this?"

I looked at him, sad to have to confirm it. "Alysto admitted it, Luka." I nodded to the bare space above my bed. "I took the dreamcatcher down and burned it that very night, and haven't seen him since."

Luka looked up and stared at the bare spot on the wall. "I knew it," he whispered to himself. "I knew there was something up with Jericho." I could finally breathe when I realized that Luka had seen the same danger in Jericho as I did. I felt relief. Luka turned to me once again. "You're sure?" He asked me as if he really wanted me to tell him it wasn't true. I wished I could have.

"Yes," I answered him. My heart ached as I saw the disappointment in his eyes.

"But why?" he whispered his question. "Why would Jericho do something like this?" His eyes narrowed to slits. "And why would Alysto want to make contact with you?"

"I don't know. Nothing has happened since that one time. I was so afraid of what would happen if I said anything, especially to Hayden. Alysto threatened that I would regret it if Hayden got involved. Luka, I'm so sorry," I whimpered.

"Evika, don't be sorry. This isn't your fault."

My face cringed. "That's the bad part, Luka. Alysto said that *I* called to him! He said my heart called to him because 'it knows what it wants.'" I paused for a moment to watch the confused expression appear on Luka's face. I was almost too afraid to tell him more as I recalled the night with the devil. "He said he can see darkness in me, Luka, that he and I are more alike than I think. Wh-what does that even mean?" It felt as though Luka and I had come full circle, beginning from the first night we'd spent together at the Cleveland bar. I found out what *tenebrae* really meant.

Luka sat back up on the bed and held me in his arms. "Evika, I've told you this before. You are nothing like him and you never will be. No matter what he told you, and no matter how awful you feel about the Seekers when you save them, it is nothing like how Alysto truly feels. The darkness in him, it's something that has never subsided, and never will."

I wanted to believe him when he told me all of that, but I didn't. I'd always felt true hatred for all of the Seekers, regardless of my coming to terms with *why* I had to save them.

Luka stood, and then started pacing. His worried expression was bothersome to me. "He's found a way to manipulate you, Evika. This isn't something we can keep from the Council."

My body jolted in fear as I heard his words. I stood up at lightning speed. "You promised!" I reminded him.

"I-I know I did," he stuttered, "but what am I supposed to do with this information, Evika? This is huge, and I could get exiled for keeping this from them."

I glared at him. "Then I shouldn't have trusted you," I shot back at him. It was the first time I'd ever been angry with Luka, and it felt strange.

I saw the defeat in Luka's eyes, the guilt that crept up on him. He let out a long sigh as he looked at me with intensity. "Why shouldn't they know?"

I started to breath easy again once he considered this. "Because I'm afraid this may start something huge. Alysto has been holding off his Drones as a favor to me. If Jericho is unmasked in any way, it may tip off Alysto."

Luka's eyes furrowed and he looked at me incredulously. "Dammit, Evika. Why now? Why couldn't you have told this to me months ago?"

I felt ashamed as I looked at the grief in his expression, and then I looked away as I answered. "Because nothing dangerous has happened since I destroyed Jericho's instrument. Because I knew you'd be subtle about finding things out no matter when I told you. And....I'm telling you now because I thought I could get you to talk Hayden out of....."

I couldn't finish the sentence. He looked away, but I could see his eyes roll.

"Putting me in the middle again," he muttered.

Again, it felt strange to have this type of quarrel with Luka. It felt surreal and unnatural for us, but necessary.

The angel's face held a somber and disappointed expression. He sighed heavily. A sigh in which, I assumed, could only be the moment he decided how to answer me.

"Well, you are right about one thing, I will be subtle about all of this, only for a while. But, like I said before, I'm not getting in Hayden's way if he makes that decision and asks me."

I made my last, failing attempt to argue. "If something goes wrong while Hayden is in transition, I could lose him forever. Just like Jack lost Lavinia," I reminded him.

Luka sighed, still not showing any sign of flexibility about the subject of Hayden's Fading. "What if he's already made up his mind, Evika?"

I looked at those crystal blue eyes; they gave me my conclusion. "You already know."

The angel's face remained expressionless for a long moment before speaking again. "The greatest gift that an angel can give to the object of their love is their choice to Fade. Evika, please don't deny him of the very thing he can do for you to express how he feels."

I moved myself to the floor by him, wiping my tears. "And what if I don't want him to?"

Luka looked me square in the eyes. "Does that mean to say that you don't love him?"

There it was, a way to get me to admit it, my feelings. He asked me so seriously, but he asked it in a way that seemed as if he was trying to prove a point. He knew the answer to that question and he knew how I felt about Hayden.

I looked away from him and shook my head in denial. "If he loves me, he'll stay invincible," I said softly.

"You know, Ev," he pulled my chin up to look at him once again, "these things that keep you from living instill so much fear in you. You need to learn to let go."

Let go. I knew there were so many things I needed to let go of. The past. The present. The determined and undetermined future. But everything seemed like such a mess.

He smiled at me sweetly, and moved my hair behind my ear. All I could do was scoot up against him and lay my head against his shoulder. His arm wrapped around me and pulled me into him snuggly. And that was when I started crying.

"It's hard for me to let go," I whispered to him.

He gave me a light, big brother-like squeeze and a kiss on the hair. "I know, Evigreen." He sighed. "But it's the only way to survive this life." He paused. "And holding on to things for too long can weigh you down indefinitely. It can be used against you."

"I can't lose any more people that I love, Luka. I couldn't take it. I couldn't take losing Hayden if-if he..." I couldn't say the word. I couldn't say "died." "I'd go crazy, just like my father," I said softly through the tears.

"And Hayden would go crazy if he knew you were attempting to coerce me into changing his mind." the angel scolded me.

"Not everything ends badly, Evika." His tone was delicate. "I know it's hard for you to believe me when I say that because you've lost a lot of people in your life, some of the most important people that were ever a part of your life, but you need to find the ability to conjure up a little bit of faith in things again. Just a little, even just in Hayden."

I took a deep breath and gazed into the angel's eyes, sky blue like the endless world above. "I'll try, Charmin," I attempted to add a little humor to my answer. He smiled, and I threw my arms around his neck and squeezed. "I don't know where I'd be without you, Luka. I really mean that."

He blushed and grinned at me. "Yeah, I love you too, Evigreen."

We both jumped at the knock on my door.

"Evika?" Hayden's muffled voice said through the door.

Luka stood awkwardly and gave me a sheepish smile. "Uh, I better go," he whispered.

I kissed his cheek and mouthed the words "thank you," and he shimmered away into thin air.

"Yeah?" I answered the door, opening to a shirtless Hayden in gray pajama pants.

He lifted his hand to give me a small wave. "Hi," he said.

I breathed a laugh at his adorableness. "Hi."

"So, uh, I just wanted to say good night."

I smiled at him before he continued. *Those emeralds will be the death of me*, I thought.

He did that thing where he ran his hand through his hair, and I melted as I watched him. "I really had a great time this weekend," he said.

"Me too." I leaned against the door frame and looked up at him. "I'm glad we went."

Hayden nodded with a simper, leaning into me a bit closer. I could see he was studying me in such depth, but it didn't feel invasive. It felt right. He lifted his fingers to my face and caressed it gently. I slowly closed my eyes and leaned my cheek into his touch. As always, he captivated me with his tenderness and warmth. I could feel the heat from his body mix with mine as he advanced a little closer.

"You are the most beautiful being I've ever known," he whispered.

I half-smiled, embarrassed. "Said the angel in my door---"

And before I knew it, his lips pressed to mine, interrupting me in mid-sentence. I let the flooding heat of that supernal kiss take me over, my senses awakened, lively. My heart pounded its drumming beats in my chest, and my pulse raced as his perfect lips kissed mine. Just like our kisses the previous night, I didn't want it to end.

He slowly pulled away from me and left me breathless as my eyes fluttered open to see him kissing me on the forehead.

"Sweet dreams tonight," he said to me, reluctantly turning to head back to his room.

"Yeah." I let out an internal sigh. "Sweet dreams."

He turned to look at me once more and smiled. I watched him walk down the hall from my doorway. I admired the smooth skin of his back, every curve of muscle. His perfection still awed me.

I closed my door after letting Beau into the room and lay down on the bed, pressing my head hard against the pillow as I tried to drive out the thoughts going through my mind. *Is this right? Me in my room and he in his? No. It's not right.* It didn't feel right to be alone, without him, after having connected the way we had. The missing piece of me was down the hall, and he was what I needed. He was my angel, and I loved him so much it hurt.

I sighed heavily, annoyed with myself for just being such a coward, and then I threw the covers off, and pattered down the hallway to his room, Beau at my flank. Hayden's door was open, and the closer I got the less muffled the sounds from his room became. It was music. I made it to the threshold and looked in.

"What took you so long?" he asked as I peered in his direction. He was laying on his side, facing the door and propped up on one elbow.

I shrugged and I crawled into the bed under the sheets, pressing my back against him and lacing my fingers through his as I pulled his arm around me. I listened to the music he had playing. I knew he'd put music on just for me. A new track started playing, and it sent chills up my spine. I couldn't suppress the guilt any longer. "A Stranger," the very song that played while I danced with Alysto.

"What do you have playing?" I asked, wondering if he'd chosen that song for any particular reason.

"Just the radio," he answered. He was quiet for a few seconds. "I know you need it to sleep."

My body slightly relaxed. "Thanks."

As if he felt my indifference, Hayden pulled me closer to him and kissed my shoulder. "I'll always protect you, no matter what. You know that, right?" he said quietly.

I swallowed hard before I answered him. "Of course," was all I could say.

I waited for some sort of elaboration to his comment-slash-question, confused as to what brought it on.

"Good. I just wanted to be sure," he said before snuggling his nose into the crook of my neck to go to sleep.

I lay there, eyes wide open, my heart pumping its guilt through my veins. What was I supposed to do? How was I supposed to tell him about the enemy invading my dreams? And worse, how was I supposed to explain to him my reasoning for keeping all of it from him? He would say there was no excuse, that no matter how awful the threats were from Alysto, I should have told him a long time ago.

But if Hayden decided to Fade, it would make him vulnerable to even more danger. Alysto would be sure to end him, just as he'd threatened. I was in a deep, deep pile of lies and deceit due to the Keeper of the Wicked, and I wanted nothing more than to close my eyes and make it all go away, to make all of the bad things disappear.

"Hayden?" I whispered. As usual, I needed a distraction from my current train of thought.

"Yeah?" his voice sounded tired.

"Do you ever dream?"

"Every night," he answered without hesitation.

"What about?"

He took in a long deep breath, exhaling with an embarrassed laugh. "You. I'm always protecting you from something," he admitted. I felt him shrug. "But it's not always bad."

"What's not always bad?"

"The thing from which I'm protecting you."

I thought for a moment. It didn't seem to make sense. I turned in the bed to face him. "So, if it's not always bad, then how come you keep protecting me from it?"

There was an instant, soundless moment created between the end of one song and the beginning of another. Hayden lifted his fingers to my hair, lacing them through the pieces. I waited patiently for his answer.

"Because whatever it is that wants you," he said softly, "is trying to take you from me." He paused before continuing with a confident grin, and closed his eyes, sighing out, "but I always win. Always."

Chapter Fifteen *The Truth About Shakespeare*

    A long morning of saves had worn me out, as usual, so I'd taken a much needed nap that continued well into the evening. I was sleeping soundly when I awoke to my angel's whispers.

    "Evika," he said softly as he crouched next to the bed, "I know you're tired, but I didn't want you to miss something."

    I rubbed my eyes. "Are you okay? What time is it?"

    "I'm fine. It's about time for sunset," he answered, then extended his hand to me. "Will you come with me?"

    I looked him over as I sat up. He seemed calm and collected. I was sure there wasn't anything wrong then. "Where are we going, Angel-man?" I asked tiredly.

He smiled solemnly, taking my hand. "Up," was all he said.

I grinned, and my excitement grew. I knew what "up" meant. It was something I'd only experienced once before with him, the day I saw the world from his eyes, an angel's eye-view.

I slid into my combat boots since they were easy to get on and off with the zipper on the side, and I tossed my dragon hoodie over my head.

Hayden placed my hand in his and led me down the stairs, out to the back porch. And just as I remembered, his magnificent, black wings spread on either side of him. It was just as amazing the second time. There was no question as to what I had to do. I walked up to him, placing my feet on top of his and embraced his body, laying my head against his chest. I felt his arms wrap around me, and I'd only taken one breath before we shot up into the sky.

This time, I kept my eyes open, and watched the landscape and the house get smaller. The yellow highlights from the sun were turning orange as the ball of fire was about to set. The roofs of the houses and the tops of the trees turned into mere shapes, blobs of color like a Monet, as we got higher and higher. I turned my head and saw the glistening tips of the waves, reflecting the broken up rays of the sun. A certain peace was blanketed over the world during this time of day; something that would always be.

It seemed as though we had to fly higher this time to reach a cloud. Hayden perched us on top of one a lot higher than I'd remembered from our last visit to the sky. He immediately sat down and placed me on his lap, locking his arms around me to keep me safe.

I looked down at his embrace and smiled. "So, what's the occasion?" I asked.

He kept his gaze on the horizon and grinned. "Last time, the sun was rising. I figured I'd show you the beauty of the sun setting this time." He paused for a moment, as if choosing his words carefully. "And I wanted to tell you about someone."

"Someone you guarded?" I asked.

"No, but I knew him very well. He is one of the most notorious writers of all time."

"Well, that could be a lot of people. Who was it?"

"Shakespeare."

I sucked air. "You knew William *Shakespeare?*"

"I did." Hayden nodded. "Did you know he was a Taurus, like you?"

"Actually," I stated, "I did know that."

Hayden chuckled.

"He was married to what's-her-name." I thought for a moment. "Don't tell me. It's on the tip of my tongue." Hayden smirked, but kept quiet. "Her name is really familiar because there is an actress that has the same name." I turned away and focused on the earth below. "Ugh, I know this. My favorite teacher taught us all about the Elizabethan times," I said as I tapped my chin. "I even did a report on Shakespeare for Literature." Then it came to me. "Anne Hathaway!" I shouted with glee.

235

I could feel Hayden vibrating with laughter and looked over at him. "I knew you'd get it." His eyes lit up as he smiled. "Do you remember any of it, the report? Wasn't that the report where you compared his relationship with Anne to his writing?" he inquired.

I nodded. "Yeah, I pulled a lot of info about how they only got married because she was three months pregnant. It was supposedly a shot-gun wedding, but my paper was to argue that he was truly in love with her. He was about eight or nine years younger than her. He was only eighteen when they got married. People also claimed that Shakespeare never really loved her because he only left her his second-best bed in his will, but I dug up a lot of information that suggested that the second-best bed was their marital bed, and the best bed in the house was left for guests. It was the normal bequest for those times, I guess." I looked at Hayden for approval. I'd wondered if I was on the right track.

Hayden nodded, smiling proudly. "Go on," he assured me. "What else do you remember?"

"Well," I continued, "I remember there were two Globe Theatres built to perform all of his plays. They called the ceiling of the stages 'The Heavens.' Another fun fact was Shakespeare actually created over thirty words that ended up in the Oxford English Dictionary, like 'bedazzle,' 'leapfrog,'....." I paused for a moment to laugh, "and even the word 'puke.'"

He rolled his eyes, lovingly. "Okay good, but what can you tell me about him and Anne?" Hayden raised his eyebrows, waiting for me to continue.

I looked at him curiously, wondering why he didn't just tell me himself. I humored him. "Anne and he had three children. There was the daughter she was pregnant with when they got married, then only a couple of years later, Anne gave birth to twins, a boy and a girl." I thought of the tragedy that I read about the twins. "The little boy was only eleven when he died, but Shakespeare kept up with his writing. It didn't stop him from continuing his work. He wrote and performed some of his plays in London, but would always come home to Stratford for a period of time every year to be with Anne. Even after he retired, he left London and permanently stayed in Stratford, where Anne wanted to live. Really though, there weren't many more facts about him outside of the rumors and allegations about his life because there was this period of time that were like the dark years for him, a length of time that no one can recall to this day. I think they were called the Lost Years?"

Hayden laughed. "You know, you really do remember a lot for having read all that so long ago."

"But, am I right?" I asked eagerly. "Was all that stuff true about him and Anne?"

The angel bobbed his head in assurance. "The fact that you argued that they were truly in love puts you completely on the right track," he praised, looking at me admiringly. "I was really proud of you when you wrote that paper, you know?"

I giggled. "You were?"

He looked at me solemnly. "Yes, I was."

We were silent for a moment, watching the setting sun. I'd

wondered what that whole trip to the clouds meant, why we were up there and why he had mentioned Shakespeare. "So, why are we talking about Shakespeare, anyway? What is this all about?" I asked seriously, still staring out at the orange horizon as I leaned into my angel.

"Because there is one huge secret that I know about him that you'll never find in any history book," he answered.

I turned in his lap and looked at him inquisitively, wondering if Shakespeare had some second life that no one knew about. There really wasn't much that historians could tell you about him that was plausible. I gave Hayden an incredulous look. "Exactly how well did you know him?"

He grinned at my question. "Evika," he said, "Shakespeare was once a Guardian, too. He fell in love with Anne and chose to Fade for her."

"What?" I was shocked. *Oh, no. We are talking about Fading.* I stared at him blankly for, what seemed like, forever. "Shakespeare was an *angel?*" The expression of disbelief didn't leave my face, I was sure of it.

Hayden nodded.

"But, how..." I paused, recalling the things I'd rambled off about my report, and then it hit me. "The Lost Years," I muttered. "That was the past that no one could explain about him. Not because of the bad documentation of records, but because he *had* no past." Saying it aloud sounded so insane, but it made total sense. I looked at Hayden for approval again. He smiled genuinely.

"He was Anne's father's Guardian, and after Richard passed

away in September of 1581, William took a trial." I watched Hayden stare off into the endless sky, to recall the story. "He spent a few months watching Anne from afar, but he knew." He smiled and turned to me. "He knew Anne was the one he wanted, and he Faded for her."

I stared at my angel in awe as he continued. "That was when all of his earliest sonnets were written. Most everything he wrote had Elizabethan pronunciation, but sometimes he'd steer away from the norm and historians would argue that Shakespeare was the wrong man to have ascribed certain writings." He held a cocky grin. "But I know the truth." He winked, then looked down at our hands, lacing his fingers through mine. "Do you want to hear one?"

God, did I ever. I nodded. "Of course, I do," I couldn't stop staring at him.

He smirked. I could tell he was enjoying my awestruck silence and lack of words. He must have been proud. He cleared his throat, looking back at the sunset once again.

"But were it to my fancy given, to rate her charms, I'd call them heaven; For though a mortal made of clay, angels must love Anne Hathaway; She hath a way so to control, to rapture the imprisoned soul, and sweetest heaven on earth display, that to be heaven Anne hath a way; She hath a way, Anne Hathaway, - to be heaven's self Anne hath a way." Hayden recited it flawlessly, as if he'd written it himself.

I watched his lips curve into a smile and I mimicked them with my own. "I've never heard that one before," I whispered, still staring into those pools of green. "It's beautiful."

"One of my favorites," he said.

"One thing I'm curious about though," I said.

"What's that?"

"How is Shakespeare a Taurus if he was never really, you know, born? I mean, how does that work? You just pick a birthday or something?"

Hayden chuckled. "His creation day was April twenty-third. He even had baptism papers made out to document the event." I looked at him incredulously, and he caught my expression. "We have lots of tricks up our sleeves." He shrugged.

"So I see. I didn't know you celebrated birthdays, er, creation days." I paused for a moment. "Actually, I never even really thought about that at all. When is yours?"

"Soon," was all he said.

I narrowed my eyes. "Hayden," I said in a scolding tone.

He cleared his throat and muttered in a hardly-audible voice. "It's sort of in three days."

"What?" My brow furrowed, and my lips pursed as I tried to calculate the day. "August sixteenth. Great. Thanks for the warning, Hayden."

"Well," he said, "last year was sort of inappropriate to mention it. There was a lot going on during that time since you were in your coma."

"Hmm. Yeah, and telling me three days before is so much better," I said sardonically. I thought about the zodiac sign at which the current date would put us and I giggled at the thought.

"What's so funny?" he asked.

"That makes you a Leo. It all makes so much sense now," I said.

"How is that?"

"Because you certainly hold true to your sign," I answered. "You're confident and vain, *love* being the hit at a party, you have an ego that demands praise and adoration." I laughed. "But you're also loyal, generous and very social. Born to be a leader, and quite the charmer."

"Hmm." Hayden smirked. "I guess that is me to a 'T'."

"Oh," I burst out laughing when I thought of another thing that his sign meant, "and your Chinese sign is the monkey."

"Nice." He rolled his eyes and laughed. "I'd rather just be the lion."

"Hey, no worries. Other than the bull, I'm a snake. I'm known as self-indulgent, greedy and, oh yeah, stubborn." I nudged him.

"But, if I'm not mistaken, you're also known to be loving, reliable, and warm-hearted, and really creative in all aspects of the arts," he added.

I smiled. "Thanks for pointing out the positive, but that doesn't get you off the hook for omitting your creation date. I'm whipping up something special for dinner this weekend, just the two of us. And, if I start now, I can plan something huge for your half-birthday in six months to make up for all of this."

He laughed heartily, shaking his head. "What am I gonna do with you?"

I shrugged sheepishly. I watched the glint in his eye that shone the last light of the sun before it set completely beyond the horizon, and then it was only moonlight that glazed the world, the clouds, only us. I watched the angel adore the scenery silently. It was as though he was making a conscious effort to commit it to memory in a certain way.

"Do you come up here a lot?" I broke his trance. "Without me, I mean."

He turned to meet my gaze and smiled genuinely. "I used to." Then he looked back to the horizon, still holding that smile while he gave a thoughtful squeeze to my hands. "But I don't need to anymore."

My body froze when he said those words. I sat there, contemplating what he meant. I was hopeful that he meant he didn't need to enjoy perching on clouds alone, without me, since I'd always liked to go with him. But in my heart, I already knew; he felt he didn't need to come up here anymore...at all. That was what his face told me, he was at peace with a decision.

"Hayden," I said his name softly, almost hoping he wouldn't hear me ask. "Why are we really up here talking about Shakespeare?" I sort of gulped after I asked, not sure that I was ready to to get my answer.

He took a deep breath, looking away just briefly. But I found the object at which he gazed; it was our hands, still laced together. He didn't answer me right away. Did I ask the wrong question? What was he really thinking? My heart raced, and my mind started to panic with questions until his eyes met mine once again, his handsome face breaking into a proud smile.

"Because I never fully understood why he did what he did for her....until you existed."

He slowly leaned into me. His hand laced through my hair, and I closed my eyes as I felt the warmth of those perfect lips press to mine. Floods of euphoric energy surged through my entire body from head to toe. I was in that state of being again, the place I never wanted to be out of. Every kiss from him was meaningful. He took his time before claiming his lips back once again, the moment I finally realized I was leaning back, his strong arm cradling my upper body. I sat up and leaned against his chest, listening to his breathing and watching the still of the world below.

Contentment. Hopefulness. Absolute nirvana. I felt all of those things and so much more just being in his arms. It was home. It was bliss. It was real.

And I was scared to death.

Chapter Sixteen *Angels Don't Bleed*

I'd been a little on edge after the next morning's save. It was a castor from the North, and the woman had died in a drowning. I'd always feared that kind of death the most, and without Hayden there to calm me, I would have lost my mind. After the save, I had to get my mind off of things and assured Hayden it was okay for him to leave the house for a while. I made Luka take him out so I could get preparations ready for the dinner I promised to make us to celebrate Hayden's creation day. Of course, Hayden wouldn't go any further than down the street, so they each took a turn on the motorcycle doing wheelies, which, I'm sure, the neighbors loved.

Since I promised a nice home-made attempt at dinner, I decided to surprise Hayden with one of the things Joel always made me for my birthdays in the past. He made the best chicken stir fry I'd ever had in my life, and if I could have duplicated it at least half as good, I'd have been proud.

I started slicing the chicken into chunks when I felt a pair of fingers lightly touch my shoulders. At that moment, I didn't think. I only reacted. Things happened so quickly. I simultaneously jumped and screamed, clutching the butcher knife and whipping it around with me as I spun around carelessly, scared out my wits. My hand, my eyes and my mind were all running at different speeds, and it was obvious that my hand reacted the fastest. I met his emerald eyes, only inches from mine, and wanted to stop the action of my body, but it wouldn't listen in that split second of time. The knife sliced across his shoulder, breaking open the material of his black shirt as it cut into his skin.

"*Ah!*" Hayden yelled, grabbing his arm where I'd made the cut. "Evika---" his breath cut short.

"Hayden!" I screamed. "Omigod!" I could hear my heartbeat in my head. "Are you okay? I'm so sorry! I didn't mean to---"

And then I saw it. I saw the blood seeping through his fingers as they covered the wound. I felt sick. This wasn't right.

"Hayden! You're bleeding! Omigod! Omigod, why are you bleeding!?" I was flustered, finally throwing the knife in the sink and grabbing the towel from the stove to tie around his arm. He was doubled over on the kitchen floor, hissing at the pain I'd caused.

Not looking up at me and remaining rigid on his knees, he let go of his arm and held out his hand to me. "Evika, give me the towel, please."

I handed it to him quickly, still not computing exactly what this all meant. He wasn't supposed to bleed. Angels don't bleed. They just don't. He told me this before. I'd felt horrible for slicing his shoulder, and for making him bleed, I felt unforgivable. I frantically looked for the first aid kit under the sink and found a square bandage.

"Hayden, I'm so, so sorry. What's going on?" I still felt my chest pounding, and my ears throbbed with that very sound. I was worried sick.

"I'm bleeding," he grunted to me as he stood to grab the bandage from my hand. He was still holding the towel tightly around the wound as he made his way to a dining chair.

"Yes, I can see this, Sherlock! But *why*?" I was frustrated, still panicked.

He pulled the towel back for a moment to check the status on his cut, then looked up at me, smirking. "Well, you were bound to find out sooner or later. What better way to find out than to cut me open, right?" he joked, trying to laugh.

I looked at him, confused. "Find out?" I hated when he didn't give me a straight answer and only said enough to give me clues. I looked at the blood-colored towel in his hand. Had he?

"Hayden, no." I shook my head, holding back the tears. I wanted him to spring up out of that chair to tell me it was all a sick joke, and the blood was only a ketchup packet squirted on his arm. I wanted to be able to just smack his chest and tell him he was a big jerk for pulling such an awful prank on me.

But he didn't. He sat there, knowing well that I'd just realized the meaning of the moment and what had just occurred. He smiled solemnly.

I started shaking my head again to the counter and leaning against it as I kept my eyes on his. "Why would you do it, Hayden?" *Too soon! I didn't want it to be so soon!*

He stood cautiously, returning my gaze and making his way over to me. "Are you not happy that I have?"

The prickling in my eyes was becoming unbearable. I couldn't contain the tears any longer. "Why would you Fade for me, Hayden?" I whispered. "Why would you choose to do that for me?"

He half-smiled, and was only inches from my face. He lowered his head, level with mine, our eyes met as he touched his forehead to mine. "Because I'm in love with you, Evika," he said to me softly.

I heard his words, shut my eyes tight and squeezed the tears from them. He said them, those words that I'd wanted to tell him as well. I choked and looked down at the bloodied towel that he'd sloppily wrapped around his arm.

"Give me this thing," I said as I took the bandage from his other hand. He grinned at me the whole time. I removed the towel. It was soaked, but I didn't let it bother me. He removed his blood-soaked t-shirt, exposing his perfect torso. Talk about distractions. Being that close to his naked chest almost made me forget about the wound entirely.

I composed myself and was able to clean the cut up with the gauze from the kit. The blood kept oozing, but I'd covered it with more clean gauze and the bandage. I was gentle with him, as if he were a child. This was all new to him, human healing. I shook my head. This angel was in love with me now, and he'd chosen to Fade; to become human because he was in love with me.

After tending to his wound, I looked at Hayden as sternly as I could. He still held that grin. "It was Luka, wasn't it?" I asked. Honestly, I have no idea why I even asked.

He wrinkled his nose animatedly. "You already knew it would be him, Evika."

I sighed. "When?" I demanded. "When did you do it?"

He smirked. "I met up with him last night after you were asleep. I gave him no choice."

Of course he didn't, just as Luka had warned me. I closed my eyes briefly, picturing the horror of those wings breaking, the sound, the sight, the pain. I was quite sure it was something I'd never want to witness. I winced at the thought and shuddered, opening my eyes to see my angel giving me a proud smile.

"And again," he continued, "I ask...." He leaned into my ear, his hot breath grazing the skin of my neck. "Does this not make you happy? Because I kinda can't take it back now." He laughed lightly.

I could have said all that I wanted, but it wouldn't have been enough. I could have shouted from the top of my lungs how wonderful I felt, how wonderful *he* made me feel, but it wouldn't have been loud enough. To show him was all I knew to do. I cupped his face in my hands and brought his eyes level with my own. I was suddenly lost in those eyes again. Yet, I felt like I'd been found for the first time in my life. He saw me. He knew me. He loved me.

"Hayden," I felt the words I'd already known inside ready to leave my tongue, "I love you." God, it felt so good to tell him. "I've wanted to tell you that so many times. I. Love. You." It was liberating.

The words poured from my mouth like a song and I wanted to sing them over and over again. It was the music I'd longed to play for him. I pulled him to me and crushed my lips against his. Jolts of electricity took over my entire body, and my senses had awakened. His soft lips stayed locked with mine and soon explored the route to my ear and down my neck. He kissed me softly, precision in every peck, down to my collarbone, across my chest along the curve of my shirt's neckline, then back up to the other side. If that was heaven, I was okay with death. Our breathing became heavy.

Hayden pulled away, but only slightly. "I was hoping you would say that, because I have something else I need to ask you."

I blinked slowly, trying to get my breathing under control. "Anything. Ask me anything."

He caressed my cheek and moved the hanging piece of hair from my eyes. "Evika Jade," he beamed, "will you marry me?"

I think my heart stopped. No, I *know* my heart stopped. For the second time in my life, it really did stop, but this time it was only because it probably leaped out of my chest and bounced around screaming on the kitchen tile. *Omigod! Did he just propose to me?* I finally felt my heart return as it beat inside me, every thump noticeable, shouting at me with exultation. I thought of how to answer him. I wanted to scream out my answer loud for the whole world to hear. *Yes! Yes! Yes!* But it wasn't enough for me. I wanted him to know just how much I meant my "yes." I locked my arms around his neck and laced my fingers through his hair, pulling him to my lips again, pressing harder than before, and wanting more of him than I could possibly ever have.

I pulled away for a short second only to give him the answer. "In a heartbeat, Angel-man."

He gave me that smile I loved, that five-hundred watt smile that shone on his face brighter than ever. He lifted me gently onto the counter, and I wrapped my legs around his waist, pulling him to me and crushing him against me just as hard as our lips. My hands explored the curves of his back muscles, while his hands played in my hair. We entwined ourselves. Our breathing become a cadence, echoing within the kitchen walls. My breathing sped while he pressed himself in between my legs. There was nothing else I wanted more right then than to give myself to him.

"Evika." He broke our heads apart, only barely, to ask. "Are you sure you want this?"

Hayden was my soul mate. I knew I wanted every part of him, and I wanted every part of me to be for him. I was finally ready.

I was lost in his eyes. "Hayden," I traced his bottom lip with my thumb, "I've never been more sure about anything else in my life. I want you forever."

He looked at me with that angel's face. "You can have me

forever."

He cautiously scooped me up, held me against him, and effortlessly walked us up the stairs to my room.

Hayden laid me gently on the bed before carefully laying his body against mine. I took in every curve of his muscles. He was beautiful, and he was mine. I was ready. I would give my innocence to my angel. My Guardian Angel.

He turned my head gently to the side and kissed my neck gingerly once again, leaving no part of my exposed skin unmarked by his lips. I felt the smoothness of his hands reach my hips and glide up under my shirt to my breasts. He squeezed them gently, making my body sing. It sent welcoming chills down my spine and through my legs. I sat up slightly as he pulled my shirt over my head, giving me his genuine smile once again. He kissed me softly from my shoulder and down to my waistline to meet my jeans. It was no surprise that he made no fumbles in getting them off so gracefully. As he slid my jeans down my legs, he gave his kisses all the way down to my toes and pulled them off entirely, managing to also unclothe his bottom half. We were then nothing but skin and passion, laying together in that bed.

I lay there anxious, waiting. Hayden then prowled up over me once again, hovering, taking in my body until he reached my eyes. He stopped for a short moment and looked at me solemnly.

"All this time that I thought I was made for you," he said, "and it was you who was made for me."

I almost cried again, but consciously made my tears relent. "You were created for me, Hayden." I whispered, holding his face.

My hands roamed around the curves of his shoulders and to his back. I could feel the scars, where his wings used to be, and I tried to put it out of my mind, the pain he must have endured for me. "I love you," I said. I felt free when I said those words. I wanted to keep telling him I loved him. I couldn't say it enough. I couldn't kiss him enough.

"Evika, I love you with my entire soul and with every beat of our hearts." Hayden took my hand and placed it on his chest. I felt it beating and his Fading became even more prominent to me. He pressed his lips against mine with a slight haste, then he buried his head into my neck, kissing and nibbling at my skin. It sent me building and gasping for air.

The rest of that night, we'd spent exploring each other's bodies and marking every part of them with kisses that we'd longed to give each other. It was as if something had finally been unleashed and we were free to express the love that we'd always meant to share with each other. I'd held onto the hopes for that moment for all my twenty-one years, and it was all for this perfect reason; my angel was my love, my life, and my destiny.

Chapter Seventeen *A Little Late*

I woke up to the heavenly feeling of Hayden's body against mine and the gentle touch of his finger tips softly caressing my bare shoulder, the light graze of each of his breaths against the skin on the back of my neck. It took me leaps and bounds past cloud nine. I turned to face him, to hold him.

He smiled brightly. "Ah, the culprit has finally awakened." He started playing with my hair.

"Culprit?" I giggled sleepily. "Me?"

"Well, you did take the innocence of one of the Creator's angels last night." He made the bed vibrate with his laughter. It was infectious.

"Oh, is that so?" My eyes dramatically scoped the room. "An angel, huh? I have no idea what you're talking about. There are clearly no angels in this bedroom."

"You better look a little harder, Miss Stormer." Hayden pulled me closer to him, his lips an inch from mine as we stared into each others eyes.

"Oh, look," I whispered to him. "You're right. I think I just found one."

Hayden grinned in satisfaction. "I'm hard to miss." I laughed, relishing the fact that I'd done nothing yet to damage his large ego. "I'm glad you're awake. I have something for you." He reached around to the nightstand behind him and held something in his palm. A ring. A beautiful, princess-cut diamond stone in a platinum band with three small diamonds on either side of it.

My hand went to my mouth.

"It was your mother's, Lavinia's, I mean. I thought it would mean more to you to have this one. I know that you're not into this kind of jewelry, but---"

My finger pressed to his lips to stop his words. "It's perfect," I assured him. And it was. Everything was. "Hayden, I love it."

He smiled at me and tugged at my left arm to reach my hand, placing the ring on my finger. It was a perfect fit.

He looked at it in delight. "This must mean that it was meant to be," he said proudly.

I pulled him closer. "I could have told you that," I said.

I observed the contours of his chest muscles, his gorgeous body that I'd been longing to touch since the day we'd met, and then grinned deviously. "So, what's it like?" I asked.

He took his gaze from my finger to look at me. "What is what like?"

"What's it like for you now that you're in this lovely vessel permanently?" I ran my finger from his shoulder down across his chest, and made figure-eights around each defined muscle. "Isn't it kind of restricting compared to what you're used to?"

He raised his brow. "Restricting?" He shook his head and laid on his back, pulling me into him. "Come here," he invited. "Lay your head right here." He tapped his chest, then pulled my body closer. I placed my ear to his chest, facing him. "Do you hear that?" he asked.

The sound of his beating heart filled my eardrum. "Yes, of course I hear it." I slid my fingers to his neck to feel the pulse beat in time with his heart.

He smiled at me solemnly. "That's the best feeling in the world. Next to having you, of course."

We lay there, still as statues. I listened to every breath he took, every beat his heart made. I began to realize the finality of Hayden's invincibility, starting to question if I was, even worth Fading for. I wondered if my father had felt the same way after Lavinia's transition. I then wondered if any of the Guardians had ever regretted their decisions to become human for another. I stayed quiet, counting a few more heartbeats before asking the question.

"So you don't regret it?" I asked too softly, almost hoping it wasn't audible.

I knew he'd heard me when his breath hitched and he sat up slightly. I turned to him to see a slight pain behind his eyes, making me ashamed that I'd even asked. "Of course I don't regret it." His hand lifted my chin. "I would do it a thousand times over, and a thousand more after that, just to prove to you that I don't, and never will, regret the decision to Fade for you, Evika."

He stroked my hair gently in a way that could have put me to sleep for days. Physical contact with him was so soothing, and an absolute addiction. He healed me, inside and out. He was made for me. I remained speechless as I watched him and as I thought about the pain I'd feel if he'd gone away. My throat closed up. I tried to hold back the tears that beckoned to fall. I wasn't scared of the pain from which he protected me. I could take that. But, losing him would hurt worse than anything I could ever imagine. I just knew it would. In essence, it would kill me. His choosing to Fade worried me to no end. It hurt me to know that he could die just like any other person. I sat up, grabbing his hands and lacing our fingers together. I looked down, and those tears finally fell.

"Hayden," I whispered reluctantly, "how does this story end…after you've become completely human?"

He smiled, gently clearing one of my runaway tears with his thumb. "Happily ever after," he said, "and that's only the beginning."

I shook my head in disbelief. "I'm scared to death that I'm going to lose you. I can't stop thinking about it," I admitted. "Hayden, if I lost you, I just couldn't live! You can't protect me from my Final Death. That death, whenever it may be, will be the one you must let happen...the way it happened when I first fell. We don't know what is to come before that moment, all I ask is that you let it happen before yours." Tears completely filled my eyes. I looked down at our hands and the blur of peach-colored skin was all I could see. "I know it's selfish of me to ask that of you. I know. I know. I *know*."

"Evika, I know you may have fears because of what happened to Lavinia, but it will be okay," he declared in a whisper. He released our hands and cupped my face, pulling my chin up. Our eyes met. He gave me a solemn smile. "As much as I'd love to make that type of promise to you, Evika, I just can't." He sighed. "After I complete the Fade, there is no telling when my time is. That is the gamble that we angels take when we decide to do this for the one we love. I don't know when my time will be. All I can hope for is to grow old and gray, with you right by my side." And it's exactly what I didn't want to hear. The unfairness, the ridiculousness of the whole idea of Fading. The complete uncertainty of the fate of an angel gone human. Then, he reminded me of something. "But, I *can* promise you this." He took my left hand and pressed it against his chest. "I will be forever yours and I promise you that we *will* go to the Council for our binding ceremony once I've completed the transition." He never ceased to amaze me with his composure, his intuitiveness. "Do you remember what I told you about the binding?"

I nodded. "We can be bound forever, even in death," I recalled.

The angel smiled with satisfaction. "Precisely."

"You promise me?" I asked in a whisper, quieting my sobs.

"Angel's honor." He winked.

"As soon as the scars are healed?"

He grinned. "If manageable, we will bind that very day. And," he leaned forward, "I promise to try my best not to let anything bad happen to myself as long as I have the power to do so." He placed his lips against mine. I closed my eyes and felt a sudden calmness extend through my nerves, silencing them. The worry was gone. My fear was gone. He pulled away slowly, and I opened my eyes, wondering where his lips had gone. He gave me one of those wide grins.

I furrowed my brow. "You did that on purpose, didn't you?"

"Did what? I just wanted to kiss you."

I rolled my eyes at his excuse, but couldn't help but laugh while I lunged toward him, knocking him down to hold him.

"So does this mean I have to protect you now, too?" I asked.

He cuffed his hand around my bicep, and wiggled my limp arm in the air. "If that were the case, we may need back-up."

I sucked air. "I'm so insulted right now!"

He laughed. I kiddingly shoved him in the chest, then leaned over him and ran my fingers through his dark hair. He was perfect. Beautiful.

Hayden grinned and pressed his lips to mine, then laid his head back into the pillow, staring at me with admiration.

I blushed. "What?" I asked.

"This moment," he took my hand, "and every moment after, I want to remember forever."

His sweet words made me melt. "Then let's make sure we never forget."

I felt a sudden grip around my hips as he placed me on top of him. "And how do you suggest we do that, Pony-girl?" he challenged, lips curling into a wicked grin. "What would you say to a little toast to our new chapter with a mimosa?"

My eyes widened. That sounded so good. "Genius idea. I would love one."

"Great." Hayden bobbed his head in satisfaction. "Then I'll go make them," he said as he gracefully slid me off of him. He whisked the covers aside and rolled over to the edge of the bed only to come to a screeching halt before standing.

"What's wrong?" I asked.

"Uh." He laughed nervously, looking down. "I'm a bit inconvenienced at the moment. Would you mind going down and grabbing everything?"

"Oh!" I realized the issue. "Say no more, Angel Man." I giggled as I threw on my black tank-top and hiphuggers. "I'll go fetch the champagne and O.J."

He lay back down onto the bed carefully and let out a sigh of relief as he beamed a smile my way. I shook my head and admired his adorable expression, one of innocence and embarrassment.

"Thanks," he said.

I leaned down to peck his lips. "Be right back."

I hustled down the stairs to the landing, excitedly turning the corner and making my way to the kitchen. Many thoughts ran through my mind. All feelings of giddiness and joy, until I heard an unfavorable voice, one that pestered, reminding me that I was soiling the perfection of the moment by continuing to keep a huge secret from my angel - my encounter with Alysto. Why, oh why did guilt surface at the most inconvenient times? I justified my actions by reminding myself that I'd told Luka, and that was good enough for the time being. There was no need to say anything further, for Hayden's own good. I let out a heavy sigh and tried to shake the feeling as I searched for the bottle of Dom Perignon. It was one of the most expensive bottles on the shelves, and I had dropped it in the shopping cart without Hayden noticing...until it was time to pay, of course. Surprisingly, he let me get away with it.

    I grabbed the orange juice and glasses, and placed everything on the breakfast tray to head back upstairs. There was a loud knock at the front door just as my foot hit the first step, startling me to the point that I'd almost dropped the tray.

    "Crap," I muttered. I set the tray on the bottom step and threw on a pair of jeans from the unfolded clothes in the hamper I'd left in the foyer. *Yesterday's laziness cures today's craziness*, I thought. I unhitched the locks, and pulled open the heavy hickory door to find a face staring at me through the screen door.

    I noted his dark, shaggy hair coming to mid-face length, chocolate brown eyes, pale skin, with a slight stubble growing in, and a cute smile plastered on his young face. The young stranger seemed familiar to me, yet still very foreign. I couldn't pin what it was. I quickly shoved my thoughts to the side before it got too awkward with the strange silence between us.

"Uh, hello," I said, offering only a slight smile.

"Hi." His hand waved to me, and then he shoved his hands back in the pockets of his gray hoodie. He studied me for a moment longer and smiled wider, captivation in his eyes. What was wrong with him?

"So, can I help you?" I hinted to get him to talk. I regretted answering that door.

"Oh." He shook his head, as if trying to force himself out of a trance, and then blinked a few times. "Uh, I'm so sorry. It's just that I didn't really think this part through. I mean, I *did*, but now I'm just sort of drawing a blank here. Rehearsal didn't really do me any good, I guess." He laughed nervously. I looked at him, still waiting for an answer to my question. "You're Evika, right? Evika Stormer?" he asked.

"Maybe," I said, folding my arms and shifting my weight. "Who wants to know?"

"Well, if you're Evika, then I'm your other half, so-to-speak." He smiled proudly. "My name is Jaxon. I'm your twin brother."

I choked on some spit in mid-swallow. "I-I'm sorry. You're my *what*?"

"Your brother," he answered confidently. "I'm Jaxon Stormer. Our father was Jack Stormer, former Warrior for the Seekers, slash, Soldier of Light. I'm assuming you've already begun the whole destiny thing, considering I found you down here in Georgia all of a sudden," he rambled. "Last place I tracked you showed you were in Cleve-"

"Hold on. Time out." I held up my hands. "Let's rewind here, buddy. My *twin*? You're my twin, as in same mother, same father, same egg, shared-a-womb-together, born-on-the-same-day kind of twin?"

He nodded slowly, befuddled, as if finally grasping the fact that I'd had absolutely no clue what he was talking about. "Wow, you mean your Guardian never told you?" he said rhetorically.

My mind went spinning again, and my mouth remained agape, refusing to confirm. My heart started pounding with an unfamiliar pain. Confusion consumed me. "H-How do you know about all this stuff? About my dad and who he was? How the hell can I have a twin?"

The stranger smiled genuinely. "Come on, look at us," he said. "Is there really any denying that we're related?" He held out his hand, palm up, lifting his sleeve and exposing his right wrist. And that was when I saw it. Without further thought and only overwhelming curiosity, I pushed open the screen door in a stupor and walked out onto the porch to grab his wrist. I saw the mark. *My* mark. His was a bit lighter than mine, but still visible. It was the negative zero.

"Is this some kind of sick joke?" I asked, pointing to the mark and looking up at him.

His expression grew solemn, and I could see into his deep, brown eyes, and saw what I had been seeing in the mirror for twenty-one years; I saw myself. He exchanged the same look and, in that split second, I could almost feel a part of me come back, a part I didn't even know was missing. A piece of me.

"No sick joke. This is real," he said, declaratively. "You really are my sister,"

"Hey, Pony-girl?" I heard a playful voice calling from the top of the stairs. "What's takin' so long?" The sound of Hayden's hurried footsteps hustled down the stairwell all the way down to the landing, coming to an abrupt halt. "Oh. Shit," was the brilliance he muttered in sync with his last two steps.

I whipped my head around to see his face in a state of shock. His face and bare chest muscles tensed. Fear filled his eyes. His comment, alone, was enough indication that our visitor was quite unexpected. I felt the prickling in my eyes as I witnessed Hayden's face become ashen. He backed away, flustered.

"What the hell have you been keeping from me, Hayden?" The boom of thunder jolted the three of us as I started to feel more irritated. My nostrils flared as I gritted my teeth. He stood there, speechless. The rain started. "Hayden!" I yelled at him, annoyed at his stupor, my voice booming throughout the entire house. "What the hell is going on?"

Still holding the stranger's wrist, I pulled him inside the house with me, getting us out of the inevitable downpour.

Hayden's hands rose, palms up. "Okay, Evika." He spoke in a calm, yet shaky voice. "I swear, I can explain all of this."

"It's true then?" I asked impatiently. "Is this my twin brother?"

His hands were still up in surrender. "Evika, please. You have to under---"

"Goddammit, Hayden! Just answer me this one thing! Is...it...true?" I was done with surprises, and this one was the biggest of them all.

I watched him take a hard swallow before he sighed in defeat. "Yes."

After hearing his honesty, I felt the fury rise within me once again, this time causing a mild shaking. "Why didn't I know, Hayden? Why?" I asked through gritted teeth.

"Because the time wasn't right yet, Evika," he admitted.

It hurt that my whole life had been a lie, that I had missed out of years of a bond with a brother, a twin brother, family.

"The time wasn't right?" I asked scathingly. "Really? When *would* have been the right time, Hayden? Did you ever think that maybe not robbing me of my own flesh and blood was something that may have called for a bit of urgency? I'd already been robbed of enough in my life, and for you to take *him* away from me---" I stopped and took a long deep breath. The heat was rising in my body. My thoughts were too scattered. "Oh, my God." I tightened my fists in pain. I was going to do something terrible if I didn't get out, or worse, say terrible things I could never take back. I threw my controlled words at Hayden. "You kept me from my twin brother."

"Uh, maybe I should just step outside," Jaxon said softly, inching his way back toward the door.

Both Hayden and I looked over at him in unison. I'd forgotten the very topic of the conversation was also our audience.

"No, Jaxon," were Hayden's first words to him. "There is no need for you to leave," he said with assurance. "There is much to discuss now that you've arrived." He then brought his eyes to mine once again. "Evika, I'm so sorry that it came up this way. I will explain everything to you both."

My brow furrowed as I looked at Hayden and felt the rage inside of me reach its tipping point. I clenched my teeth. I knew he was going to spew off a list of rules or commands that were given to him by the Council. Free will? How did this not tamper with anyone's free will? As far as I was concerned, angels were just as imperfect as humans, and probably worse. I knew there was going to be a list of excuses Hayden would rattle off; I didn't want to hear them. None of them.

No matter what I did, the words were going to pour from my mouth. "You know what, Hayden? I don't want to hear what you have to tell us. Fuck the rules and fuck this life!" I gave him my most deadly glare. "Nothing. *Nothing* like this should be kept from someone. I don't care what your damned Council says. Your mission is over. You're done. *I'm* done!" I headed for the door and tugged Jaxon by the hood of his sweatshirt. "Come on, Jaxon. We're going out."

Jaxon stumbled on his feet. I hadn't realized the severity of the tug I gave him. I finally let go so he could make his way out the door first. I was sure I'd made enough of an ass of myself.

"No." Hayden rushed past me and blocked the door with his arm before I could get out. "Evika, you need to hear this. Both of you. There was huge danger in keeping you two together, and there still is."

"*No!*" I held up my hand. "Just save it. Get the hell out of our way." I grabbed my army boots and jacket, planning on throwing them on after I was outside.

"You're not going anywhere right now," Hayden said sternly.

I glared. "The hell I'm not, Hayden! You can't fix this. No matter how hard you try, you just can't!" I yelled, seething, shoving him hard in the chest.

He made an advance toward me, and I shoved him even harder the second time. "Don't you dare touch me, Hayden!" I screeched. "I swear, you will regret it!"

He backed away. Concern, hurt and shock washed over his face. Defeat.

I opened the screen door and guided Jaxon to step out first. I looked at Hayden. "And don't even think about sending Luka after me. He kept this from me too." I held my penetrating glare. I saw the frustration in his face before I turned to leave.

"This was everyone's secret to keep, Evika!" he called to me. "Even hers! She kept this from you, too. You don't understand. We *all* had to! You're making a huge mistake." I could hear the desperation in his voice. It was his last attempt at calming me down. He knew that I might think twice if my mother was mentioned. But it only made the rage in me spill over.

"Mistake?" I bore into Hayden's eyes, my nostrils flaring. "The only mistake I ever made was trusting you," I said to him scathingly. "Be out of this house by the time I'm back tonight."

"E-Evika," Hayden projected devastation in his tone, "you're just upset. You don't mean---"

"I do mean it, Hayden!" I screamed at the top of my lungs. "I want you out!"

I could almost hear the rip I tore into his heart – the new heart that had just started beating less than twenty-four hours ago – as I said those words. I could almost feel it break. Or maybe it was my own. I saw the agony in his face. I was so livid, I'd only cared that I'd hurt him and was satisfied to know that I truly had. Maybe there really was a darkness inside of me that was trying to win.

Beau started barking after me as I stepped out, a reminder of the past, one full of lies. "No, Beau. You stay here. I gotta go." The words came out brokenly, each of them stinging as I said them, making me feel as if I was abandoning him.

I just knew I needed to clear my head, and the only way to do that was to get Hayden out of my sight. But, I was certain that my contempt spread far beyond just Hayden. It went deeper than that. It included the Council, all Guardians, Alysto, my father, even my mother and, worst of all, God. It felt like there was no one left to trust.

Just when I thought I had all of the pieces to my life put together, just when I thought I knew who I really was, who I was becoming, a whole new curve ball was thrown. My whole life had been a lie.

I felt guilt blanket over me as I pulled the door closed with such a force that it shook the entire porch. I stared at my bare feet, still clinging to the jacket and the boots, breathing heavily in anger after the echo of the slamming door dissipated, leaving only the sound of the rain drops plummeting menacingly onto the porch roof. Hardly prepared, with head spinning, I slowly raised my tear-filled eyes to meet those of my own flesh and blood...my twin brother, Jaxon.

Made in the USA
San Bernardino, CA
15 September 2016